AN OMINOUS EXPLOSION

A Regency Cozy

LYNN MESSINA

potatoworks press • greenwich village

Cover design by Jennifer Lewis

ISBN: (eBook): 978-1-942218-43-2
ISBN (Paperback): 978-1-942218-44-9
ISBN (Hardcover) : 978-1-942218-59-3
ISBN (Jacketed Hardcover): 978-1-942218-80-7

Published 2022 by Potatoworks Press

Never miss a new release! Join Lynn's mailing list.

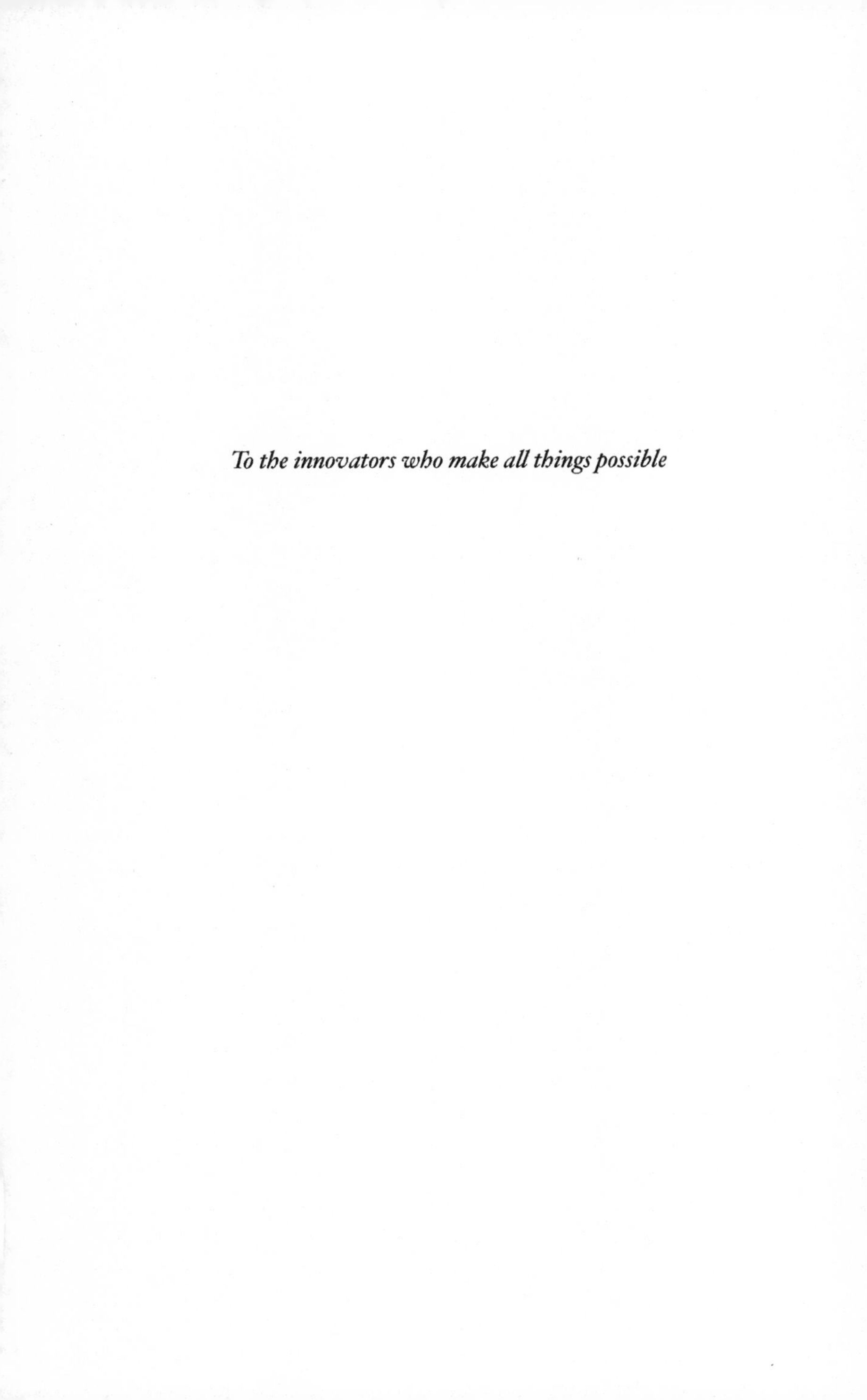

To the innovators who make all things possible

Chapter One

Although Vera Hyde-Clare was not a particularly large woman, possessing the gently rounded figure common in a matron of six and forty, she was still too big to disappear into the wingback chair she currently occupied.

She made a noble effort, however, pulling her shoulders together as tightly as possible as she scrunched one side of her body against the leather. At intervals, she closed her eyes, like a small child who thought she could not be seen if she herself could not see, and opened them wide, incapable of not gaping at the spectacle of the Duke of Kesgrave arguing with his grandmother.

Noting her aunt's discomfort, the duchess—formerly Miss Beatrice Hyde-Clare—thought the reaction did not accurately reflect the events currently unfolding before her. In particular, the disagreement, which hardly rose to the level of spectacle. During the quarrel, which had grown quite heated in the twenty minutes since Bea's aunt Vera had arrived, the dowager maintained an expression of polite good humor and Kesgrave kept his tone smooth and even.

Without imbuing his voice with undue emphasis, the duke informed the septuagenarian that he would escort her to Cambridgeshire to attend the burial of his uncle. As her other grandson, Mortimer Matlock, had already left the capital in the company of his father's body, the duty fell to him, and even if he did not desire the responsibility—which, to be clear, he did—it was morally incumbent upon him to assume it.

Firmly, her grace disavowed the existence of any such obligation.

Kesgrave frowned.

The dowager grimaced.

Mrs. Hyde-Clare cringed.

Poor Aunt Vera!

Having allowed herself to overcome four decades' worth of reticence and awe to pay a condolence call on the highest-ranking peeress of her acquaintance—no minor feat for a woman who genuflected before finely veined marble—she was now forced to endure an exchange best conducted in the privacy of a secluded room, preferably one with very thick walls so that not even the servants could overhear.

It was the very devil, for the situation had already been so awkward, what with the deceased getting himself bludgeoned to death for behavior unbefitting a gentleman.

Bea's aunt would never go so far as to imply that Lord Myles Matlock deserved the ill treatment, for nothing justified murder, especially not the sort administered via candlestick, but his lordship *had* descended into trade. What else did one expect to happen when one sullied one's hands with the ownership of a drinking establishment?

And then to sink further into degradation by setting up an operation to *produce* the liquor oneself.

The scion of one of the oldest families in England making gin!

'Twas a wonder Kesgrave House was still standing, for, in truth, the walls should have disassembled themselves stone by stone in shame.

The fact that the duke and his grandmother were quarreling in front of a personage of Mrs. Hyde-Clare's ilk—gentry, yes, but in possession of only an indifferent plot of land in some unheralded corner of Sussex—testified to the insidious effects of iniquity, for clearly it corrupted everything it touched, even these exalted beings who had seemed as impervious as oak trees.

"You must consider your bride," the dowager said, and although this seemed like a benign enough statement to Bea, it caused her aunt to press her cheek against the fine upholstery of the chair. "You have been married so briefly, and your leaving town would cause tongues to wag. People will say you have abandoned her, and at such a time. She has barely recovered from a monstrous attack on her life. They will consider it a harsh judgment on her activities."

In light of the circumstance, this claim was patently false, for even the most zealous gossip could not entirely dismiss the reality of a dead uncle. Lord Myles's brutal murder had reverberated throughout the beau monde, and even people who knew the enmity between the two men had felt compelled to offer their condolences.

Nevertheless, Kesgrave addressed the concern as if it were a legitimate worry, assuring her that Bea would accompany them on their journey as well. "She has never seen Haverill Hall and has lately developed a keen interest in its pinery."

But this reasonable solution dismayed the dowager as well, for she could brook no interference with Bea's rigorous training schedule. "Her fencing skills are so deplorable, Carlo still walks with a slight limp, and I comprehend her speed could withstand considerable improvement. During your foot pursuit on Wednesday, she fell well behind you and some hefty log of a man easily overtook her."

Kesgrave narrowed his eyes suspiciously. "Comprehend from whom? My groom? Have you taken to gossiping with the servants?"

"Nothing of the sort," the dowager replied blandly. "I served tea to Jenkins. I believe my granddaughter calls that an interview." She turned to Bea for confirmation. "Or was it an interrogation when you entertained the Mayhews' housekeeper in the drawing room at Kesgrave House during your investigation into Mr. Réjane's death? I am not yet conversant in the subtle distinction."

Although this tidbit was already known to everyone in the room, for it had been contained in Mr. Twaddle-Thum's extravagant account of the new duchess's investigation, which had been published in the *London Daily Gazette,* Aunt Vera tightened her features as if discovering a new unsavory detail about her niece's proclivities.

Indeed, her shock appeared to be so great she actually straightened her posture and pulled away from the corner into which she had been burrowing.

Bea, anticipating a sharp rebuke, marveled at how deeply Aunt Vera's disapproval ran. Truly, the only thing that would allow her to forget her mortification at the scene unfolding before her was condemnation of her former ward's behavior.

She simply could not help herself.

As if to prove Bea's point, Vera scooted to the very edge of her seat and said, "I shall go with you."

At this announcement, three sets of eyes turned to look at her.

All displayed surprise.

Only Bea's goggled with utter befuddlement as she sought to make sense of what her aunt had just said.

It *sounded* as though she was offering to accompany the dowager.

But that could not be right.

Clearly, Bea heard it wrong.

Her aunt had said *high* or *sigh*.

Or maybe she meant *aye* or *eye*.

Quickly, as if aware she had said something untoward, Vera added that the dowager could not go alone. Then she flinched at the unwieldy confidence of her own tone and stammered that of course the dowager could go alone if that was what she wanted. "I do not mean to tell you what you should do, for you are an old woman...that is, a woman who is old enough to know her own mind. If you genuinely desire to go on your own, then you must. But it is a difficult circumstance, and you would want family with you," she said, immediately shaking her head as she rushed to correct a potential misunderstanding. "Not that *we* are family. Obviously, I know that I am not *your* family. I would never presume to claim a kinship with a family as illustrious as yours...or, rather, any family not my own. I do not mean to present myself as the sort of person who goes around society rooting about for relatives, for that would be vulgar. And strange. Yes, that would be quite strange. But we are *like* family, for my niece is married to your grandson, so there is a connection, and I would like to be of service if I may. I comprehend that there are quite a lot of family members who could attend to you, but it appears as though most of them annoy you. No...no... no, not *annoy* you. But try your patience. Yes, they appear to try your patience because you know your own mind."

As articulate as this explanation was—and representative of her relative's harried, self-conscious thinking—Bea still could not fully comprehend the words she was hearing. Aunt Vera *wanted* to spend hours and hours alone with the Dowager Duchess of Kesgrave? Given the older woman's age, the pace of travel would be slow, with the sixty-mile drive spread over two, possibly three days.

Aunt Vera would have to *put up* in a posting house with her.

She would have to eat her meals at the *same* table as her.

She would have to sit across from her in the *confined space* of a coach.

Surely, Mrs. Hyde-Clare would disintegrate from all that exposure to grandeur.

Aunt Vera could barely sit in a drawing room with the newly minted duchess without swooning from nerves and she had spent years treating the girl like an unpaid companion.

The dowager, taken aback by the offer, looked at her granddaughter-in-law as if to ascertain her opinion, and it was all Bea could do not to lift her shoulders in a shrug.

Truthfully, she had no idea what to make of the proposal.

Vera, either noting the dowager's confusion or feeling as though still more needed to be said, added that she would also like to see the pinery, for she could not imagine anything more indulgent than growing a tropical fruit on English soil. Then, fearing she had insulted either the duke or the lavish splendor that was his birthright, she explained that pineapples were obviously a necessity for someone of his wealth and position. "*I* would not like it at every meal because my palate is plain and undeveloped and suited only to simple English fare such as roast beef or plum pudding. I do, of course, enjoy a nice ragout when it is served to me, but I find nothing so favorable as a humble bowl of stewed meats with an assortment of sturdy vegetables."

Anticipating an ode to boiled mutton to swiftly follow, Bea was surprised when her aunt paused in her speech to allow the dowager to respond.

Verily, she affirmed the worthiness of turnips, carrots and onions, and asserted the ingenuity of the pinery. "You will be

very impressed, I think, when you see how pineapples are cultivated. And your understanding of the fruit is correct. It does require an effort to be liked, as I recently explained to your niece. I am confident by the time we return to London, you will like them as much as I do. My chef is particularly adept at preparing dishes incorporating pineapple and I will have him send an assortment to Portman Square for your own cook."

Vera, intrepidly bearing the weight of this oppressive generosity, dipped her head in a dignified nod and owned herself grateful for the opportunity to acquire a taste for the exotic delicacy. "I shall devote myself to the task."

And that was all she said.

Despite her habit of rambling through a seemingly endless supply of caveats, she made no attempt to clarify the extent of her proposed devotion or provide its precise dimensions. Bea, observing her restraint, thought Aunt Vera might indeed be the solution to a rather thorny problem, for the dowager was determined to go without Kesgrave and no amount of cajoling or coaxing could convince her to relent.

It was baffling, her refusal, for she was fond of her grandson and Bea assumed she would desire his consoling presence at such a painful time. Lord Myles had been a terrible human being in every way imaginable, seeking the removal of his own nephew to clear the line of succession for himself, but he was still her child. No matter what he was, she could not help loving him, if only for the small, endearing, innocent little boy he must have once been.

His death was a terrible blow.

Surely, Kesgrave could help soften it.

And yet, Bea knew, it was impossible to account for the vagaries of grief, and even if they could not comprehend her wishes, they could at least abide by them.

The duke's understanding of the situation varied greatly

from hers, however, and he remained ardently opposed to any outcome that did not involve him. With a brisk nod, he thanked Mrs. Hyde-Clare for her kind offer, then firmly rejected it.

At his curt rebuff, Bea expected her aunt to redouble her efforts to disappear into the furniture, for Kesgrave's tone had been brusque if not harsh, but she held her position at the edge of the seat. Then, in what her niece considered an unfathomable event, she replied that the right of refusal belonged to his grandmother.

Her courage held for one breathless moment.

Doggedly, she kept her eyes steady as if daring the duke to disagree.

Then her pluck seemed to desert her, and she rounded her shoulders as she added in a quivering rush, "I am sure your counsel is invaluable to her. You are so wise and learned, she could not possibly make a decision without taking your thoughts and opinions into consideration, for they are known to be better than everyone else's. Your intelligence and discernment are widely admired, and her grace is fortunate to have you to advise her. But in the end, we have to trust that she knows what is best for herself and allow her to make that decision. I hope it goes without saying that *I* believe your companionship is vastly superior to mine and I would be delighted for the opportunity to accompany you on your travels."

But that would never do, for Vera Hyde-Clare to invite herself on a journey with the Duke of Kesgrave, and she explained that she was speaking only in hypothetical terms. "Our actually traveling together would be highly irregular and inappropriate. I cannot imagine what the *ton* would say if such a thing were to occur. And where would we be going? Not abroad, I hope, because I cannot stand foreigners, with their incomprehensible languages. It is bad enough when

Flora and her father speak Latin. Regardless, anywhere we went, Bea would come with us, even if it meant she would have to miss her fencing—"

Abruptly she broke off and looked at her niece in confusion. "I am sorry, but did the dowager say you are taking *fencing* lessons?"

"She did, yes," Bea said, amused and relieved by Aunt Vera's return to form. The digression into coherence and kindness had been as shocking as it was unsettling and forced her to entertain the highly disconcerting notion that she had underestimated her relative. For years, she had assumed she knew every frivolous and disapproving thought that flitted through the other woman's head, and to allow now for the possibility that she might have been wrong was almost more than she could handle.

It was not only the obligation of a sweeping reappraisal that unnerved Bea but also the horrifying possibility that Aunt Vera might be the victim of a grave disservice. Having endured gross misjudgments herself, she was appalled at the prospect of inflicting them on someone else.

Fortunately, her aunt's gasp at the confirmation of her fencing lessons indicated that a comprehensive overhaul was not in order.

Perhaps only a slight reevaluation.

"And what did she mean about your being overtaken by a lug of a man?" Aunt Vera asked. "Were you *running* in a public street?"

"'A log of a man' is the term she used," Bea explained, "and she was referring to Mr. Trudgeon, who was also chasing the man who killed Lord Myles."

Now Aunt Vera pressed against the leather of the chair as if too exhausted to hold herself upright. "Does Mr. Twaddle-Thum know about this foot race of yours?"

Although Bea could have objected to the use of the

possessive, for she did not consider the pursuit of justice to be her exclusive domain, she chose not to belabor the point. Rather, she confessed that she had no idea what the scurrilous reporter did or did not know. "But considering how resourceful he has been in the past, I imagine it is only a matter of time before we read about it in the *London Daily Gazette*."

Appalled at the prospect of yet another newspaper report detailing her niece's ghastly activities, Vera fanned herself with dramatic vigor, as if trying to ward off a faint. Although her intent clearly had been only to further censure the unruly young duchess, her theatrical display eased the tension in the room, and instead of issuing the cutting set-down that had been on his lips, Kesgrave told Mrs. Hyde-Clare that she was correct.

"It is for her grace to decide," he agreed, before turning to look at his grandmother and asking her why she would not allow him to accompany her. His tone was mild now, more curious than hurt, as if he was seeking merely to understand her intransigence, not overcome it. "I assure you, it is not an inconvenience to me or Bea in any way. He was my uncle, after all, and it is right that I should be there, and even if he were not, I am very fond of you and wish to provide my support."

Ordinarily forthright, the dowager lowered her gaze to her hands, which were clasped tightly in her lap, and stared silently at her clenched fingers for several long moments. Despite these signs of agitation, her voice was matter-of-fact when she finally replied.

Even so, she kept her eyes tilted resolutely down, unable, it seemed, to respond while looking at her grandson. "It is because he *was* your uncle. He was *your* family, *my* blood, and I could exert no control over him. He was horrible in every way, without a drop of decency in the end, and there was nothing I could do about it. Every attempt I made to dissuade him from his course, whether threats of penury or pleas for integrity, only further entrenched his hatred. He blamed me for every setback he suffered going back to the day he was born, for he deeply resented being a second son. Your father did not make it any easier on him, but I do not hold him responsible for Myles's spitefulness—for other things, yes, but not that," she said, continuing in the same mild tone, as if making a vaguely interesting comment about that evening's diversion. "I was given two opportunities to raise honorable men and I failed on both accounts. I feel that failure always, and nothing I do makes it better. But having you there, with your surfeit of decency, will make it worse, and that is more than I can bear."

Kesgrave wanted to quarrel.

Oh, yes, Bea could see it in his eyes, the determination to make the counterargument that his presence could provide his grandmother with solace and succor, that his surfeit of decency, as she called it, was nothing more than affection and concern for her well-being.

It was, Bea thought, an understandable impulse—and a lovely one at that—but she could not allow him to indulge it. The dowager had enough with which to cope without having to console the wounded vanity of her grandson.

Consequently, she announced that it was the shoes.

All three occupants in the room turned to look at her, but only the duke's face twisted with irritation at the heavy-handed attempt at diversion.

He did not appreciate her changing the subject.

Undaunted by his disapproval, she said, "During the chase to apprehend Lord Myles's killer, I was encumbered by a pair of silk booties while Kesgrave and Trudgeon had the advantage of sturdy boots. I am confident that if they had been forced to contend with flimsy swaths of satin, their performance would have been no more impressive than mine. It is the very devil, which Kesgrave knows, for I have pleaded with him several times to commission his boot maker to make me a pair of Hessians and he adamantly refuses. It is because he knows I would beat him in a race if properly attired, and he hopes to preserve his dignity."

At this rallying speech, the duke's expression lightened, and he assured her that he had surrendered his last shred of dignity at the altar when the minister asked him for the fourth time if he was *absolutely certain* he wanted to take her for a wife. "But you are not entirely wrong, for I do hope to preserve something and that is my relationship with Hoby. If I dared to ask him to make boots for a woman, he would cut me off without a second thought and I would be forced to buy my shoes from Poole in Cheapside."

But Bea shook her head, for she had heard this argument before and had no patience for it. "Hoby does not require chapter and verse of every pair you purchase. And if he does ask about the wearer, you can invent a young cousin lately arrived to the capital hoping to acquire a little town bronze. If telling even that small lie offends your sense of honor, then surely there is a young man of that general description knocking around your family tree whom we could dragoon into service."

Now the duke grinned as he contemplated her with amusement. "Yes, because Mr. Twaddle-Thum would not immediately root out that deception. If left to your devices, I would be banned from every shoemaker, bookmaker, cobbler and cordwainer in London."

Bea, shaking her head with exaggerated sadness, heaved a hefty sigh and said to the dowager, "It is always like this, for your grandson harbors a crippling fear of the servants. It is always, 'No, Bea, we cannot search my housekeeper's quarters for a suspected clue at midnight,' or 'No, Bea, you cannot

hide under the butler's bed.' It is bewildering to me that a man who was raised with so much privilege could be so wary of his own staff. If he felt an inkling of concern for the neighbors' servants, I would understand it better, but he was happy to trudge through the Mayhews' kitchens."

"Happy, no," Kesgrave replied mildly. "Resigned, yes."

The dowager smiled at these antics, as Bea had intended, while her aunt gawked like a fish suddenly exposed to air, her lips flapping wildly as her eyelids fluttered.

Pressing her hand against her bosom, as if trying to still her suddenly racing heart, Vera fervently assured the duke that Bea had not learned such appalling behavior in Portman Square. "Neither Mr. Hyde-Clare nor I would ever countenance such a want of conduct!" she said, then gasped as the implication struck her and she rushed to clarify that her niece could not have learned it at Kesgrave House either. "Books! Yes, yes, of course, obviously, that is the source, for she often had her head buried in one Gothic or another, and you know how those people comport themselves, always sneaking through hidden passages in the middle of the night and pretending to be ghosts."

"Your reading material sounds charming," the dowager said to Bea, her hands unclasped now that the matter had been settled. "I do hope you can lend me some of the more salacious titles for my journey. It is generally too bumpy for me to read in the coach, but one of the horses will throw its shoes and we will be forced to dither by the side of the lane or in a posting house for hours."

Aunt Vera flinched at the inevitable discomforts of the journey but smiled gamely and asked Bea to recommend some books for her as well. "I would hate to pester the dowager with conversation when her attention is engrossed elsewhere."

Bea, who knew her relative's reading preferences leaned

toward flipping absentmindedly through *La Belle Assemblée* while criticizing her children, promised to have several weighty tomes delivered to Portman Square posthaste.

"You are too kind," Vera said, smiling stiffly.

The dowager, determined to get an early start for their trip, instructed Mrs. Hyde-Clare to return to her home and commence packing. She would send a footman to pick up her luggage in four hours. "Unless your maid can accomplish it sooner? I would like the coach with the bags to leave at first light to ensure that it arrives before we do. We do not have to depart until seven in the morning," she announced, her mood vastly improved by the requirements of the journey.

As her grace catalogued the many tasks to which she had to attend before she could leave for Cambridgeshire, Aunt Vera's complexion grew increasingly pale until she was practically ashen.

In making her generous offer, Mrs. Hyde-Clare had failed to consider the rigors of travel, and reminded now of how little she enjoyed the road, she appeared to sink into herself. Despite her efforts to once again hide in its depths, the wingback chair remained as impervious to her needs as ever. Kesgrave, noting her distress, owned himself grateful for her willingness to stand in his stead at the funeral and proffered his arm. Momentarily taken aback by the kindness in his voice, she flushed prettily, then simpered with delight.

Accepting the duke's escort, she promised to be ready to depart at six forty-five in the unlikely event her grace wanted to leave a little earlier, then rattled off a list of the many things she herself had to see to, the majority of which consisted of sending notes to various friends and acquaintances to alert them to the fact that she would be traveling with the dowager duchess as a personal favor to the duke.

Kesgrave indulged this turn, nodding at regular intervals and suggesting other people she might inform, such as Mrs.

Ralston, who was among the most accomplished gossips in London.

Short of sending a missive directly to Mr. Twaddle-Thum, it was, Bea thought, the most effective way of notifying the *ton* of her increased significance to the Matlock family.

Delivering Aunt Vera to her carriage, the duke thanked her again for unhesitatingly offering her assistance and asked if there was anything he could do to help while she was away.

Ardently, she demurred, noting at length that he had far more important business to oversee than the minor details of her life. He persisted, and although she remained stridently opposed to his performing any service for her, regardless how small, she admitted that she could bear to accept a tiny favor from Bea.

"If you could find time in your busy schedule to have a peek in on your uncle, that would be remarkably calming to my mind," she said. "You know how he gets when I am not around."

Indeed, Bea did—and it bore little difference from when his wife *was* around. Accustomed to her prattle after decades of marriage, he was particularly adept at ignoring her entirely and every morning enjoyed his eggs and newspaper as if she were not sitting directly across from him at the breakfast table. She had yet to notice his lack of attention because she typically passed the meal in a flurry of anxiety, reviewing the prior day's events and making mountains out of the molehills with which her children continually supplied her.

"I am happy to visit with my uncle," Bea said.

"Thank you, my dear," Aunt Vera said. "You relieved my mind greatly."

Alas, it was only temporary, for she had no sooner said the words than her brow furrowed with apprehension and she voiced her concern about Flora, who had been acting strangely ever since suffering a terrible bout of food poisoning.

"Do look in on her as well and make sure she does not eat any more rotten eggs," she said. "I cannot believe Mrs. Emerson is at fault and can only assume the poor girl has a special sensitivity. 'Tis highly vexing! Nonetheless, perhaps you could look over the menus for the week and confirm there is nothing that will cause a bother."

Although she knew her cousin's recent spate of gastric issues was the product of subterfuge, not spoiled food, Bea readily agreed.

"And Russell," her aunt added. "He has a tendency to get into mischief if I am not there to guide his actions. If you could perhaps play a few hands of piquet with him for ha'penny a point to satisfy his desire to gamble. It is vital that you win, so that he can feel dreadful about owing you money, and although I would never condone cheating per se, you should feel free to tweak the cards while he is not looking to ensure you prevail. I find pointing out an imperfection in his tailoring, whether real or imagined, is sufficient to distract him."

As her aunt was far from subtle, Bea had to assume her cousin's vanity was so overweening as to allow this deception to succeed. "Piquet with Russell. Check."

Relieved, Aunt Vera permitted Kesgrave to hand her into her carriage. As she perched on the bench, her lips pursed and she said, "Oh, and then there is Aileen."

"Aileen?" Bea asked, puzzled.

"The new upstairs maid. She is from Edinburgh and having a terrible time settling in," her relative explained. "It is her family. She misses them dreadfully. The only thing for it is to keep her too busy to brood. So, if you would not mind making sure she has enough to do? Mrs. Emerson, bless her heart, is a dear, but she lacks the ingenuity necessary to fill every minute of the poor girl's day. The linens, for example. Just because they were reorganized on Monday does not mean they cannot be reorganized on Thursday. We all know how insidious dust is. Honestly, I see no reason why the closet should not be reorganized daily, other than the fact that the maids cannot be incessantly folding linens. There is already so much to do around the house!"

Stifling a smile, Bea assented to this request and to the entreaty, issued sotto voce so that Kesgrave could not hear it as well, that she examine the western wall in the dining room for cracks because she feared a leak in the window casement was causing irreparable damage.

Graciously, Bea pledged to inspect the plaster and to even make sure that Flora did not read the new issue of Ackerman's before her mother did because the wretched girl always turned down the corners of the pages she liked.

She drew the line, however, at paying a call on Aunt Susan, who had been slow in recovering from the cold that had laid her low the week before.

Aunt Vera sighed dramatically, as if her niece were being unreasonable, and resolved to content herself with sending her sister a note.

Chapter Two

When Bea arrived at Nineteen Portman Square two days later, she expected to find the members of her family enjoying the calm interval that typically followed breakfast. Uncle Horace would be in his study, either finishing the *London Daily Gazette* or attending to his correspondence. Flora would be in the drawing room ostensibly plying a needle to the sewing pattern she had been working on for months but actually reading a fashion magazine. Russell would be in his bedchamber grumbling over his poorly tied cravat.

Briskly, she would dart from room to room, confirming at a glance that everyone was well, then pop down to the kitchen to consult with Mrs. Emerson. After approving the menus for the week and discussing the new maid's responsibilities, she would dash into the dining room to examine the west-facing wall for damage caused by water.

None of it was necessary, of course, but having given her word to her aunt, she was obligated to keep it.

Morally, yes, because a promise was a promise.

But more pressingly as a matter of straightforward practicality, for Aunt Vera would bemoan her omission for weeks if not months to come.

'Twas far better to devote thirty minutes to the pointless mission now than to lose hours to her relative's petulance later.

Instead of the quiet lull, however, she was greeted with a flurry of activity, as Russell hailed her from the bottom of the staircase, which he had been on the verge of ascending. "Bea, dear, you are just in time. Huzzah!"

Flora flew out of the breakfast room with a piece of toast in her hand to berate her brother. "You dolt, you are saying it all wrong. It is *huzz*ah."

Accustomed to her criticism, which was frequently indiscriminate, Russell held firm to his pronunciation. "I am certain I am correct. Huzz*ah*!"

His sister rolled her eyes at this display of misplaced confidence. "Do excuse him, Bea, for he cannot help being ignorant."

"Is Bea here?" Uncle Horace asked, strolling down the corridor from the back of the house, where his study was situated, and smiling when he caught sight of her. "Very good. Huzzah."

Russell looked at Flora with the gleam of triumph in his eye. "See? It is precisely as I said. Huzzah!"

"No, it is huzzah—*huzz*-ah, with the emphasis on the first syllable," Flora replied before turning to her father. "Tell him, Papa."

But Uncle Horace shook his head blithely and said he would tell his son nothing. "Your mother is not here so I do not have to pretend to care about your squabbles."

Taking his sire's abstention as an endorsement of his pronunciation, Russell thrust out his chin in victory, then announced that he had to return to his room to finish dressing. "I just need to perfect my cravat."

Flora, calling after him as he skipped up the stairs, said that if they had to wait until he achieved perfection, they would never go.

"Go where?" Bea asked, puzzled by the bustle.

"To see Mr. Huzza," Flora explained as she took another bite of her toast. "Mr. Peter Huzza. He is the inventor of a new steam carriage that he is demonstrating for investors this morning, and we are attending. As you know, my father is fascinated with technical inventions."

In fact, Bea knew no such thing and she imagined her cousin had only just discovered it herself, for neither one of them had ever had an extended conversation with the gentleman until recently. Like most men of his class, he spent a large portion of his day either at his club or in his study, doggedly avoiding the delights of domesticity.

"Uncle Horace has never mentioned his interest to me," Bea said, "so I did not realize he was seeking opportunities to invest in steam carriages."

"Seeking opportunities to invest in steam carriages?" Flora repeated with a trill of laughter. "Of course he is not. You know Mama and how cautious she is. She would never countenance a venture with any risk attached to it. She would be vehemently opposed to our attending a demonstration expressly designed to entice investors, for she would be terrified that Papa would allow his enthusiasm to overcome his good judgment. But as she is not here to object...."

Flora trailed off meaningfully and licked toast crumbs off the tips of her fingers, something else she would never dare to do if her mother were in residence.

"Do say you'll come, Bea," her cousin continued. "I know it sounds horribly dull, but last month I went with Papa to see a demonstration of Mr. Tarwich's steam carriage and it was engrossing. Truly! And Mr. Holcroft thought so too, for he was there, at the same exhibition, although I could not know it, for we had not yet met."

At the mention of Flora's beau, who had left the city several days before to spend time with his family in Norfolk, Bea felt her understanding of the situation sharpen. Her cousin was either secretly wishing Holcroft would also be in attendance or hoping to gather information with which to woo him back to town.

Whatever pleasures Norfolk offered, surely they could not compete with the technological wonders of Mr. Huzza's advanced steam engine.

Although imperfect, this plan was an improvement on her previous one, which involved embroiling Holcroft's disgraced cousin in a murder investigation.

To be fair, Flora's intention had been merely to coax Mr. Caruthers into going for a drive with them in Hyde Park and had pivoted to paying a call on a former associate only when he remained impervious to her cajoleries.

Having pitched the errand as a matter of life and death, she had not believed it would actually involve the latter.

And yet somehow that was precisely the result, for when they arrived at the solicitor's office, there was Kesgrave's bludgeoned uncle lying on the floor.

Poor Mr. Caruthers!

He had desired nothing more than to pass through the world unnoticed and then fate—or, rather the Duchess of Kesgrave—compelled him to call on his former colleagues and ask them questions about Lord Myles's homicide.

If Bea had not been so worried about the duke and his murdered relation, she would have felt awful about sending him off to do the exact thing he dreaded most.

Despite his reluctance, Caruthers acquitted himself beautifully, conducting the interviews without complaint and discovering pertinent information. He had even sent Bea a polite note formally conveying his condolences to the family and seeking to confirm she had suffered no ill effects from the shocking experience.

She did not know what Holcroft thought of their misadventure, for he had yet to reply to her cousin's missive explaining her intention and apologizing for its unanticipated outcome, but Bea assumed his judgment would not be harsh. Given his excessive rationality, he could not hold Flora responsible for the actions of a killer and Caruthers appeared to have emerged from the ordeal unscathed.

Still, Flora fretted, Holcroft was protective of his disgraced cousin, whose ignominy he had a hand in exposing, and might resent her for subjecting him to danger.

Before Bea could politely decline the invitation, Uncle Horace appeared in the hallway and exhorted her to come. Tucking his watch into the fob pocket, he insisted that as a devotee of the scientifical method, she would find the experience edifying. "I believe you will discover Mr. Huzza's machine represents a huge leap forward in our understanding of steam power. It is an impressive advancement on Mr. Phillips's invention, which was once revolutionary. You own shares in it through your father. It was your mother, if I am remembering correctly, who urged him to make the investment after attending a demonstration like this one. I believe she first came across information about the engine in a newspaper article. Clara was quite studious and able to recall great amounts of information. In that way you take after her."

Bea, who knew very little about her parents, felt her heart flutter at the comparison, for it was so very bittersweet to discover she shared one of her most enduring character traits with her parent.

'Twas delightful as well to know her father listened to and valued her mother's opinion.

The refusal on her lips died, for the prospect of following

in her mother's footsteps was too compelling to resist, and she owned herself happy to attend.

Pleased, Uncle Horace smiled and said, "Good. I am certain you will enjoy it and look forward to hearing your thoughts."

"We're just waiting on Russell now," Flora said, raising her voice as she tilted her head upward to make sure her brother could hear her complaint two stories up.

Marveling at how little had changed in the six weeks since she had removed to Berkeley Square, Bea excused herself to inspect the dining room wall. Even with Russell's inexpert neckcloth fumbling, there was not enough time to confer with Mrs. Emerson regarding the menus and Aileen's tasks for the week, but she could at least gauge the damage caused by the leak.

Flora, cheerfully chattering about Holcroft's opinion of the Tarwich engine, followed her cousin into the dining room and immediately fell silent when Bea positioned herself in front of the wall. After a few moments of contemplation, she said, "It was David."

Taken aback by the pronouncement, Bea turned to look at her. "Excuse me?"

"The mark on the wall that has Mama convinced the house is about to fall down around our ears," Flora said as she stepped forward and pointed to a brown-colored stain a few inches from the corner. "It was David, the footman. He tripped on the edge of the rug and spilled tea. It was a very minor amount, more like a splash than a spill. I know it because I saw it happen. Papa as well. We were both sitting at the table, but Mama will not hear a sensible word about it. No, she insists that the walls must be moldering from the inside and spends about ten minutes a day staring at the stain. The poor dear, she worries so! I do wish Papa would hire a builder to inspect the room and bring her peace of mind, but

he refuses to condone the expense. He says he will not dignify her foolish anxieties by spending money on them. Perhaps he will change his mind when he learns her concern is so acute she enlisted the Duchess of Kesgrave into minding the wall for her. I am sure he thinks as I do that there are much better ways for you to spend your time."

Amused as ever by Aunt Vera's nonsense, Bea examined the marks, which were no larger than a ring for her little finger and noted that they did indeed look like faded splatters of bohea. "Could you not just wash them away?"

"Oh, yes, very easily, I think, but Mama is insistent that we leave them exactly as they are so that she can track the damage," Flora explained. "You are such a darling to indulge her, for I know she has done nothing to deserve it. Her offering to attend to the dowager is without question a *step* in the right direction but not the whole journey."

Bea, who remained baffled by Aunt Vera's offer, found Flora's assessment intriguing and wondered if could be accurate.

It was difficult for her to imagine because her relative was so set in her ways.

And yet suffering the discomforts of travel to lessen another person's burden was already out of character for her.

At least, Bea believed it was out of character.

Now, as before, she found herself disquieted by the prospect of having to reconsider everything her aunt had ever done.

It was so much easier to simply assume she knew the other woman's every miserly thought.

These musings were interrupted by the sound of Russell's voice as he loudly announced that *he* was ready to leave. "I do not know where Flora is."

Affronted, Flora huffed loudly and called out that she had been waiting an age for him. "And so has Bea, who is far too important to be left cooling her heels as you primp in front of the mirror. She is a *duchess* now."

Russell scoffed at the implication that he did not know his cousin's rank and complained that he had been trying to use it to his advantage for weeks to no avail. "Weston refuses to extend me credit, even with the connection!"

Aunt Vera, who considered sharing a tailor with the prince regent the height of impertinence, would never approve of such an immoderate expense and would be utterly mortified at the prospect of her son going into debt to fund the presumption.

Uncle Horace chided his son for daring to exploit the new duchess, then scolded his daughter for laughing, before apologizing to Bea for both of them. "I would not mind siring heathens if they were educated heathens, but they are dreadfully ignorant on top of it."

"*Homines dum docent discunt,*" Flora said in an attempt to disprove the sentiment by displaying her proficiency in both Latin and the production of topically relevant historical quotations.

Russell, whose understanding of the language was usually inadequate, somehow managed to recognize the Seneca reference and insisted it was an insult to their parent. "If men learn while they teach, then the only conclusion to be drawn here, Father, is that Flora thinks you have much more to learn."

His sister hotly denied the charge as they left the house, and Bea, amused by their bickering, most likely because she no longer had to live with it, did something she had never done before in the whole of her life—threaded her arm amiably through her uncle's as they strolled down the walk to his carriage.

The site of the demonstration was in Bloomsbury, off Melton Street, which was not very far, and during the short ride, Uncle Horace tried to facilitate an edifying discussion about the differences between low- and high-pressure steam, but Russell kept returning the conversation to the only aspect that interested him, which was boiler explosions.

"Not every steam engine explodes, you dunderhead," Flora said peevishly. "Papa and I went to a demonstration of Mr. Tarwich's new carriage, and the boiler behaved superbly, did it not, Papa?"

"*You* are the dunderhead," Russell retorted, "because everyone knows that low-pressure steam does not cause explosions. Only strong steam poses a risk."

"Yes, and that was precisely the type employed by the Tarwich," Flora replied huffily. "Steam that was strong enough to power the pistons. Do explain it to him in terms simple enough for even my brother to understand, Papa."

Alas, Flora was the one who required clarification, for strong steam was the same thing as high-pressure steam.

"The Tarwich uses low-pressure steam," Uncle Horace explained. "The elder Mr. Tarwich's great innovation was the placement of the cylinder, which turned the wheels directly, removing the need for gearing. The new carriage improves on that basic innovation, making the engine more efficient without significantly changing the design. Engines that use strong steam are rare because there is the risk of explosion, and most inventors choose to give it a wide berth. Years ago —in 1803, if my memory is correct—a high-pressure stationary pumping engine exploded near Greenwich, killing four men. The devastation was so staggering, it was as though a gunpowder mill had detonated."

"Now *that* would be a spectacle to see!" Russell said approvingly.

His father, incapable of suppressing his impatience at his son's unsatisfactory response, added that the accident depressed interest in strong steam for more than a decade.

"That had to do in some part with Watt, who spoke at length against it for the hazards it poses and even proposed making its use illegal. Naturally, he could not remain silent on a subject with which he was so well acquainted."

Bea, who had silently listened to this exchange, bent her lips in a cynical twist. "James Watt of the Watt engine, which uses low-pressure steam?"

Uncle Horace conceded her point but insisted Watt and his partner, Boulton, had done the only thing they could in the situation, for the public deserved to be saved from the perils. "A government inquiry was held on the tragedy, and while it did not find Trevithick to be at fault, ascribing the blame to neglect on the part of a worker, it did prohibit the use of cast-iron plates in the production of boilers. Only wrought iron was allowed going forward. All of this, however, is what makes the *Bright Benny* so exciting. With it, Huzza has solved the problem of strong steam once and for all. You see, he designed an ingenious plug made out of a material that melts when the temperature in the boiler rises above a dangerous level, thereby releasing the pressure and averting tragedy."

"Yes, precisely," Flora murmured, nodding officiously, as if this were the adjustment she herself would have made.

Unimpressed, her brother scoffed and sought more details about the Greenwich explosion. "Were a great many people injured? Were they horribly mangled? Did they lose arms and legs? Did their eyes pop out of their sockets?"

Noting the eager bloodthirstiness in his tone, Bea thought perhaps his mother was correct to deny him lessons with Gentleman Jackson.

If Uncle Horace also found it off-putting, his calm reply gave no indication. "The casualties were held to a minimum because most of the workers were away at dinner at the time."

Before Russell could digest this disappointing fact, the carriage arrived at the foundry. His mood immediately improved, however, when his sister, rising to his taunting "Huzzah!" corrected his pronunciation yet again.

Gleefully, he explained that in this instance he meant it was an expression of approbation. "Huzzah for Huzza!"

Flora rolled her eyes at what she considered to be a juvenile display and congratulated him on his witticism. "I am sure a child in leading strings could not have done better."

Uncle Horace sent them both a quelling look, and the pair fell silent as they proceeded to the site of the demonstration.

It bore, Bea noted with interest, a disconcerting similarity to a fairground, with musicians playing a lively tune as they passed through the opening in a low fence and a gaily decorated platform to the left of the entrance. On the other side was a yard, wide and deep, with a large building at the far end, its gabled roof augmented with skylights to allow sunshine to flood the factory floor. The vast space was exposed to the crowd via broad swaths of wood that slid along a track like the doors of a barn. A brightly colored banner over the entrance announced the grand debut of the *Bright Benny* steam carriage.

A large crowd milled around the engine, obscuring Bea's view, and she waited with Flora and her uncle for their opportunity to inspect it up close. Russell, impatient with the queue after barely a minute, had wandered off to greet the father of a school friend.

"About time," Flora murmured as the woman with the high-plumed hat in front of them finally stepped aside to provide them with unimpeded access to the prototype.

It was, Bea noted, a large barrel of a machine with three pairs of wheels and a vertical pipe. It was surrounded by ornamental ribbons hanging like garlands from wood posts to ensure that spectators did not draw too close, and a serious-looking man was feeding the firebox. He was about thirty, possibly a little younger, with closely shorn blond hair, and despite the beads of sweat trickling down the sides of his face, he wore a heavy cloak and thick gloves. Both were generously streaked with black from the lumps of coal, which he added by hand.

To her surprise, she discovered she wanted to touch the carriage, for it had an appealingly mechanical look about it, with its long water tank encased in smooth wood planks and black chimney extending several feet in the air.

Having read her mother's letter to Lady Abercrombie detailing the technological wonders of the Phillips engine, she had a general understanding of how steam power worked. She knew the coal heated the water to create the steam, which moved the pistons back and forth, thereby propelling the wheels to turn.

It was fascinating indeed, as her mother had written, to contemplate traversing great stretches of land with the same effortless grace as sailing the ocean.

The specifics of the process eluded her, and she could make only approximate guesses as to where things went and in which space they occurred.

Having attended the demonstration of the Tarwich, Flora naturally considered herself an expert on the matter and pointed to various features, all of which were patently obvious to any onlooker, such as the firebox. Had he been present, Russell would have found her air of proficiency intolerable, but Bea was as amused as ever by the authoritative note in her cousin's voice.

Leading them around the engine, Flora described how steam collected above the water, forcing it to travel through a pipe that led to the cylinders. As informed as she was about the main section of the mechanism, she was at a loss to explain why the middle pair of wheels had cogs while the

other two sets were smooth. It was not a feature incorporated by Tarwich in his steam carriage, and as such she was inclined to dismiss its importance.

Consequently, she proposed that it most likely served a decorative function, a suggestion that amused a gentleman standing behind them so much he felt compelled to interrupt their conversation to set her straight.

Chapter Three

Turning, Bea observed that the word *decorative* applied to the gentleman as well, for he was brightly dressed in an overly large cocked hat and vibrant jonquil waistcoat. In his hand he clutched an ebony walking stick with an ornate gold knob. A large signet ring glinted on his finger.

Taken as a whole, his outfit was cheerful and discordant—an unusual combination to attempt for a man well into his sixth decade.

Smiling enthusiastically, with no self-consciousness for interrupting a private conversation, he explained that the cogged wheels were pinions. "That typifies the shrewdness of Mr. Huzza's invention. The gear teeth on the pinion slot into the teeth on the rack, which is attached to the rails. That keeps the engine in place and propels it forward. His previous model was too heavy and crushed the cast-iron rails it traveled on. So he made his next version lighter and developed the rack system to help with adhesion. Those pinions keep the engine on the rail even when going up a steep hill, which makes it the first of its kind. Even the Tarwich carriage, which I think is the best model available for reliability and efficiency, cannot go up steep inclines," he said, before laughing awkwardly. "Oh, dear, am I talking too much? Pestering you with my knowledge? I know I should keep a dignified silence, but I find it impossible to allow anyone to wallow in their ignorance—especially when there are wonders like the *Bright Benny* to behold! Do say you forgive me."

Flora obliged at once, assuring the speaker that she suffered from the exact same fault. "Why, I was explaining to my cousin all the ways Mr. Huzza's invention differed from Mr. Tarwich's, the demonstration of which I was fortunate to attend a few weeks ago. Were you there as well?"

"I was, yes, and *thought* it was a marvelous carriage," he replied enthusiastically. "As I said, it is very reliable and efficient. It does not have the thrills and excitement of something like the *Bright Benny,* but that is because low-pressure steam is so consistent and safe. I had planned to buy those for my factory in Stockwell, but then I read that Huzza planned to debut an engine that utilizes strong steam and knew I had to see it for myself. If it is as wonderful as the newspapers describe, then I shall invest in the company as well, not just in its machines. Am I slightly concerned about the dangers? Perhaps a little, for I am human, am I not? But high-pressure steam is the future and low pressure is the past. Therefore, the Tarwich is the past. Even if it's perfect, it is still mediocre. I assume you share my opinion."

Verily, she did.

Previously, she had been impressed with the Tarwich precisely in accordance with Holcroft's admiration. Now her thoughts aligned with her new acquaintance's. "Low pressure is where the steam engine started, not where it is going."

The gentleman shook his head, as if awed by the insightfulness of this simple observation, which only amused Bea further, for her cousin had merely repeated his own idea back to him in different words.

"And what do you think, Miss..." he began, then trailed off expectantly.

Obligingly, Flora said, "Your grace. Do let me present to you my cousin who is as dear to me as a sister, Beatrice, Duchess of Kesgrave. And I am Miss Hyde-Clare. And who may you be?"

"Ah, you see, the *Bright Benny* is so exciting it entices the interest of duchesses!" he cried triumphantly, before lowering into a bow. "I am Grimes, Mr. Hubert Grimes, and as delighted as I am to meet you and your cousin, I am also deeply unsettled by the duke's interest. I had not realized word of Mr. Huzza's fame had spread so far and wide. If a man with the duke's resources decides the engine is worth his time, he might just gobble up the whole thing—firm, patents, engine, workshop, everything—leaving nothing for the rest of us. I must beg you to introduce me to your husband at once, your grace, so that I may describe to him at length the engine's many design flaws. The pinion-and-rack system, I understand, is prone to breakage."

Bea smiled at this extravagant reversal and explained that the duke was not present. "I am attending in the company of my uncle and have no intention of investing, so you do not have to malign a worthy machine to protect your own interest."

Grimes, sighing dramatically, announced himself relieved. "But what of your uncle? Do I have to worry about him buying an undue number of shares?"

"You do not have to worry about him buying any number," she replied.

But this information did not please him either and he stared at her aghast. "Not invest! An infamous notion if I ever heard one. You must present me to your extraordinary relative at once so I can set him to rights. Not invest in the *Bright Benny*! For what is he waiting? The esteemed Mr. Watt to come out of retirement to improve upon his own invention?"

Flora rushed to disabuse him of this notion, assuring the gentleman that her father would not invest in a new steam engine by even the estimable Mr. Watt. "Mama would never allow it. She is very careful with her money and believes the only secure investment is the funds."

This discouraging reply did little to dampen Mr. Grimes's confidence, and he swore he could persuade Mr. Hyde-Clare to purchase shares. "I feel it is an act of public-spiritedness because an opportunity of this scope will likely not arise again. As I said, the *Bright Benny* is the future! Now do let us find your father so that I may plead my case before the presentation begins."

Although Bea had not finished her inspection of the engine, she allowed herself to be led away by Flora, who spotted her parent across the yard. As they hailed him, he gestured excitedly to a man large in both height and girth who was bedecked entirely in white and identified him as the inventor. Huzza, his broad face split by a giddy smile, stood in the middle of a circle of admiring spectators.

"And there"—now Uncle Horace pointed to a mustachioed man who had lowered to one knee to get a better look at the tracks—"is a lieutenant-colonel in His Majesty's Armed Forces. Such illustrious company underscores the momentousness of the occasion. We are very lucky to be here."

Mr. Grimes, noting the astuteness of this observation, eagerly introduced himself. "A momentous occasion is precisely how I would describe it myself. And you must be Mr. Hyde-Clare, as only a man of discernment could have such a shrewd daughter."

Uncle Horace, who had never heard anyone apply that

description to either of his children, was momentarily perplexed. Then he graciously, if hesitantly, thanked him for the compliment.

"Mr. Grimes is an enthusiast," Flora explained. "He also attended the Tarwich demonstration last month."

"Guilty as charged," Grimes said with a nod of his head. "And I am too enthusiastic to allow you to miss the opportunity to invest in the *Bright Benny*. You must let me persuade you."

But Uncle Horace could not. Mindful of his wife's ardent disapproval of speculation, as well as his own cautious nature, he rattled off a list of reasons why the investment was too risky to even consider.

Undaunted, Grimes hailed the venture's uncertainty as its most valuable asset. "With great risk comes great reward. A man of your intelligence knows that! Nothing wondrous has ever been achieved away from the looming shadow of failure. Huzza could amass a huge fortune selling his marvelous steam carriage to every mill, colliery and ironworks in the country. But he knows there is more to life than money. He wants to create something entirely new that the world has never seen. That is why he is looking for investors to fund a tramroad from London to Whitstable."

"Whitstable?" Flora asked, puzzled by the non sequitur.

"The seaside," Bea said.

"Yes, your grace," Grimes said with approval. "The seaside! Can you imagine it? A steam carriage that brings passengers—dozens of passengers at one time!—to the beach so they may enjoy the briny air and the water and the elegant repose of sea-bathing. It is an audacious vision, I know, and perhaps it will fail, precisely as Mr. Hyde-Clare supposes. I do not think it will, but I cannot dismiss the possibility, for the majority of enterprises disappoint. Even so, I defy you to propose a more noble way to lose your last shilling than on the dream of taking hundreds of happy revelers to the sea. It is glorious!"

The notion that a person could use any favorable adjective to describe penury, let alone one as stirring as *glorious,* confounded Uncle Horace and he gaped at Grimes with unassailable dismay.

Noting his expression, Bea thought that Grimes, for all his determination, was not particularly adept at assessing his listener's temperament.

Ah, but even as his argument struck horror in Mr. Hyde-Clare's heart, it sparked excitement in Flora's. Swearing she could not think of a more satisfying reason to invest in a company, she lamented the fact that she lacked funds to give in support of Mr. Huzza's venture.

Her father gaped at these words, and Bea imagined Flora's monthly pin money allotment shrinking by one-half or three-quarters.

"What an idyllic vision! It is indeed glorious, like the sun," Flora added merrily, then her eyes widened as an idea occurred to her. "Oh! Is *that* why it is called the *Bright Benny*? Because it is as bright as the sun and Benny...hmm...Benny...." Here, her ingenuity failed her, and she scrunched her nose as she contemplated what the source could be. "Perhaps it is short for the *benefit*—that is, the benefit one derives from being at the seashore on a gorgeous day?"

Russell, who had joined the small group in time to hear this last comment, pooh-poohed her theory and said that it was very clearly a person's name.

"Mr. Huzza's son Benedict," Grimes confirmed. "He died tragically in the war. Mrs. Huzza followed suit just a few months later."

"How desperately sad," Flora said, her cheerfulness dimming. "The poor man."

Her brother, however, scoffed at the needlessly morose

nomenclature and declared that Matthew Murray had had it right by naming his steam carriage after the Battle of Salamanca. "Wellington's great victory—that is the way to do it!"

"I think that is a despicable thing to glorify, for thousands and thousands of brave English soldiers met their death on that battlefield," Flora said.

Russell replied that the Battle of Salamanca actually saved lives because it forced the French to abandon Madrid and temporarily withdraw toward their border. Before Flora could counter—perhaps with some broader point about the nihilism of war, although more likely with an insult for her brother—the musicians ceased to play and a man mounted the platform. When he arrived in the center, he raised his hand to indicate he wished to speak.

"That is Leopold Lynch," Grimes said. "He is a manufacturer and Huzza's business partner."

While the hundred or so spectators in the yard gathered near the platform, Lynch, a white-haired gentleman with rounded shoulders and a ruddy complexion, stood patiently. The hush that fell over the crowd descended slowly, and although he was content to wait, Huzza felt no such compunction. Climbing the platform's steps, the inventor called out in greeting and thanked everyone for attending.

Then he positioned himself to the right and slightly in front of his partner and said, "Mr. Lynch planned to begin these proceedings with technical specifications and to bore you with the details of how the *Bright Benny* works."

"Not bore," Lynch interjected defensively. "Inform."

"His intent might be to inform," Huzza allowed with a sly grin, "but the result will be to bore. I know of what I speak, for I have spent many hours listening to him review our finances, and all of them have been tedious."

Beside him, Lynch smiled to show he was unbothered by these comments, and yet Bea noted a resigned acceptance in the slant of his shoulders that indicated he was frequently teased in this manner.

As if to affirm her thought, Huzza quickly added that he was only jesting. "Mr. Lynch is a godsend to me, and if it were not for his timely money, I would have given up my dream after my last attempt ended in failure and returned to Scotland to dig canals. Yes, I know, I am not supposed to discuss it so blatantly. Mr. Lynch, in his speech, was to make subtle reference to our need for investors if we are going to fulfill our vision of replacing every low-pressure steam engine in the country with our vastly superior high-pressure model while also constructing the world's first tramroad for passengers, not coal. But I say 'bah!' to being subtle. We would like your money, so please give us your money. After you see the amazing *Bright Benny* in action, I think you will be begging me to take your guineas. And have no fear: I will accept!"

Lynch laughed along with the audience, but Bea could tell that he was not amused. He had prepared a lovely little speech that he would not get to use, for Huzza was now inviting the spectators to join him as he demonstrated the wonders of his marvelous invention. He urged the entire throng to enter the foundry, but the space was too tight and Lynch begged the onlookers to arrange themselves along the large circular track.

"But not too close!" he rushed to add earnestly. "It is for your own safety. Embers flying out of the chimney can spark and catch fire. We have a fire brigade standing by in case anything goes awry, but everything will be fine if you keep a good distance from the track."

Few heeded his suggestion, instead following Huzza into the foundry, where the *Bright Benny* now spewed puffs of smoke. The blond-haired man continued to feed the firebox, and the inventor removed him from his position so that he could take over the task.

As the other man stepped down from the platform, Huzza introduced him as Martin Rhodes. "Do give him a round of applause, for he is the true hero of the piece. For several years, he has painstakingly helped me fabricate my designs. He has been beside me for my many failures, and if you are reluctant to give money to me, then I urge you to give it to Mr. Rhodes. I assure you, he has worked hard for it. Indeed, he is far too important for menial work like feeding the firebox, which is why I will do it myself. You see how humble I am? Does that not endear me to you all? I am sure you want to give your money to a humble man," he said, then looked around with exaggerated interest. "Where is Mr. Lynch to scold me for talking about money again? Oh, I see. He is in the yard scolding the crowd for standing too close to the track."

In fact, Lynch was now at the entrance of the foundry, exhorting people to please step back. He enlisted the help of the firemen in his endeavor, and slowly the crowd moved away. As Bea turned to follow her uncle to the far side of the yard, she saw Huzza refuse the use of Mr. Rhodes's gloves.

"How bold he is," Flora said admiringly, "performing such a filthy task whilst bedecked in white. I would not have the courage."

Russell rolled his eyes and said Huzza would be able to buy a dozen new tailcoats with all the money he would raise from investors. Scoffing at the implied censure of this response, Flora insisted that the inventor's candor was commendable.

While her cousins squabbled, Bea considered Huzza's ambition to build a tramroad to the beach at Whitstable and decided it was very clever. Hauling coal from Middleton to Leeds was all very well, but its utility was limited. There were only so many tons of coal and coke one could extract from the earth before nothing remained.

All mines were emptied eventually.

But people desiring a holiday by the seashore—that was an inexhaustible resource.

If Huzza could contrive to get them there en masse at a price they could readily afford, then the sky was the limit.

And the adventure!

What a wonderful way to go on holiday, via steam carriage.

As Lynch continued to move the crowd back to a safe distance from the machine, Bea felt her anticipation grow and imagined describing the scene to Kesgrave, with its cheerful banners and merry music and air of excitement. He would be amused, to be sure, by the irrepressible absurdity of her relations, from her uncle's enthusiastic exploitation of his wife's absence to Russell's vexing determination to mispronounce the inventor's name. But it was the innovation itself, the leap forward in knowledge and what was possible in the world, that he would find compelling.

Steam—that wisp of a thing that wafted out of kettles—creating power equal to the strength of a horse.

No, not one horse.

Many horses.

It was all so remarkable.

Ah, but maybe he would not find it fascinating at all, she thought, as another notion occurred to her.

Perhaps for someone like the Duke of Kesgrave it was all very mundane, these mechanical improvements that augured fantastical things for the future.

With his vast wealth and innumerable properties, he might already own his own plateway somewhere in the north, attended by an engine of relatively primitive design. It was possible, she thought, for the dowager had intimated that the Matlocks owned land in half the counties in England. It was

not difficult to conceive a parcel containing coal to be extricated and brought to market.

The truth was, she had no idea.

Despite the intimacy of their bond, there was still so much she did not know about her own husband.

His parents, for example.

After carefully avoiding the subject for several weeks, she had finally asked him about his childhood and discovered an assortment of disturbing details about his upbringing: nasty father, grasping mother, murderous uncle.

But the problem was not limited to his past, for aspects of his present eluded her as well. Recently, he had made a significant investment in a theater company without her having the least notion of it—and she had been sitting next to him while he did so.

That she had failed to comprehend his intentions at the Particular continued to bedevil her, for it meant she had underestimated him. Even holding him in high esteem, she had still assumed he had played fast and loose with the theater owner's expectations. It had not struck her as malicious because they were in pursuit of a murderer and access to the company had to be gained in the most efficient way possible.

She had felt bad for Miss Drake and wished it could be different but had decided her disappointment was a reasonable price to pay to bring a killer to justice.

But Kesgrave had decided it was not.

He had negotiated the deal in good faith and would abide by it.

What had Lady Abercrombie recently said about him?

You are so very good, Damien. You have always been decent, but since aligning with Bea you have become good.

Although her observation might have been accurate, the countess attributed the change to the wrong source. It was not Bea who exerted an improving influence over the duke but the situations to which an association with her had exposed him.

She had merely provided him with more opportunities to demonstrate his goodness.

Considering how easily Kesgrave had invested in the Particular, Bea thought Grimes was perhaps correct to be wary of the duke taking an interest in the *Bright Benny*. He could indeed buy the entire enterprise on a whim and leave his steward to sort out the details.

Bea smiled as she pictured Mr. Stephens cataloguing all the tools and machinery in the foundry. Given his penchant for detail, he would probably relish the assignment.

A gust of wind blew through the yard as Rhodes, accepting the futility of removing Huzza from his post at the firebox, joined the firemen in moving onlookers away from the building. Not satisfied with the track as a marker, he pushed the audience back toward the fence that encased the courtyard. A few minutes later, pleased with the arrangement, Lynch called to the musicians, who began to play "Heart of Oak." Then, over the noise of both the band and the *Bright Benny*, he made the prepared remarks that had been preempted by his partner.

"What is he saying?" Flora asked. "I cannot hear him from here. We are too far back. This distance was not necessary at the Tarwich demonstration."

"Now he is telling us the capacity of the boiler," Bea said with amusement. "Previously, he told us the radius of each of the wheels."

"Boring technical specifications," Russell said with disgust. "When will the demonstration start? I am tired of waiting."

"Presently," Uncle Horace said as Lynch gave the length of

the flue in inches. "Huzza just took hold of the steering lever."

"Ooh, I think it is beginning now," Flora said, clapping her hands excitedly.

"Huzzah!" Russell said.

And the foundry exploded.

Chapter Four

The ringing, the black.

The ringing, the black.

It was all Bea could hear or see, a dull *ding, ding, ding*, chiming with sickening repetition deep inside her head, and the smoke-filled air, both bilious and billowing, briefly blocked every ray of light so she did not know in which direction to run.

So she stood there as still as a statue.

Like the sphinx on the bank of the Nile, she thought, suddenly feeling as though she were made of sand and might blow away grain by grain.

Daylight returned—swiftly, starkly, as if someone had tugged open the drapes in a dank cellar.

All at once sunshine was everywhere, and Bea could see people yelling even if she could not hear them over the ringing in her ears.

Blankly, she stared, struggling to pull herself together, to gather up the granules that comprised her arms and her legs and her torso.

And then Russell was there, grabbing her shoulders and shaking her gently as he spoke in a stranger's voice, garbled and drowned.

Then abruptly, it changed, as if they had emerged from a deep well of water and shuddered with breath. "Bea! Bea! Are you all right?"

He was composed, she thought.

Her cousin Russell, the scapegrace of the family, thoroughly composed while the rest of the world screamed in terror.

That, too, was odd and confusing.

Even so, she understood enough to respond. "I am, yes, I am fine."

Clearly relieved, he grasped her shoulders in a display of bracing comfort and said, "Good. That is good."

What a thing that was—a reassuring squeeze from Russell!

"You see to Flora," he said with unprecedented authority, "while I look after my father."

The shrill ringing dulled to a piercing trill as she turned to her cousin, whose pale face was half hidden by her right hand, which clutched her mouth as if holding in a shriek. Bea's stomach roiled at the expression of despair, and following Russell's lead, she clasped the girl by the shoulders and noted they trembled.

Murmuring softly, Bea assured Flora that everything was all right. "You are unharmed. I am unharmed. Russell is unharmed. Your father"—a glance in the other direction confirmed his condition—"is unharmed. We are all unharmed."

As she spoke, Bea realized the words were true. Everyone around her, the scores of spectators, were without injury. She saw chaos and smoke, panic and terror, but no blood, no bodies. The foundry itself still stood.

At least the section of it she could make out through the smoky haze and rushing swarm of bodies.

But the damage could not be minimal.

No, the destruction from a blast of that intensity had to be immense.

Huzza was gone.

His body ripped to shreds by shards of iron and wood and steam so hot it annihilated everything in its path.

With a look at Flora, who was now reassuring herself that her father was all right, she took a step toward the building, then another and another until she was halfway across the yard. Her gaze was focused straight ahead, on the wide entrance to the foundry, of which she had only glimpses.

Was that the front of the *Bright Benny* or a fire engine?

She narrowed her gaze just as a gust blew thick smoke in her face, obscuring her view, and she ducked down to get underneath the plume. From her low vantage point, she looked up and noted the skylights of the foundry were intact. The wall to the right, the one closest to where Huzza had stood, was burning and firemen frantically pumped water to extinguish it.

The wind changed directions, and she rose to her feet, drawing ever closer to the scene, still uncertain of what she was seeing.

It was the remains of the *Bright Benny,* she thought, an abomination of twisted metal and charred wood and cinders.

Heaps of cinders.

Was Huzza among the cinders?

Bea felt a wave of nausea overcome her as she tripped over the track.

About to topple over, she found herself steadied by Grimes, who looked at her with a mixture of shock and concern.

"Your grace!" he cried in alarm. "The exit is behind you.

You must leave at once. This is no place for a lady. Or indeed any person. Come!"

In her head, she argued.

Stridently, silently, she protested the heavy-handed treatment, for she was not a child to be bear-led from danger. If she wanted to inspect the damage wrought by the horrible accident, then that was her prerogative.

She was an adult fully grown!

And yet Bea knew it was childish, the impulse to see more, for there was nothing she could add to the awfulness, nothing she could do to mitigate it. Without any purpose, her interest was mere curiosity, which made her every bit as ghoulish as Mrs. Norton had accused her of being all those weeks ago.

She did not belong there.

None of them did.

"Bea!" Flora screeched, her voice shrill with relief as she grabbed her cousin's wrist.

"I found her wandering aimlessly," Grimes explained.

"No, I was not—" Bea began, then broke off because the alternative sounded worse. Instead, she thanked him for his assistance.

A moment later, Uncle Horace was at her side as well, his own visage quite pale as he examined her in the hazy light. "Thank God you're all right. Kesgrave would have thrashed me within an inch of my life if anything worse had happened to you," he said, then turned around to call to his son. "She is here! We can leave."

Russell declared himself relieved as well, which troubled Bea a great deal.

What a fright she must look if her entire family was worried about her.

"I am all right," she said, promptly earning herself an

impatient pish-posh from Flora, who insisted that none of them were all right because Mr. Huzza had just disintegrated before their eyes.

Uncle Horace concurred, echoing her *pish-posh*.

Having never heard the patriarch of the Hyde-Clare clan use such juvenile language, Beatrice burst into laughter. Her cousins quickly followed.

Deeply concerned now for all four of them, Grimes urged the small group to leave at once.

Bea, the ringing in her ears subsiding to a hum, agreed there was no reason to linger. They would only get in the way of people who could actually help. She slipped her arm through her uncle's and began to lead them to the exit.

It was not easy, weaving through the crowd of spectators, who moved in unexpected ways as they tried to figure out what to do next. The majority settled on leaving as well, creating a glut of bodies at the gate, and it was several minutes before they drew near enough to pass through.

Finally, they were outside, and the relief Bea felt just stepping onto the pavement was immense. The fence was barely a barrier—she could still hear the shrill clamor of the courtyard—but the acrid smell was not as intense.

She drew her first steady breath in what felt like hours.

Reasonably, she knew it could have barely been fifteen minutes.

The shuddering boom of the explosion had torn through the quiet neighborhood, and a throng gathered near the entrance, their necks craned as they tried to get a glimpse of the catastrophe. One man threw his elbow into Bea's side as he shoved past her, while another grabbed her sleeve to halt her progress.

"Something 'orrible 'appened, didn't it?" he asked, his voice a growl of suspicion as he glared at her. His breath, hot against her cheek, smelled of onions. "I knew something 'orrible would 'appen. It goes against nature, using steam to replace 'orses."

"On the contrary," Russell said sternly, stepping forward and putting his body squarely in front of his cousin's, "harnessing the power of steam is using the gift nature has bestowed. Now unhand the lady so that we may be on our way."

The authority in his tone was undeniable, and it was impossible to say who was more taken aback by it: the man who accosted Bea, Uncle Horace or Russell himself.

Regardless, the stranger responded to it at once, dropping his hand, lowering his head and issuing a fractured apology.

Russell, who was inclined to savor his small victory, watched the man disappear into the press of people gathered at the gate and said, "I trust he will learn some manners."

Flora rolled her eyes but refrained from comment and continued toward the street to find their carriage. Amid the confusion, locating it was no minor accomplishment, and by the time she settled into the conveyance, Bea was ready to admit that the hum in her ears was really an exasperating ache.

Inhaling so much smoke had not helped the matter.

Her relatives, either suffering from a similar malady or finding the events too upsetting to discuss, said very little during the journey to Berkeley Square. Russell commented on the weather, which appeared to have taken a turn for the worse, then fell silent.

As they passed through the gates at Kesgrave House, her uncle spoke for the first time, announcing he would accompany her inside to apologize to the duke for wantonly exposing her to danger.

Baffled by the sentiment, Bea refused to allow for the

necessity, as there had been absolutely nothing wanton about the exposure. Having attended a previous demonstration of steam power, Uncle Horace had every reason to believe the presentation would be a calm and impressive display of technical innovation.

It was a tragedy, she insisted, precisely because nobody could have predicted it.

An ornery expression overtook her uncle's face, and Bea stiffened her shoulders to argue further even as the throbbing in her head intensified.

She was fully supportive of her family taking responsibility for their actions, especially the twenty years during which she was treated with little affection, but she had no desire to see them assume responsibility for things over which they had no control.

Seeing Bea's exhaustion or perhaps feeling his own, Uncle Horace fell back in his seat and said he would pay a call on her the next day to make sure she had recovered from their ordeal. "You are far too pale for my comfort."

It was, Bea thought, a particularly amusing observation considering that description could apply to all of them, and smiling gently, she advised her uncle to consult a mirror when he returned to Portman Square. "We are fortunate my aunt is not here to see it, are we not?"

Uncle Horace shook his head. "Fortune has nothing to do with it. If my wife were home, we would never have attended a demonstration of a prototype engine—which is how I know the exposure *was* wanton. Tell Kesgrave to expect a note from me this afternoon."

As avuncular affection was still a novelty for the former Beatrice Hyde-Clare, she lowered her eyes and nodded, touched, she realized, by his determination to hold himself to account.

"Yes, uncle," she added meekly.

Russell, displaying an equal level of concern for her, climbed out of the carriage and provided escort to the front door. It was a sweet gesture, although unnecessary as the distance was barely a full yard, but she did not have the heart to quibble. His composure in the immediate aftermath of the explosion was unprecedented, and she remained deeply grateful for it, which she told him as they approached the steps.

Startled, he blushed at her kind words and said with all due modesty that he was just glad everyone was safe. "That is, I mean, everyone in our party. I know not everyone at the demonstration is safe," he added quickly, displaying his mother's tendency to reconsider his words as soon as they were spoken. And just like with her, the color in his cheeks deepened as his embarrassment at the slight faux pas grew. "Mr. Huzza obviously. He suffered the worst fate possible, and I cannot say with any degree of confidence that Mr. Rhodes is not gravely harmed. There might be other casualties as well because I do not know the state of all the attendees. Should I know?" He paused for a moment to consider the question, then shook his head, deciding firmly in the negative. His first duty was to her and Flora's safety, for they were but frail and delicate women who had to be protected from the world.

"Well, no, not *you,*" he said with particular emphasis. "You are not delicate, fending off the Earl of Bentham while he tried to smother you to death in your sitting room. There is nothing frail about you. You are a Trojan! Which is not to say you are mannish or unfeminine. You are no Incomparable, for your features are not at all balanced like Miss Petworth's and your shoulders are strikingly broad, but you have a certain appeal that is...is...appealing."

He finished his rambling speech on a sputter of uncertainty, and unlike his mother, sought to correct the situation by openly acknowledging it. "If I may, Bea, I would like to amend my answer to say thank you."

Although tempted to laugh, she kept her features even as she acknowledged his reply and advised him to have a bracing glass of port in a quiet room when he arrived at home.

"The same to you, my dear," he said before bidding her good-bye.

Bea assured him she would as she watched him skip down the steps, but upon entering Kesgrave House she decided alcohol would do little to improve her headache.

The quiet room, however, enticed her greatly, and as she passed through the marble entry hall, she tried to recall if she had any appointments for the afternoon.

No, no, of course not, for she and the duke were in mourning. Although Lord Myles's death was not regretted by either of them, they had enough respect for social custom to withdraw from gaiety for the length of time deemed appropriate.

Ordinarily, an uncle required three months' sequestration, but she assumed an allowance would be made for a nephew whose relation had arranged for his violent and premature death.

The *ton* was rigid in its codes but not wholly unreasonable.

Relieved to have no obligations, she greeted Marlow as she passed him on the way to the staircase and asked him to send up a tray with food.

But the thought of eating anything with the acrid smell of smoke clinging to her roiled her stomach and she requested a bath be drawn.

Although it was evident to anyone who looked at her—or inhaled her scent—that she had undergone an ordeal of one sort or another, the butler revealed no curiosity as he replied, "Yes, your grace."

"Thank you," she murmured, grasping the handrail as she began to climb the steps.

Her exhaustion, which had been faint but oppressive when she entered the house, overwhelmed her as she arrived at the landing. Wearily, she allowed her maid to lead her to the dressing room, where Dolly removed her garments with gentle fingers, seemingly incapable of believing, despite her mistress's assurances, that she was unharmed.

Fresh from her bath, Bea retrieved her book from the table in the sitting room to read while awaiting the delivery of the tray. She knew it would be sent up soon, and she did not want to fall asleep during the interval. Eschewing the alluring comforts of the bed, she settled herself on the settee and marveled again at the extent of her fatigue. It did not seem right that the explosion, which was, by any account, a horrific event, should make her so tired. It was a horrible thing that happened near her, not to her.

Bentham's attack in the sitting room, by contrast, had been perpetrated directly against her person, and afterward she had maintained her ability not only to keep her eyes open but also to ask her would-be murderer a series of pertinent questions.

Determinedly, she opened *The Life and Death of Cardinal Wolsey* to where she had left off that morning, just a few pages past the prologue, and forced herself to finish three paragraphs before allowing her lashes to flutter shut.

A few minutes' rest, she thought, before Joseph carried in the tray.

Opening her eyes a short while later, she was disconcerted to discover it was in fact a long while later, for now she was in the bed and the sun no longer poured in through the room's southern exposure. Disappearing behind a copse of trees at the far end of the garden, it had begun its steady descent.

Bewildered, she stared at the tray, which sat on the night

table, a half-finished rout cake perched on a plate toward the edge.

Had she taken a few bites before falling asleep?

Surely, she would recall eating before her nap.

She had not been *that* tired.

The duke, then, she thought, tilting her head toward the sitting area and meeting his amused gaze over the newspaper, which he held firmly in his grasp. Idly, he lowered the broadsheet to the cushion next to him and rose. "If I ever doubted that I come in second in your affection to your beloved rout cakes, the look of longing on your face as you contemplated the half-empty platter would remove it entirely."

Bea, shifting her position so that she sat upright, expressed surprise at his need for confirmation. "I thought for sure the hierarchy was readily apparent to everyone. After all, there is no office of Kesgrave enjoyment."

His eyes gleamed with delight as he settled one knee on the bed next to her, leaned forward and brushed a stray lock behind her ears. "Oh, but isn't there?" he asked softly, seductively, pressing a kiss against her cheek, her jaw, her shoulder. "Is this not it?"

In response to his query, Bea had no reply—and not because the touch of his lips undermined her ability to think clearly. Desire had the disconcerting ability to cloud her brain, to be sure, but its effects were not so severe that she could not recognize a valid argument when its fingers toyed with the bodice of her gown.

It had been revelatory to discover there were some activities more wonderful than rout cakes, a good book and silence by which to enjoy them.

Kesgrave, shifting his weight forward, settled on the mattress next to her as his lips traveled up her neck to capture her own.

No longer stunned by his ardor, she was still baffled by it.

Six years of languishing on the fringes of society had been instructive, and the lesson she had learned over and over was that beauty was the only power a woman possessed. It was the most important thing she could be, and while Bea did not tremble in awe at Incomparables like Flora did, she certainly felt overshadowed by them.

Standing next to a diamond of the first water like Lady Victoria, she might as well have been a lump of coal.

And yet for all her lumpishness, she was not massively surprised by Kesgrave's ability to look past her drab appearance to the nimble ember flickering inside, for there was now, in retrospect, an air of inevitability about it. Accustomed to the best of everything, he had grown bored with perfection.

Of course he had, for there was an unremitting sameness about it, like a pattern that endlessly repeated, and the Duke of Kesgrave already owned the finest collection of delftware in the country.

No, what had amazed Bea was the way he succeeded in bending reality to his will, somehow perceiving a woman of great beauty when he beheld her plain features.

She had not believed him, not at first, when he insisted her impish grin was the single most beautiful thing he had ever seen. She had assumed he was being kind or appeasing her vanity or spouting the foolish nonsense of a besotted lover, but six weeks of marriage had convinced her otherwise.

Inexplicably, it was the truth.

The inner light had become an outer glow, and when he held her like this, the weight of his body pressed against hers, it flared into a conflagration.

And that was the thing that confounded her—how his desire for her always felt all-consuming. It burned hotly, intensely, with a feverish determination of which the prim and polite Miss Hyde-Clare had seen no hide nor hair during her many years of extensive reading. Having found no inkling of the pleasures of the marital bed, she marveled at the veiling of such wonders, for they seemed well suited for poetry, and she succumbed now as she succumbed often, giddy with happiness and grateful for the absurd machinations of fate.

Chapter Five

As eager as Bea was to discuss the steam carriage explosion that ended Mr. Huzza's life, she realized the least she could do was allow Kesgrave's breathing to return to normal before introducing the topic.

How long that would take, she did not actually know, for she had not made a study of it during their marriage. Usually following such activities, she was pleasingly limber and content to luxuriate in the embrace of her husband.

In truth, she had no idea with what speed the racing of her own heart subsided.

A few minutes, perhaps.

That was not an intolerable amount of time to wait.

Except now that she was rested and her head finally clear, she was unsettled by how little she comprehended the events of the afternoon.

She had a firm grasp on the basic elements of the incident: The pressure in the boiler had grown to an intolerable degree, causing the engine's tank to blow apart and end Mr. Huzza's existence.

But the details eluded her.

Part of the problem was how quickly it had happened: Only a fraction of a second separated Mr. Huzza from obliteration.

One moment everything was fine—the music, the sunshine, the air of anticipation—and the next it was not.

Smoke, noise and terror were everywhere at once, choking the courtyard, and Russell was urging them to leave, and Grimes was urging them to leave, and every instinct Bea had was urging them to leave.

And then time had altered again, seemingly slowing down as they sluggishly made their way through the dense crowd, trudging out to the pavement, where another crush of people met them.

But the disorienting pace of the incident contributed only partly to her confusion. The larger component was her lack of familiarity with the subject. If only she knew enough about steam engines to picture for herself how the event had unfolded.

And the fusible plug—that was another perplexing mystery.

From the way Uncle Horace described it, the new valve was supposed to resolve once and for all the various hazards that bedeviled high-pressure steam.

Obviously, her relative had been unduly optimistic in his outlook.

As had Mr. Huzza.

She recalled now the way the plug was supposed to have worked, by melting when the temperature inside the boiler grew too hot, thereby releasing the pressure inside the tank.

Was the problem, then, that the plug did not melt or that something else blocked the hole after it did?

It had struck her as such an ingenious solution, simple and infallible, and yet the *Bright Benny* had exploded like a bomb on the field of battle.

Boom.

Bea shuddered, hearing the explosive roar sound again in her ears, and she wondered if the duke would have any insight. He knew a great deal about a surprising number of things, usually in stultifying detail, and his wide range of interests had been useful in her previous investigations.

The still, for example.

Examining the swirling scribbles made by Lord Myles, she had had no notion she was looking at a device modified to produce gin more efficiently than its predecessor.

But Kesgrave had.

One glance and he perceived immediately at what he was looking.

Recognizing its potential, he had charged his steward with submitting a patent application so that its inventor could retain ownership of his innovation—although the man in question would not have the pleasure of spending any of the profits earned from it. At that very moment, Tyne was confined to a dank, dark cell in Newgate to answer for his crimes. But he had parents who lived cheaply in Biddlesden Street and would be grateful for the funds, and there was a younger sister as well. Currently, she worked as a scullery maid in Mount Street, but with the proceeds from her brother's modified column still, she could train in a profession.

Bea's impatience to discuss the explosion with the duke, however, did not stem from a desire to learn information from him.

Naturally no, for that was the purpose of books.

Rather, she had discovered during the course of their acquaintance that reviewing the facts with Kesgrave improved her understanding of them.

Possibly, it was just the effect of saying the words out loud or maybe it was the result of hearing them said back to her.

Regardless, conversing with the duke had the unexpected benefit of clarifying her own thoughts.

And that was why she was so eager now.

Kesgrave, unaware of her avidity—which was, she conceded, fair enough, as he had exerted himself quite a bit on her behalf—displayed no interest in rousing himself. He pressed a soft kiss against her collarbone and sighed languidly.

A lovely shiver passed through her at the feel of his lips, and she told herself another minute would not hurt.

After all, it had barely been one.

Shifting slightly, she stretched her arm toward the night table and picked up the forlorn remains of the rout cake. Delivered hours before, it disintegrated in her hand and small pieces dropped onto the sheet.

Uh-oh, Kesgrave was perfectly beastly about crumbs in bed.

Brushing frantically at them—yes, she knew that only spread out the problem, not solved it—she bit into the pastry and then squealed.

"You villain!" she cried, twisting free of his embrace as she raised herself fully and pointed accusingly. "There is not a hint of pineapple in that cake!"

Without revealing even the smallest trace of contrition, he smiled.

He presented a picture.

Oh, indeed he did: the delighted grin, the amused blue eyes, the tousled blond hair, the broad chest rippling with muscle as he sat up in the bed.

Nevertheless, he answered the charge soberly, swearing on his grandmother's life he had stopped eating the rout cake the moment he realized it contained no pineapple. "I left the rest for you."

Far from appeased by this explanation, she pointed out

that more than half the pastry had been consumed. "You are a man of privilege who has enjoyed every advantage wealth and breeding have to offer and can list all fourteen ships—"

"Fifteen," he interjected.

"—that fought against Napoleon in the Battle of the Nile in order of their appearance and yet it somehow took you three or four bites to discover the rout cake was without pineapple flecks, chunks or slabs?"

Although her tone dripped with both suspicion and contempt, Kesgrave's grin widened as he replied, "I do not think you properly understand what it means to be a duke. It comes with land and a coronet, not a heightened sense of taste."

She scorned his excuse. "I had barely a nibble and noticed at once."

"Ah, but you, my dear, are a remarkable creature," he said, his voice growing softer as he threaded his fingers through hers, "which I have just finished demonstrating. But I am happy to repeat the performance if you are in any doubt."

Her heart tripped lightly in reply, for in fact it was he who was remarkable, even with the worrying limitations of his palate, and she was tempted to succumb.

Always, she wanted him, and the sickening boom of Mr. Huzza's fate was not going anywhere. It would be there, in the back of her mind, when her senses returned.

But the reverse was true as well, and she was genuinely discomforted by the gaps in her understanding. Furthermore, she had already done the hard work of waiting. If she submitted to the duke's attentions now, she would have to start counting the seconds all over again.

Consequently, she pulled back, freeing her hand from his as she took another bite of the deliciously bland rout cake. Then she lifted the teapot and discovered it was still full. After so many hours, the brew was cool to the touch but nevertheless quenching, which was welcome after her long nap and delightful awakening.

Kesgrave regarded her silently as the liquid touched her lips, then rose from the bed and disappeared into the adjacent room. Returning a few moments later, he held out her dressing gown, which she slipped into. Then he tied the belt snugly at the waist, pulled her toward him and held her for several long seconds, his grip perhaps a little tighter than intended.

His tone was gentle, however, as he spoke. "I suppose it was very awful."

Bea, startled that he knew the details of her afternoon, recalled his disconcerting ability early in their courtship to suddenly appear where she was, as if blessed with omniscience. The explanation for his presence then was always mundane, if sometimes impressively deductive, and such was the case now. Her uncle had promised to send around a note.

Clearly, he had.

With a nod of agreement, she stepped back from his embrace and led him to the settee so she could see his face while they conversed. Tossing the newspaper to the side—well, onto the rug because the sofa was not large enough to accommodate two adults and a broadsheet—she sat down. Kesgrave retrieved the periodical from the floor and placed it on the night table next to the teapot. Then he settled onto the cushion next to her.

Adoring his meticulous soul, she waited a moment for a lecture on respecting the manifold responsibilities of the upstairs maid and when it did not come, said, "Russell recovered his wits first."

Fully cognizant of the improbability of that development, the duke lifted a curious eyebrow. "Did he?"

"While I was contemplating life as a sphinx, he regained his faculties, then turned his attention to recalling me to

mine," she replied, still confounded by her inability to remember the moments immediately following the blast.

There was the roar of the explosion and then...and then...

But her mind remained frustratingly blank.

Her memories picked up again with the ringing in her ears and the glare of sunlight through the smoke.

"For future reference, shaking me by the shoulders roughly works well," she said. She made the observation lightly but in fact was quite serious. Having lost the ability to think clearly once, she thought it wise to allow for the possibility that it could happen again. "Russell did not have to do it above three or four times."

Kesgrave, noting it dutifully, suggested that perhaps the more pragmatic solution was to keep away from exploding steam engines.

It amused her deeply, the confidence of his response, as if Providence were an unruly dog to be brought to heel by stubborn practicality.

Obviously, it could not, but his outlook was not inexplicable, for his standing afforded him an unusual amount of control over everyday events.

And yet even a duchy had its limits.

Earnestly, she promised to keep a safe distance from all steam engines, even little toy models that contained no internal mechanism. Then, gently prodding him, she added, "But tell me, your grace, what shall we do about all the other devices that may fail to function properly? Carriage wheels that snap off their axels mid-journey, for example, and candles, which have a troubling tendency to fall over and cause fires. Or horses. Even the tamest among them is still a wild animal at heart and could behave in an unreliable—some might say *explosive*—way at any minute."

"You are mocking me," he said, seemingly unbothered by the prospect.

Nevertheless, she shook her head and insisted she was not. "No, your grace, not even a little. It just struck me as an opportune moment to remind you that it is impossible to account for every outcome. I take full responsibility for the reckless decisions that have endangered my life, many of which we have discussed before and I am happy to catalog again, now if necessary, but I cannot accept blame for random occurrences, however tragic and awful. Sometimes terrible things happen, and it is nobody's fault. Attempting to anticipate them is a fool's game, and the one thing you are not is a fool."

Even so, there was a condescending edge to her tone, as if explaining something to a young child, and she would not have been surprised if he took offense.

Instead, he instructed her to ask him about Robert Johnson.

Baffled, she stared at him. "Who is Robert Johnson?"

"I have no idea," he replied.

Stranger and stranger, Bea thought, for not only was it unusual for the duke to introduce non sequiturs to their conversation but he also purported to know everything. "A remarkable development, to be sure, but I am certain Mr. Stephens will be happy to rectify the situation if you assign him the task."

"It would be an easy assignment, for there is an article about him in the paper today," Kesgrave said. "I know this because I have been staring at it for the better part of the past two hours. He is a Whig who aspires to be prime minister, at least according to the *Gazette,* but I have been unable to digest a single word because I have been sitting on this settee contemplating the vagaries of fate."

"Well, you have managed to digest one word if you know Mr. Johnson's party affiliation," she pointed out.

But the duke was in no mood for humor.

"From almost the very beginning, I have been troubled by your recklessness, the way you bound heedlessly into danger, determined to investigate murders that have nothing to do with you," he said smoothly, calmly, as if they were indeed discussing the career prospects of a Whig politician in whom he had a passing interest. "I sought to curb this habit by gaining your pledge to stop doing it and we both know how that turned out. But then I realized that you were not solely the problem, for much of the danger to which you were exposed came through me. The events of this afternoon, however, have forced me to confront a far starker truth: The world itself is the problem."

Bea smiled faintly at the allegation, for only a man accustomed to having control would seek to level blame for the lack of it.

Before she could comment to that effect, he added, "I do not like it, Bea."

It was a petulant thing to say.

Even though he spoke in that matter-of-fact way, as if noting the color of the drapes or thanking a servant for delivering a tray, it sounded childish and churlish, like a little boy refusing to submit to a bath.

A smile rose immediately to her lips, and try as she might, she could not suppress it.

If she had had the merest inkling that this moment would one day exist during that interminable dinner party at Lakeview Hall when he was holding forth on one tedious subject after another, how different their history would be. Incapable of holding herself back, she would have mortified her family and secured a spot in an asylum by hurling herself bodily at him.

As it was, it was extremely difficult not to lean forward and kiss him. She resisted because it was clear to her that he still had more to say.

"I have had very little worry in my life," he continued mildly. "The only person I have ever cared deeply about is my grandmother, and my concern has always been tempered by knowledge of her age. I bedevil her constantly about taking care of herself and heeding her physician's advice because I love her and want her to be around as long as possible. Be that as it is, I am reconciled to the inevitable, for she is old and has perhaps a dozen years left if I am lucky. But now there is you."

How resigned he sounded!

Bea's airy sigh was full of exaggerated pity. "But now there is me."

He did not rise to the bait and merely shook his head. "Realizing that I can lose you at any moment to a stupid and senseless accident is a thoroughly unpleasant revelation for me. I never imagined I could feel this way, and if I had had an inkling of what was in store, I would never have knocked on your window."

Confused again, she said, "My window?"

Now he smiled faintly as he reminded her of his visit to her bedchamber during their stay in the Lake District. "It was the evening you discovered the truth about Mrs. Otley's affair with Wilson. At dinner, you fluttered your eyelashes wildly at me to indicate you had something important to share, so I climbed up the tree outside your window to discover what it was."

She remembered the evening in question.

Oh, yes, she did, for it was one of her most cherished memories. In the quiet of the night and in the glow of the firelight, they had discussed suspects in the spice trader's murder with the congenial accord of colleagues.

The unprecedented show of respect had warmed her heart.

Indeed, it warmed her heart still.

She doubted, however, that Kesgrave was referring to that amicable exchange. His experience was too broad for such an unremarkable conversation to make an impression.

Nevertheless, something else had struck him as memorable from that night.

And it involved the window.

Fascinated, she said, "And that was the moment that sealed your fate? Perched on a branch outside my window?"

"You were reading *The Vicar of Wakefield,*" he replied.

Bea laughed, recalling how she had struggled to finish that tiresome novel, with its heavy-handed morality and clumsy plotting. "*Reading* is a generous term. *Contemptuously slogging through* is more accurate."

"Yes, I know," he said.

"How could you?" she asked, taken aback by his conviction. "I have never shared my opinion of the book with anyone, as I did not think it was worth the breath it would require."

"The expression on your face," he explained. "Your lip was curled disdainfully, and you kept raising your eyes to the ceiling as if requesting divine assistance to continue."

This, too, was startling, for she had not imagined him lingering on the tree outside her room for more than the time it took to settle himself safely on the limb. "I would not have taken you for a Peeping Tom, your grace."

"No," he said softly, "me neither. And yet even as I raised my hand to tap on the glass, I found myself curiously transfixed by your expression. Perched on that branch, I wanted to know what you were thinking. I wanted to know it so badly, Bea, that when I returned home, I read *The Vicar of Wakefield* so that I may converse with you about it."

Thoroughly nonplussed, she stared at him.

"I even decided in advance what I was going to say to you, which I had not done since my first year at Oxford and was trying to impress my classics tutor with my erudite opinions," he continued, his lips twitching at the admission. "I did not comprehend yet what it meant, you understand, the desire to know your thoughts. I believed it was intellectual curiosity. What could that exasperating woman who refused to mind her own bloody business have found so offensive in Goldsmith's famously benign tome that she was compelled to throw it across the room in disgust? Now I recognize it for what it was: The moment the die was cast."

Even back then, she thought, he had been taken with her.

It was almost too stunning to contemplate.

She believed, yes, that there was something fated about their relationship, as if he was always going to succumb to her impish impudence no matter how or when or why they met.

But she knew that was pure fancy, the story a besotted heart told itself.

And yet, listening to his confession, she could not help but believe it was true.

It was a little overwhelming, she thought, surprised by how unsteady she felt. For some reason, realizing just how ordained her relationship with the duke was made her weepy.

Dissolve into a puddle of overwrought tears?

That would never do, no.

Determinedly, she cast about for a wry and sardonic reply, something that hinted at sentiment but did not wallow in it.

Taking aim at his earlier surliness, she arranged her features in a moue of concern and said with excessive sympathy, "You wretched darling, condemned to suffer the indignity of emotion like an ordinary human. How unfair! A man of your stature should by nature be exempt. I am certain this would never have happened if you had had the good sense to marry Lady Victoria. If only you had taken the time to properly consider Tavistock's proposal before rejecting it out of

hand. He did everything in his power to save you from this miserable fate, if you recall."

"I do recall, yes, brat," he said, linking the fingers of his right hand through hers and tugging her closer. "And I will admit now that it was terribly shortsighted of me not to fully contemplate the advantages of a marriage of convenience. Think of all the hours I could have passed in sublime indifference."

"All the aspiring prime ministers with whom you might have become familiar," she said with a regretful sigh.

Kesgrave shuddered in exaggerated horror. "Yet another reason to be grateful Tavistock's plan did not prevail."

"Poor Mr. Johnson, besmirched and maligned for having the misfortune to appear in the *Gazette* on the same day you realize happenstance is a damned inconvenience," she said, settling comfortably against his chest. "He is probably a beguiling creature, and I will be sure to encourage Mrs. Palmer to invite him to her inaugural political salon so that he may become as inured to the opinions of a sensible female as his colleagues."

"As he has been a backbencher for three years, I am sure that disgust is already well honed," Kesgrave replied.

"Yes, because *Parliament* is where men learn to scorn women's opinions," Bea said satirically. "Speaking of opinions, what did you think of *The Vicar of Wakefield* and why did you abandon your plan to subtly raise the topic with me to satisfy your intellectual curiosity?"

"I intended to broach the subject when I called in Portman Square to express my condolences on the loss of your erstwhile betrothed," he replied with lilting amusement.

But Bea protested the description, which she found insulting, and reminded him that Mr. Davies had merely been the love of her life. "I would never be so gauche as to engage myself to a lowly law clerk even in pretense."

"When I arrived at your address, however, I saw you leaving with your maid in tow and followed you to Montague House, where you proceeded to berate a librarian—"

"A preening windbag!" she insisted.

"—into providing you with access to Sir Walter's papers, and that delightful sight was enough to remove all thoughts of Goldsmith from my mind," he explained. "By the time I remembered it, I was too angry at you for breaking your word to me to pay you the compliment of my attention. If you had honored your pledge, you would know that I found the book to be so facile and didactic that in the end I was rooting for Squire Thornhill, who, though a caricature of a villain, was at least interesting."

It was, to be fair, an uncommon opinion, for Mr. Goldsmith's opus had been almost universally admired since its publication, most recently by Edward Mangin, whose essay praised the work at great length, extolling, among other attributes, the delicacy with which the vicar's story was related.

But it was not so radical as to justify the enthusiasm of Bea's response—the seductive curl of her body, the forceful press of her lips—and yet hearing him echo her exact thoughts stirred her in a way she could not control.

It was the Mangin review that made her susceptible, she decided, for it had been particularly fawning.

A performance which contains beauties sufficient to entitle it to almost the highest applause.

Unqualified drivel.

Kesgrave, suspecting the source of her ardor, said, "It was overly sentimental."

Bea pressed firmly against him.

"Excessively melodramatic," he added softly.

She slipped his dressing grown off his shoulders.

"Painfully high-minded," he murmured, his own fingers busily at work.

Given the very low esteem in which the duke held the tome, it was quite some time before she was able to compliment him on his excellent taste in books.

It was another long while later before they discussed the accident that had killed Mr. Huzza. Not wanting to disturb the convivial atmosphere established by their rigorous discussion of literature, she waited until after dinner. Then, comfortably ensconced in her favorite nook in the library, she relayed the details of the horrible explosion.

Kesgrave listened without interrupting, contenting himself with squeezing her hand and grimacing at intervals. He lamented the tragedy, wondered if the fusible plug had failed, agreed that keeping the fact of their attendance from Aunt Vera was the best course of action and revealed that not only did he not own a plateway somewhere in the north, he had never contemplated acquiring such an asset.

"Why?" he asked curiously. "Do you want one? I am sure Stephens could arrange it if you wish to procure one. It is precisely the kind of project he enjoys."

Bea refused the extravagant offer with a dismissive laugh, although in truth she found the reminder of his wealth highly disconcerting. He had a way of doing that, casually making a suggestion available to only a select few with immense wealth —previously, he had advised her to found her own charity organization if she could not find one that met her requirements, as if it were no more remarkable than buying pansies at the market.

Chapter Six

Bea was still thinking about lavish fortunes and grave misfortunes a few hours later as she lay in bed trying to sleep. Well rested from her long afternoon nap, she could not get her mind to settle. Instead, it lurched from topic to topic, from Mr. Grimes's fear that the duke would gobble up all the shares to Russell's unprecedented composure to Uncle Horace's description of the fusible plug.

But always, always, it returned to that deafening bang, the black smoke, the ringing in her ears and Mr. Huzza's decimated corpse.

It simply escaped her comprehension: how he could exist one moment, a single corporeal being, and be incalculable fragments the next.

In her brief career as an investigator, she had stood over several corpses, and although the lack of animation unnerved her, it was a concept she grasped intellectually.

A cadaver was a hollow thing, its soul long gone.

A body rupturing in a flash of heat—that defied her understanding.

She literally could not picture it.

To be sure, she knew it was no great mystery.

Any soldier who had stood on a battlefield while mortars exploded around him had the image irrevocably seared into his head.

Truthfully, it was not that strange.

But this was London, not Belgium, and telling herself that Huzza's death was ordinary did little to quiet her thoughts.

Frustrated, she sighed heavily and threw back the blanket.

It was useless to keep trying to sleep when she was not the least bit tired.

Slipping smoothly out of bed so as not to wake Kesgrave, she wondered where her book was, the one she had been reading when she had fallen asleep earlier. If it had slid onto the floor, Kesgrave would have retrieved it.

On the table, then.

There it is, she thought, as she raised the candle to improve her view. She began to step toward it, then decided she was not interested in finishing the chapter.

Wide awake and fitful, she wanted to discover what she could about steam engines.

Tying her dressing gown firmly around her waist, she put on her slippers and crossed silently to the door.

It was strange, stepping into the corridor at that hour, well after midnight, all by herself. In the weeks since she had taken up residence in Berkeley Square, she had never done it.

She had yet to have cause, for anything she needed was either readily available or easily attained. It astonished her that such a large establishment could function so smoothly—a reaction that was as banal as it was mortifying. If money could secure anything, it was comfort and efficiency.

Reaching the staircase, Bea contemplated who else might be awake. Mr. Stephens, perhaps, for he struck her as the sort of diligent man who would lose track of time while engrossed in a project. Or if he was entering information about soil composition in his ledger, she could imagine him remaining stubbornly at his desk until the last figure had been recorded.

Marlow, she wondered, making one last sweep of the house to ensure all persons and items were in their proper place?

Surely, two a.m. was too late for that?

Maybe if she and Kesgrave had attended an event that evening, such as a ball or the theater, he would still be at his post.

It was also too early for any of the kitchen staff to prepare the fire for breakfast.

Most likely, she was the only one wandering the halls, a condition that had occurred frequently during her years at Welldale House. Visiting the library in the middle of the night was a necessary evil if she desired to find something interesting to read. Otherwise, she was forced to endure the input of her aunt, who always insisted she waste her time on more worthy works, such as a treatise on the civilizing effects of etiquette or the collected sermons of James Fordyce.

Once, in a desperate attempt to distract Bea from a two-volume dissertation on how a nation compiled its wealth, Aunt Vera threw William Beckford's *Vathek* at her.

It was in the original French, which would have made comprehending the contents difficult for her relative, but Bea's command of the language was impeccable and she thoroughly enjoyed the Gothic.

Nevertheless, she snuck back down several hours later to retrieve the books by Adam Smith.

Aunt Vera had never explained why she was so unsettled by her niece's erudition, but Bea knew now that it derived from her belief in Clara Hyde-Clare's moral debasement.

Education and depravity went hand in hand.

Stepping into the library, Bea felt the familiar sense of welcome, even in the darkness. She lit a sconce near the doorway and then one along the wall toward the back left corner, next to a bust of the second duke (or third duke or perhaps the first earl—to be honest, she had been too busy gawking at the splendor of the room to pay attention to the tour).

She had not lived here long enough to familiarize herself with the entire collection but had a general sense of how it was organized. Novels were at the north end of the room, poems and essays to the east, and texts exploring various phenomena, both natural and man-made, were grouped near the duke (or earl).

Thoughtfully, she held up her candle to the top shelf and read the titles to orient herself.

There was Gaspar Schott's *Technica Curiosa.*

"Very good," she murmured, pleased that the compendium of scientific advances indicated she was in the right general area.

Just the wrong time period, she thought, noting the work had been written in 1664.

On the shelf below was *The Century of Inventions* by the Marquess of Worcester. Hopeful, she turned to the title page and saw that had been published almost a decade earlier, in 1655.

That was the wrong direction.

Bea crossed to the other side of the bust and examined the spines.

Continuation of New Experiments by Denis Papin seemed promising.

1680—still too early.

Ah, but next to it was *A Course of Experimental Philosophy* by John Theophilus Desaguliers. It dated to 1734 and contained a chapter on the Newcomen atmospheric engine, which was one of the first successful steam engines.

That had potential.

Curling up in her favorite armchair, she skimmed the table of contents, then the first several chapters until she found an explanation of how the device worked. The atmospheric engine was a relatively simple machine: Coal heated the water, which created steam. The steam rose and entered the chamber beneath the piston, pushing it up. The steam was cooled with water, condensing the steam and creating a vacuum. The atmospheric pressure then pushed the piston down.

The process was illustrated with a series of neat drawings, which made it easy for Bea to picture the action. She could see the piston darting up and down, causing the beam attached to it to likewise bob, which in turn pumped water out of mines.

Over the course of the next few decades, various improvements were made on this basic design, including changes to the valves and the addition of a second chamber.

Confident in her understanding of steam power's central premise, she slid *A Course of Experimental Philosophy* onto the shelf and looked for a book that addressed more recent innovations. James Watt introduced his steam engine in 1776, and Nathan Phillips's model debuted fifteen years later.

She could find no tome that discussed either.

Clearly, an egregious oversight, to which she would alert the estate's librarian immediately.

But that did not help her now, she thought with a heavy sigh as she looked at the next book on the shelf, a slim volume detailing the short life of a steam engine called the *Puffing Devil,* built by Richard Trevithick.

Trevithick, she thought, recognizing the name from their

discussion in the carriage en route to the demonstration. It was his pumping machine that had exploded in Greenwich.

The *Puffing Devil* preceded that accident by two years.

Designed to traverse roads and turnpikes like a coach, it made its debut on December twenty-fourth, 1801, when Trevithick took several friends for a drive on his invention to demonstrate its efficacy. They traveled a good distance, from Fore Street up Camborne Hill and across to Beacon, a small village nearby.

Intrigued by this stunning success that was followed so closely by abject failure, she carried the book to the chair and settled in.

Although not very long—the work comprised barely one hundred pages in total—it provided an in-depth account of Trevithick's history. Briefly, she read about his childhood in Cornwall and his aptitude for math. For a time, he was a neighbor of William Murdoch, a Scottish inventor responsible for the oscillating cylinder steam engine. A detailed description of that innovation followed, and although Bea did not doubt the machine was vital to Trevithick's story, she considered it incidental to her own and impatiently flipped past it to an early drawing of the *Puffing Devil.*

That was more like it, she thought, noting how similar the steam engine looked to the *Bright Benny,* with its horizontal tubular boiler, as thick as a barrel, and the straight vertical pipe. Like Huzza's device, it used high-pressure steam to move the piston.

"Thank you very much," Bea murmured as the author launched into a brief overview of the changes Watt made to Newcomen's design. By adding an apparatus that condensed the steam via cool water, he eliminated the need to heat and cool the cylinder with each stroke. As a consequence, the engine was far more efficient, using only a fraction of the amount of coal of its predecessor.

Improving the Newcomen further, Phillips—ah, there was Clara's favorite!—eliminated the need for the main beam by flipping the steam cylinder upside down over the pump. This tweak reduced the amount of space the machine needed by half and made it safer to operate.

The adeptness of Phillips's model—a minor alteration leading to a huge improvement—appealed to Bea's sense of order and it pleased her to know her mother admired it as well.

Having relayed a general history of steam power, the book turned its attention to the *Puffing Devil*, which looked harmless in black and white, its wide body trimming to an elongated neck, like an exotic beast from a fairy story. The cylindrical shape allowed the boiler to withstand greater pressure, which was essential in a machine that used strong steam. The advantages of using high pressure were incontestable. Without the need for cooled steam to push the piston down, Watt's condenser could be removed, making the machine even more efficient.

It was little wonder, then, that Watt had eagerly disparaged high-pressure steam in the wake of the Greenwich explosion and sought to prohibit its use.

His financial success depended on the innovation's failure.

Examining the *Puffing Devil* now, Bea thought there was no hint of the tragedy to come. Its design was simple, with a U-shaped conduit inside the boiler to draw the heat of the fire evenly through the tank when the flue was open. Increasing the temperature caused the water to boil, producing the high-pressure steam needed to move the piston up and down, which propelled the wheels to turn.

Despite its triumphant debut, the elegant machine came to an ignominious end only a few days later, when a deep gully in the road caused it to tip over. After righting it with the help of passersby, Trevithick and his party retired to a nearby tavern to console themselves with food. The *Puffing Devil,* unattended and its fire still burning, boiled through the water that remained in its tank, causing the metal parts to grow so hot, they set fire to the wood sections.

Trevithick's invention was destroyed.

This sequence of events made sense to Bea, who crossed her legs in the commodious chair in a way that would horrify her aunt. If one left a kettle on the fire long after the liquid boiled away, it would eventually cause a disastrous mishap.

What it would not do, she thought, was create a deadly explosion.

Obviously, that formulation was not directly analogous because a pot was a simple device and a steam-powered engine was endlessly complex. Perhaps when the water dropped to a low level in a boiler, it caused an explosion.

That, too, seemed reasonable to Bea.

And yet that precise circumstance produced only a fire in the *Puffing Devil.*

What, then, would result in a blast?

Too much pressure.

Naturally, yes, but something had to create that intolerable increase, for the machine itself was built to withstand a tremendous amount of it. The *Bright Benny* was designed to sustain up to sixty pounds of pressure on the square inch—twelve times as much as Watt's engine, which could tolerate only five.

Again, she thought of Huzza's fusible plug, which was meant to regulate the extent of the pressure. Safety valves such as these were vital to the operation of high-pressure steam engines. The one in Greenwich had failed because a worker had tampered with it so he could leave the machine unattended to disastrous effect.

What had Uncle Horace said about the devastation?

It was as though a gunpowder mill had detonated.

The scene he had described was brutal: six men injured, four of whom died, and the large machine blown to pieces by the massive explosion. The casualty count would have been far greater if the incident had not occurred while the majority of workers were at dinner.

Bea was struck by the description—how dissimilar it was from the ordeal she had endured earlier that day.

Or, rather, yesterday, she thought, as the clock chimed four.

All those people there, such a thick crowd of onlookers, and only the inventor was fatally harmed.

It helped, yes, that Lynch and Rhodes had pushed them back toward the fence, ensuring they were a safe distance not only from the tracks but also the foundry. If the spectators had gotten the close-up view they had sought, then the carnage would have been immense.

As though a gunpowder mill had detonated.

But would the casualty count have been so high? She wondered, recalling the minimal damage suffered by the building itself—and the possibility that some portion of the *Bright Benny* was intact. She could not say for sure because her view of the destruction had been impeded, first by the smoke and crowd, then by Mr. Grimes, who refused to allow her to draw closer.

Her understanding of the scene was all so vague and hazy, and she did not know if she had caught sight of a remnant of the machine itself or one of the fire engines.

But the foundry, she reminded herself.

She had noted how remarkably unscathed it was by the blast. So much destruction and yet the skylights held firm.

That meant the explosion did not travel up.

In fact, it had barely traveled out.

So very definitely not a gunpowder mill, at least not as she conceived of one.

In that case, the two disasters were not comparable.

What was the difference?

The source of the explosion?

Considering, Bea decided it was likely.

Again, the cause of the Greenwich blast was known to be the valve, which had been fixed in place by one of the workers. Without any way for the steam to escape, the pressure inside the boiler grew to an unsustainable degree and when it was too great to be contained, it exploded with so much propulsive force it destroyed everything in its immediate vicinity.

That was significant—the utter decimation.

If the *Bright Benny* explosion had been caused by a fusible plug that had failed to work properly, then the destruction of the boiler would be absolute. The tank's cylindrical shape ensured that pressure was applied evenly to the inside of the container.

But the furnace could not be the culprit either because the timbers did not ignite. If the accident had been caused by a low water level, then the *Bright Benny* should have burned the way the *Puffing Devil* did.

What did it mean that it had not?

Nothing, she thought, other than the source of the explosion was unknown to her, which was hardly a startling development, as she was not an engineer, inventor, ironworker or instrument maker.

Sighing, Bea dropped her head against the back of the chair, closed her eyes and listened to the ticking of the clock. Although there was no logical reason why she should expect to understand something so thoroughly outside her scope of knowledge, she was nevertheless frustrated by her lack of comprehension.

If only she had gotten close enough to examine the engine!

Oh, yes, that would have made a wonderful impression.

Smoke everywhere, the crowd in a frenzy, Mr. Huzza in fragments, his associates frantically trying to salvage something while dousing flames with buckets of water—and she, the Duchess of Kesgrave, pulling out her sapphire-encrusted magnifying glass to get a better look.

Do not mind me, my good fellows. I shall just poke around over here while you try to sift through pieces of your fallen colleague.

Even if something about the incident had struck her as unusual, she would never have had the nerve to elbow her way to the center of the fracas to make an inspection. Her compulsion yesterday to draw closer to the fire had been an unthinking one, and she was certain that if Mr. Grimes had not halted her progress, her own sense of decency or decorum would have.

But now she regretted his interference, for if she had been left to her own devices, she might have a much better sense of the damage that had been done to the *Bright Benny*. His impulse was entirely natural, of course, for not only was the foundry too dangerous for spectators with the fires still burning but it was also the site of a hideous mutilation.

The Duchess of Kesgrave could not walk among that muck.

And yet she had walked among it, several times, in fact.

Struck by the thought, Bea wondered if Grimes had known that.

They were no secret, her proclivities, and Mr. Twaddle-Thum had made every effort to ensure they were broadcast far and wide.

Perhaps Mr. Grimes, upon realizing the infamous investigative duchess was in their midst, sought to cover up the truth by refusing to allow her to examine the evidence.

Other strange things occurred to her, such as Mr. Lynch's implacable resolve to push all the spectators away from the track, ultimately settling them along the perimeter of the yard. He claimed it was to protect the onlookers from stray embers that might be expelled from the flue, but Flora, who had been to a previous demonstration, found this caution unnecessary. It also seemed antithetical to the purpose of wooing investors. Rather than keeping them at a distance, one would want to draw them as close to one's remarkable invention as possible.

It made sense, however, if one wanted to ensure they were safely removed from the explosion.

Exasperated with her own nonsensical ramblings, Bea shook her head in disgust. What an utterly ridiculous creature she was, weaving elaborate plots whilst sitting in lavish splendor simply because she was too awake to fall asleep like everyone else in the house.

The mechanical complexity of the subject under consideration made her speculation even more preposterous. The idea that she—a woman who had learned the difference between the Newcomen atmospheric engine and the Watt steam engine a scant hour before—had somehow noticed an inexplicable strangeness to an event that everyone else in attendance thought was an accident was beyond risible.

Did she actually hold herself in such high esteem?

Only months ago, she was a reticent spinster, barely capable of offering a benign reply to a remark about the weather, and now she was a confident investigator sifting through a horrifying tragedy to find a murder plot.

Oh, but she was so very clever, was she not?

Bea shook her head, amazed that she had learned so little from her confrontation with Bentham. Pandering to her belief that she was as astute as any Runner, he had used her own vanity against her. He had known in advance every move she would make because she had been so blatant in her self-regard.

It was easy enough for him to pull her strings.

Discovering how susceptible she was to manipulation should have been enough to humble her.

Indeed, she thought it had.

And yet here she was, unable to smother the insidious little seed that seemed to lodge itself deeper into her mind with every passing minute.

The clock ticked and ticked and ticked.

Bea assured herself she was wrong.

Oh, but that boiler, the fragment of doubt.

The foundry still standing—not leveled to dust like a gunpowder mill.

Shaking her head as if to dislodge a particularly unpleasant thought, she unfolded her legs, which were stiff from inactivity.

It was just exhaustion, she told herself, noting that it was now almost five in the morning. She had been reading for more than three hours and the weariness was finally catching up to her.

The niggling suspicion would dissipate as soon as she got some rest.

But as she rose to her feet, she was forced to admit that her mind was remarkably clear. Usually, fatigue was accompanied by a woolly-headedness, an inability to follow a line of thought from beginning to end.

At the moment, all the lines were sharp.

Indeed, she could even picture the *Puffing Devil* on its maiden voyage, its wooden beam darting up and down as the wheels turned.

As a result, it was difficult to convince herself that her conclusions were outlandish or irrational.

Not correct either.

No, she was far from certain her suppositions were accurate. She merely thought the circumstance was suspicious enough to warrant further investigation.

What that entailed exactly, she was not sure, but she rather supposed it started with a visit to Bloomsbury. As less than twenty-four hours had passed since the calamity, she assumed the scene would be undisturbed.

The question was, how to gain entry.

Her title, of course, would open doors but would also draw attention—and not just the perplexingly all-seeing gaze of Mr. Twaddle-Thum. Her interest might alert the killer. So, too, would Kesgrave's, for he had shown himself to be indulgent of his wife's bizarre habit.

Really, the only option was to proceed in secrecy.

The duke would object on some grounds pertaining to the rigid code that governed a gentleman's behavior, such as sneaking into a foundry to ascertain the extent of the damage caused by an exploding steam engine was a gross violation of privacy.

It amazed her how much deference gentlemen showed each other and how little they displayed toward everyone else.

No matter, she thought as she crossed the room, he would simply have to find a way to overcome his scruples. His proficiency at unlocking secured doors was far too useful to waste on asymmetric morality.

Resolving to rouse him at once so they could take full advantage of the hour, she stepped into the hallway. She did not know what time workers would show up at the foundry under normal conditions and could make no guess for the strange circumstance. Maybe they would not come in at all. Perhaps they would arrive early to continue cleaning up.

The more likely scenario, she thought, was that Lynch would visit the foundry to take stock of the destruction. He would want a sense of what could be repaired and how much it would cost. The time and expense of rebuilding would depend on the cause of the accident and the extent of the damage.

Rhodes, too, might attend to the site.

Considering that their friend and colleague had died horribly the day before, she thought it reasonable to assume they would arrive a little later in the morning—say, eight or nine o'clock.

That gave them almost three hours.

Kesgrave would require at least fifteen minutes to dress.

Or was that overly optimistic?

Surely, he would not insist on starched shirt points to illicitly sift through the wreckage of a burned-out steam engine, although, perhaps, if one did get caught in the middle of such an endeavor, presenting an intimidating posture would discourage the asking of awkward questions—and there were few things more daunting than a well-executed Mail Coach.

Bea also had to find appropriate attire for skulking, which she could do quickly enough, assuming she could evade her maid's own rigid standards. Dolly had become difficult of late, allowing her grace to rise from the dressing table only when every silken strand of hair was in place.

And then there was breakfast.

Kesgrave would insist on eating something first.

Uncertain how long that would take, she allotted another fifteen minutes.

Then, allowing for travel time from Berkeley Square and supposing it would not take the duke above five minutes to pick the lock, she figured they would have a full—

Her calculations were abruptly cut off when she realized Marlow, his mien as imposing as ever, was standing directly in front of her.

Just as startled as she, he furrowed his heavy black brows

first in confusion, then in annoyance, before adopting his customary pose of bland impassivity.

He greeted her smoothly, bidding her good morning with mild familiarity, as if he often encountered her wandering the halls of Kesgrave House at five in the morning.

By any measure, it was an impressive showing, and considering how her own heart still pounded from the butler's unexpected appearance, an enviable skill.

Prior to learning of his history as a bare-knuckled boxer and protector of the young Duke of Kesgrave, Bea had attributed his impregnable composure to several generations of butlering. Since she had discovered the truth, her opinion of him had undergone a radical change, and although she had so far resisted the urge to offer her gratitude for keeping Damien safe when he was too young to defend himself against a murderous uncle, she certainly felt it whenever she was in his presence.

Consequently, she greeted him warmly now and said he was precisely the person for whom she was looking. "The duke and I intend to make an early start to our day, so please ask Mrs. Wallace or one of the kitchen maids to send up tea as soon as possible. We will require something to eat as well, but it need not be elaborate. I am sure toast with jam will be fine."

"Very good, your grace," Marlow said calmly. "Will you be taking the carriage?"

It was, Bea thought, an excellent question, for she had not considered what effect arriving in a conveyance easily identified as their own would have on the surreptitious nature of their mission.

A negative one, presumably.

And yet she had no idea how difficult securing a hackney cab would be so early in the morning.

"I am not sure," she said.

The butler nodded and said he would have it readied regardless.

"Thank you, Marlow," she said sincerely.

He nodded in acknowledgment and asked if she required anything else.

Bea was halfway through a negative reply when a strange daring overcame her—fostered, she was convinced, by the mysterious intimacy of the early hour—and she broke off abruptly.

Swiftly, before she lost her nerve, she said, "The rout cakes from yesterday afternoon did not have pineapple."

For a moment he seemed on the verge of offering an apology, but he managed to hold himself in check. "The anticipated delivery has been detained and is now expected to arrive tomorrow."

Ah, so that explained it.

Arranging her features in a frown of dismay, she said, "I trust it goes without saying how very disappointing I find that."

Marlow lowered his head as if accepting a rebuke. "Yes, your grace."

The uncommon effusiveness of his response made Bea feel wretched, for she knew the staff showed their regard for her by ensuring her favorite fruit was incorporated into every meal. It was a lovely gesture, one as thoughtful as it was sincere, and she was loath to do anything that might convey dissatisfaction.

Truly, she was so very touched by their consideration.

And yet, after two weeks of dishes, she abhorred pineapples.

Naturally, the only way out of the fix was by cowardly laying the blame elsewhere.

"I fear the duke will think otherwise," she said, before quickly adding that her observation was mere speculation based on his enjoyment of the previous day's rout cake. "He had eaten half of it before I even noticed the tray had been delivered."

This was, she assured herself consolingly, nothing but the truth.

"As his comfort is of the utmost importance to me, I think I must forgo the pleasure of pineapple, at least for the immediate future," she continued, striving for an appropriately sad note. "If you could please advise the chef to return to using the usual amount of pineapple in dishes, I would be very grateful. And do make sure to tell him it is *my* request. I would never want him or any of the staff to think less of the duke, especially in a matter of such importance as his gustatory preferences. As we all know, liking pineapple requires a certain industriousness and persistence."

And there, she thought, the duke was absolved of all blame. The responsibility for the decision rested solely on her shoulders.

Might the act of selflessness burnish her own reputation among the servants?

Possibly, but that was an unavoidable consequence and if she had to bear the weight of unearned esteem, then she would do so with grace and humility.

Kesgrave would not suffer for it.

The staff already adored him with disconcerting fervor, and his having the wisdom to choose a solicitous wife who put his needs before her own could only deepen their regard.

Marlow, displaying unprecedented sympathy, reminded her that she would still have the pleasure of daily pineapple slices at breakfast.

Devil it, Bea thought, she had forgotten about that specific request.

Nevertheless, the conversation had worked out primarily

to her benefit and she was pleased that her day was already off to a bright start.

"That is perfect, Marlow, thank you," she said, before returning to her calculations as she continued to the staircase.

Chapter Seven

Given Bea's deep and abiding respect for Kesgrave's intelligence, she could only conclude that his inability to grasp the facts of the situation was the result of being rudely awakened at five-thirteen in the morning.

His lids still heavy from sleep, he considered her with a disgruntled expression and said, "You want to examine the steam carriage because you think Huzza was murdered."

Having already answered this question twice before, she shook her head impatiently. "I have no thoughts whatsoever regarding the true nature of Mr. Huzza's death. I merely find several aspects of his demise to be in need of more explanation."

"Such as a man asking you to stand away from the tracks," he replied.

"Well, yes," she conceded, for she had indeed included this occurrence in her list of curiosities, although as the very last item, which indicated it was of low importance, "but no. The skylights were undamaged, which is more revealing."

"Because all the windows in the gunpowder mill in Greenwich shattered," he said.

"A corn tide mill on the banks of the Thames," she corrected with huffy exasperation, for he should have immediately grasped the situation. It was early, to be sure, but was not rising at first light to catch the early grouse or trout or whatever wild creature stalked the landscape his milieu? Or joining a race to the next posting house as the sun crept over the horizon?

What good was a Corinthian if he could not rise at dawn, fully awake and alive to all the possibilities of life?

Unperturbed by her growing annoyance, Kesgrave swept his hand through his hair and advised her to try simplifying her account. "Perhaps if you shared only your conclusion rather than all the minor deductions you arrived at on the way there."

"Oh, so now the pedant thinks a methodical description of my thought process is too much detail?" she asked, tut-tutting with disapproval at the violation of one of his most dearly held principles. "I do hope you remember this moment the next time you decide to lecture a roomful of people on the variety of fish found in ponds in northwest England."

His lips twitched as he said, "Bea, I can hardly recall it now. Honestly, I am still not sure what is happening."

Before she could launch into yet another explanation, a knock sounded on the door and she bid the servant to enter. Dutifully, Joseph carried in the tray, which he placed on the low table next to the settee. "Breakfast will be ready in twenty minutes. Toast as you requested, your grace, but also eggs and muffins."

"Excellent, Joseph," she said gratefully, "and do thank Mrs. Wallace for going above and beyond. As well, please inform the duke's valet that his assistance is needed."

"Already done, your grace," he replied. "Harris is waiting

in the dressing room."

After Joseph left the room, Bea turned to the duke and said cheerfully, "There, your grace, everyone in the household understands the urgency of the situation except you. Now do get up before you fall even farther behind. You will note, I am sure, how I am now appealing to your sense of competition to spur you to action. I cannot believe the Duke of Kesgrave can withstand unfavorable comparison to his third footman."

As she shifted her legs to stand, he grasped her hand and tugged her forward so that she landed on his chest. Settling her comfortably against his shoulder, he pointed out that Joseph was in fact second footman. "Which I know you know."

"Yes, well, failing to anticipate your premature descent into senility, it did not occur to me to request that Edward deliver the tea," she replied demurely. "You may be assured, however, that I will bear it in mind for future episodes."

"Will there be many?" he asked curiously.

"Given that you are asking the question after I have impressed upon you the need for haste, I can only assume yes," she said.

And yet his grip remained firm. "Plainly, Bea, so that even my sleep-addled brain can understand it: Do you think Huzza was murdered?"

She sighed, feeling perfectly absurd. "I do, yes."

"Very well, then, let us visit the foundry," he said, releasing his hold and shifting to climb out of bed.

"But that is based on flimsy evidence, a limited understanding of how steam accumulates in a boiler and a random comment made by my relative," she said perversely, as if striving to undercut his resolve.

Kesgrave halted his progress and turned to look at her with a skeptical expression. "If the relative is Russell, then I am going back to sleep."

"'Twas Uncle Horace who compared the explosion of Trevithick's stationary pumping engine to a gunpowder mill," she replied.

"Since the damage caused by *Bright Benny* was not nearly as extensive, it could not have been caused by the boiler exploding," he observed with an affirming nod. "Lacking another explanation that could account for it, you suspect it was caused deliberately."

Listening to this neat summation of her argument, she smiled at him fondly and said, "Aw, Damien, you are not senile after all. Only insufficiently Corinthian."

"I never claimed membership to that set," he replied as he rose to his feet.

Bea, her back resting comfortably against the pillows, rolled her eyes at this patently false assertion and began to list his accomplishments: regular bouts with Gentleman Jackson, a deft whip hand, an excellent seat, ruthlessly tailored clothes with a pleasing austerity.

"Need I continue?" she asked.

"If you wish to arrive at the foundry sometime after noon, yes," he said, striding to the door that led to his dressing room. "But as I am obligated to demonstrate that I am at least as useful as Joseph—"

"Edward," she corrected.

"—I cannot allow you to distract me. You may have nothing in particular to do today, but I have a steam engine to examine posthaste."

Bea was relieved that he found her vague misgivings enough to launch an investigation because she was not sure she could have defended her point of view more robustly. Grateful, she allowed his impertinent comment to pass without reply and retreated to her own dressing room, where Dolly was laying out a dress.

Seemingly unaffected by the earliness of the hour, the

maid greeted her cheerfully, but her bright smile dimmed when Bea requested a plainer gown.

"Plainer?" she repeated, as if confounded by the notion.

"Plainest," Bea amended, recalling that much of her trousseau had been selected by the Countess of Abercrombie, whose tastes ran toward excessive ornamentation.

Dolly nodded as if she understood the notion, but her furrowed brow indicated otherwise. Nevertheless, she applied herself to the task, returning a few minutes later with a sprigged muslin dress. The confection was, by Portman Square standards, elaborate, with its silk trim and flounced hem, but her maid insisted it was a bland garment suitable only for answering one's correspondence or reading in leisure.

It was never meant to *leave the house*.

Bea deemed it acceptable if not ideal for her purpose, and Dolly, seeking to compensate for the pitiful simplicity of the gown, arranged her mistress's hair in a style that was inappropriately intricate for a morning outing. As she could not explain to her maid that the excursion consisted of unlawfully entering a foundry to ascertain the extent of the damage to a steam carriage, she submitted to this treatment without complaint.

As a result, she arrived at breakfast a good fifteen minutes after Kesgrave, whose appearance was far more suitable for furtive lurking.

Taking her seat at the table she was struck yet again by how unfair it was that she had to contend with the constraints of female attire while men had the comfort and ease of trousers. Learning to fence in skirts was a particularly daft occupation but not as silly as running through the streets of London after a suspected murderer with her dress hiked up to her knees.

It was a shame Madam Bélanger did not make clothes tailored to the requirements of the upstart lady investigator.

For a short while, Bea had worn an outfit she had liberated from her cousin Russell's closet, but Flora had stolen it weeks ago and so far demonstrated no interest in giving it back.

Since the duke was finishing his coffee just as she was sitting down, she refused to linger over her own beverage, taking several quick, deep sips of pekoe, which was slightly too hot for the activity. Then she buttered two pieces of toast, wrapped them in a serviette and announced she was ready to leave.

The housekeeper, whose expression revealed both fascination and dismay at this behavior, offered to pour some tea in a pint mug so the duchess could take that with her as well.

"You are so very thoughtful, Mrs. Wallace, but I'm sure it is not necessary," Bea replied, standing with purpose. "We must be on our way."

Kesgrave called for the carriage, which was brought around to the front at once despite Bea's concerns that it would draw undue attention to their undertaking. Although he could not believe it would be a problem, as it was only six-fifteen, he proposed alighting a few streets over and walking the rest of the distance.

As they stepped outside, Bea allowed it was a fair compromise.

Dark gray clouds hung over the morning as they made their way to Bloomsbury, where they disembarked to Jenkins's staunch disapproval. Although he had no more idea about the reason for their visit than the rest of the staff, he knew enough to suspect it was either dangerous or would lead to something dangerous. Muttering with displeasure under his breath, he agreed to stay with the horses.

"That is another reason to take a hack," Bea observed as they turned the corner onto Melton.

"To spare us his grumblings?" Kesgrave asked.

"To spare his feelings," she corrected. "The poor man worries about us."

"Perhaps you should invite him to your next lesson with Carlo, so he can see how proficient you are with a blade," he said.

Bea appreciated the suggestion but insisted it would not prosper, for Jenkins's preferences were well-known. "He respects only brute force and cannot observe me until I have mastered the art of bare-knuckle fighting."

"That is not among your lessons," the duke reminded her, for they had had this conversation several times before. "You will use gloves or forgo boxing instruction entirely."

In a placating lilt, she rushed to assure him she understood perfectly, as would, she was certain, the next villain who sought to end her life in the comfort of her own sitting room. "He will happily hold off attacking me while I fetch the proper accoutrement."

"If your goal is to make me regret encouraging you to engage in further investigations rather than wrapping you in cotton, do please continue to discuss future murder attempts on your life," he said coolly. "If not, I suggest you slyly change the subject to something insipid in hopes of distracting me."

Perceiving the wisdom of his advice, Bea glanced upward and, noting the heaviness of the clouds, asked if he thought the weather would remain dry until after Mrs. Dalrymple's garden party that afternoon.

"Very insipid," he murmured admiringly.

"I should hope so," she replied as they arrived at the tall gate that enclosed the foundry's courtyard. "Six seasons on the fringes of society have to be good for something."

Retrieving a slim tool from his pocket, Kesgrave asked her to keep an eye out for passersby while he picked the lock. She agreed, of course, but she was too beguiled by his skill—the way his fingers skillfully plied the instrument—to perform her task with any diligence.

Prinny himself could have strolled past, and she would have been none the wiser.

A little more than a minute later, metal clanged as the duke pulled open the door. "After you, your grace."

Shaking her head in wonder, Bea marveled at the usefulness of having a matrimonial partner who could unlock any door with ease and dexterity. "Truthfully, I had no idea at all of the advantages, or I would have assuredly added it to my list of requirements in a husband."

Amused, Kesgrave pointed out her list had been quite spare. "From what I understand, it had only two items: mild temper and a modest library."

"Yes," Bea replied as he closed the gate behind them, "and Aunt Vera considered that already too picky."

"If only she had thought to look in Cheapside for a law clerk," he replied.

Bea shook her head. Poor Mr. Davies, reduced to being no more than an overused plot device! She led Kesgrave to the spot where she had stood for the demonstration. Without the crush of onlookers, the yard looked bigger, and she noted with dismay how very far away the building actually was.

In her memory, it was much closer.

Surely, this distance was far too great to make any reasonable judgment regarding how much of the boiler remained. The smoke had been so thick and black, she had barely been able to see Russell only a few inches from her nose, and yet she believed she could accurately assess the state of a contraption several dozen yards away.

That was arrogance, was it not? The unqualified belief in her own convictions. She had known enough to doubt her understanding of the science itself, but what she had seen with her own two eyes—her faith in that had been unshakeable.

And now they were here, at the foundry only an hour after sunrise, about to discover how very misplaced her confidence was.

It mortified her, truly, fully, deeply to her soul, because she knew how this had happened. The former Beatrice Hyde-Clare was so desperate to perceive herself as an investigator that she spotted murder everywhere she looked—like a small child seeing ghosts in the shadows.

'Twas bad enough when she insisted on knocking on neighbors' doors and demanding access to their decapitated chefs. But this—constructing a fantasy out of whole cloth and wisps of smoke—was an appalling new feat of determination.

She had willed it into existence.

And the houseful of servants wrested from their slumber to appease her ego—that was particularly painful to contemplate.

Clearly, she deserved to be banished to an empty room to embroider quietly by herself.

Well, no, that was a little too harsh.

Banished to a room to read, then.

But definitely alone.

She did not deserve the ineffable comfort of Kesgrave.

Recalling the duke, she felt her humiliation rise, for she had not pursued this ludicrous notion alone. Foolishly, she had insisted on bringing him along.

Oblivious to her increasing qualms, he examined the tracks with curiosity as he drew closer to the foundry doors.

She thought about calling him back and explaining that it had all been a stupid misunderstanding on her part, but allowing the scene to unfold naturally struck her as the only fair resolution.

Let him see for himself the depth of her pathology.

Let him comprehend thoroughly the extent of her folly.

It was all his fault anyway, for if he had not bolstered her confidence at every turn, she would still be a drab spinster sputtering through banalities.

A ghost of a smile crossed her lips as she acknowledged the flimsiness of that argument, for she had required no outside encouragement to continue with her investigations. Kesgrave's attempt to curtail her habit by coercing a pledge to cease it added a sense of righteousness to her investigation into Mr. Wilson's death, to be sure, but she would have pursued his killer regardless.

And the duke made it clear that his interest in her had been fixed during their sojourn in the Lake District, so he would have sought her out during the season regardless of her activities.

Patently, they were always going to end up here, at the foundry.

So be it, she thought, marching toward the building.

The real damage would come from him examining the scene and understanding once and for all how close she had come to annihilation.

It was as though a gunpowder mill had detonated.

He would tear up her training schedule and enfold her in reams of cotton.

The acrid smell roiled her stomach as she drew closer to the building, and she noted her heartbeat tick up. It was anxiety, she knew, but she could not determine if it was apprehension over what Kesgrave would think when he saw the engine or what she would.

Something about the explosion felt closer to death than Bentham's hand over her mouth.

It was, she supposed, the thunderous boom.

By the time you heard it, it was already too late.

You were dead.

Or a sphinx.

The wide barn-like doors to the foundry were closed, shielding the vastness of its interior from her view, and Kesgrave deftly applied his tool to unlocking the smaller entrance to the right. A few moments later, he slipped the device back into his pocket, gripped the handle and opened the door.

And there it was—black iron mangled and mounted on a charred frame.

Ah, but there *it* was.

Half the boiler, perfectly intact, just as she had pictured.

Her heart pounding wildly, she drew closer and raised her hand to touch it, her movements cautious, as if it might still burn. But it was cool, of course, the fire long extinguished, the floor still damp from the hundreds of gallons of water employed to douse the flame.

Bea exhaled sharply and closed her eyes for a moment, allowing herself to feel the lightness of a weight lifting. It was, she knew, an inappropriate response. A man died gruesomely only a few feet from where she stood and yet her first thought was of herself and the relief of knowing her cognitive ability had not been undermined by her success.

Even so, she gave it a few seconds.

In the end, it made no difference to Mr. Huzza.

Hearing the clang of metal, she opened her eyes and saw Kesgrave examining the firebox end of the boiler, which had been decimated. The chamber had been blown open, its sides either melted by the explosion or shot like shrapnel into the air. It was the window nearest it that had shattered, the wall encasing it charred so extensively by fire that daylight peeked through a narrow hole. But the skylights, she affirmed, glancing up, had emerged unscathed.

It was, she knew, deeply significant.

"I see what you mean," Kesgrave said with a thoughtful nod. "My understanding of boiler explosions is as imperfect as yours, but it seems uncontestable that the problem was with the firebox. That is what exploded."

"Huzza was here when the explosion happened," Bea said, positioning herself beside the firebox, opposite the contorted remains of the flue. The small platform on which he had stood to feed the fire while the steam engine was in motion had burned almost entirely away. "When we arrived, the fire was banked. The coals were hot, but I do not think the water had begun to boil yet because the flue was not open. It emitted no black smoke. At that point, we were allowed to get close to the machine, and Huzza was moving among the spectators, talking to different groups. Then his partner, Lynch, tried to settle the crowd enough to make introductory remarks, and Huzza commanded the stage, making his own speech while the other man waited. He urged everyone to invest in the *Bright Benny,* then came to stand here, on the platform, displacing the engineer, a man called Rhodes, who had been tending the coals."

It was strange, she thought, describing the scene of death as actual fact, not speculation. So often she had to rely on other people's account of what happened.

Fazeley was the exception.

He had dropped dead at her feet as she was exiting the offices of the *London Daily Gazette,* and the advantage to witnessing his murder was immediately apparent because she recognized the dagger protruding from his back.

That carved jade knife was the clue from which the whole mystery unfurled.

"He stood here, and spectators were there," she said, pointing to the yard on the other side of the wide doors. "They tried to draw closer, but Lynch insisted they move several feet away from the tracks to remain clear of debris from the flue. Mr. Huzza tended to the fire, and it was comical, really, the way he looked, dressed all in white, waving to his admiring audience while Rhodes tried to switch positions with him. After a few moments, Rhodes gave up and assisted Lynch in pushing back the crowd. Huzza had just taken hold of the steering lever when the explosion happened."

Kesgrave dropped to his haunches and examined the charred remains of the platform, lifting a bent bar of metal as if something might be hiding beneath it. "I do not see anything that looks like it might have been a shovel."

"No, you would not," Bea said thoughtfully as she lowered herself beside him. Her dress billowed slightly, causing ash to scatter and mar the pristine hem of her day dress. "He did not use one. The platform he was standing on was too narrow for a mound of coal. He was taking lumps from a pile in a basket, which I do not see either. Presumably, it burned in the fire."

Even so, she dirtied her gloves by picking up a partially burned beam and using it to sift through the wreckage for a remnant of the hamper.

"He was feeding the fire by hand?" he asked.

"Throwing a few coals in at a time and then closing the firebox door," she replied. "As I said, my scientifical understanding of steam power is incomplete, but nothing I have read explains why the firebox would explode. Either it grew too hot, in which case the timbers would have ignited first, or it caused the pressure to increase too much, in which case the boiler would blow up and the foundry would look as though a gunpowder mill detonated. But it does not, so the explanation must be sinister."

Kesgrave, his expression suddenly arrested, stared at her unblinkingly for several seconds. Then he shook his head and said, "Gunpowder, Bea."

She was confused at first, believing he was merely

repeating something she said, but then she recalled her own thought about mortar fire.

That was what the explosion had reminded her of—accounts she had read of mortar fire.

Bea looked again at the vestige of the firebox and knew a small bomb was a plausible theory for why the chamber—and only the chamber—had exploded.

Slipping it in among the coals would be easy enough.

Did it look different from the coals surrounding it?

Inevitably, yes, because it was a bomb, not a lump of coal. But its size would be similar as would its shape, and a superficial likeness was probably all that was necessary in the situation. With all the fanfare of the demonstration—the clamoring crowd, the raucous music—Huzza would be too distracted to examine each piece as he tossed it in the fire.

And even if his attention was focused on the duty at hand, why would he notice a particular lump?

It was coal.

But was such a thing possible?

Kesgrave insisted that it was, yes, and launched into an explanation of how he would do it. Although he described the process in great detail, in fact it entailed only three significant steps: filling a small iron casing with gunpowder, plugging the hole with more iron, coating it with pitch to make the coal dust stick to it.

Bea, taken aback to discover the duke was such a munitions expert, told herself it was not particularly surprising, for anyone who would memorize all the names of the ships that enjoined the Battle of the Nile clearly had a well-developed interest in war.

Not just memorized the names but also the order in which they appeared. It was, she thought, an impressive level of commitment.

Unless, of course, all students at Eton and Oxford were

required to know it for their course of study. The glories of British naval dominance seemed like exactly the sort of subject you would teach to the most privileged of English youth to keep their sense of superiority well honed.

Kesgrave, concluding his lecture, looked at her expectantly, and Bea, realizing it was her turn to speak, lauded him on his extensive knowledge of weapons production.

His lips quivered at this response, which revealed quite plainly that she had not been listening for some time, and he said he had not been seeking a compliment. "I asked if you thought any of Huzza's colleagues possessed the skills to make the bomb."

"Oh, I see, yes," she replied, apologizing for the misunderstanding. "It is just that you have displayed insecurity regarding your position as my investigative assistant in the past, and I thought you were seeking affirmation. But you have no cause to worry, for it is not as though Flora will come flouncing in here with her air of worldliness and begin spouting conclusions."

Nevertheless, they both turned their heads to look at the doorway as if that might actually happen. For one humming moment, they waited.

Then Kesgrave said, "Even so, I do think a petard-like bomb was a noteworthy deduction."

Beatrice raised an eyebrow as she examined him with amused interest. "To be clear, your grace, now you *are* seeking a compliment?"

Although his eyes glinted, he dipped his head in shame and said, "It is the depths to which you have sunk me."

She was about to counter that outrageous claim when a muffled clank sounded in the large space. Startled, she darted her head to the right and took one step forward as Kesgrave clasped her elbow as if to keep her in place. Although she had not intended to go dashing off in pursuit of an intruder and possibly the villain, she understood his concern.

Holding his gaze as she pointed in the direction of the noise—the back left corner of the foundry—she said, "That was not my intention, for I am trying to hold you to a higher standard."

Kesgrave nodded and indicated that he would approach the area directly while she arced around to creep up on him from the side. "Your commitment to improving my character is humbling," he said, skirting a pile of wood as he walked toward the back.

Bea stepped carefully around broken glass from the shattered window. "Ah, so that explains the undue humility."

The duke made no answering reply, for he was now close enough to the target that his voice would reveal his proximity. Bea, passing a beam anchoring several pulleys that hung over the floor, heard a sudden crash and looked over in time to see Kesgrave dodge pieces of falling pottery. The intruder had knocked over a crate, which broke a shelf.

Echoing footsteps indicated he was near, and Bea saw a flash of brown coat as the prowler toppled another stack of crates to impede the duke's progress. Then he ran to the left, toward the charred wall, with its narrow slit, and Bea, calculating his trajectory, untied a rope to release the pulley.

It dropped onto the man's head.

Stunned but unharmed, he paused just long enough to wonder what had fallen and allow himself to be apprehended.

"Nicely done," Kesgrave said admiringly as he tightened his grip on the intruder's arm. Then, tugging him across the floor, he turned the man around and Bea saw his face for the first time.

Mr. Grimes!

Chapter Eight

More confused than surprised, Bea stared at the factory owner from Stockwell and assumed some terrible misunderstanding on his part had caused him to return to the foundry mere hours after the horrific explosion that claimed the inventor's life.

Fleetingly, she wondered if he had never left—if, in his determination to be helpful, he had remained throughout the night, extinguishing fires and scraping pieces of Mr. Huzza from the walls.

Ah, but no, for he looked different.

Gone were the garish waistcoat and gaudy walking stick and in their place was a plainly cut suit in a subdued brown.

Before she could draw a reasonable conclusion, Grimes cried, "It is not what you think!"

Designed to preempt judgment, the statement had the opposite effect, leading her to conclude his behavior was more nefarious than she had supposed, not less. If he was in some way involved in the explosion, then he would be there to remove evidence—which was not the direction in which her mind had originally gone.

Skeptically, then, she said, "Is it not?"

"I am here to collect my pay," he insisted. "That is all! I merely sought to be compensated for services rendered in good faith. I was not stealing! I would never steal. I am an honest man, not a thief."

More confused than ever, for this information did little to improve her understanding, Bea introduced Kesgrave to his captive. "This not-thief is Mr. Grimes, whom you may recall from my account of yesterday's events. He presented himself as an enthusiastic investor in the *Bright Benny* and claimed to own a factory in need of engines, something I begin to suspect is not the truth. Tell me, Mr. Grimes, what service did you render that requires compensation?"

"Enthusiasm," he said, shrugging as if to dislodge the duke's grip and then immediately apologized if the gesture appeared rude. "I was seeking to ease a crimp in my neck."

"I am not familiar with enthusiasm as an employable skill," Bea said.

"You wouldn't be, no," Grimes said with agreeable ease, "because you are not engaged in trade. Those of us who have a product to sell find that it helps increase our profits if a person with no apparent connection to the item demonstrates enthusiasm for it. It persuades others to make the investment. Sometimes all a reluctant man needs is one last little push."

"Does he?" she murmured curiously, recalling how he had inserted himself into her and Flora's conversation the day before. He had certainly been enthusiastic to discuss the many wonders of the *Bright Benny*.

"I have made a small study of it, you see, and perfected my technique," he explained. "The secret is not to apply too much pressure. Nobody wants you to make up their mind for them. They simply want you to validate the decision they are already inclined to make. It is a skill few have mastered."

In this, Bea was inclined to agree, for the ability to manipulate did not come naturally to most people. "Persuasion is how you earn your living?"

"Enthusiasm," he corrected.

She acknowledged the semantical distinction, which was ultimately meaningless, with a nod. "And you go from demonstration to demonstration convincing people to invest for a fee?"

With a regretful sigh, he admitted that there were not enough opportunities for a peddler of enthusiasm to draw a regular salary. "I also work in an office as a clerk, copying letters for my employer, filing documents and keeping records. This is something I do only from time to time. My real name is Garfield, Elias Garfield. I realize this must sound highly irregular to you, your grace, but I am confident the duke—and I trust I am right in assuming this is the duke—can confirm that business is often conducted in sly and unexpected ways."

Kesgrave, alas, did not affirm this statement, asking instead if it was also a common business practice to collect one's wages at six in the morning from an empty building. "It bears a striking resemblance to stealing, which you have already assured us you are not doing."

Garfield's expression tightened as a blush crept up his neck. "A fair observation. Very fair! And I know how this looks. But you were not there yesterday, so you cannot know what it was like, the horror of the explosion, the chaos of the aftermath. Nobody knew what to do or think. Her grace, for example, was wandering around the yard like a ghost, her complexion as white as marble. Fortunately, I found her and returned her to her family, but anything could have happened. It was that frenzied. Mindful of my obligation, I helped disperse the crowd and treated the injured. I provided my assistance in a variety of ways that were outside my purview. But I was not compensated for my labors, which is not remarkable given the situation. Still, an honest day's work deserves an honest day's pay, and given all that has happened, I do not expect Mr. Lynch will have the presence of mind or composure necessary to deal with business matters for several days, if not weeks, to come. To spare him the trouble, I decided to just pop in here and settle the account myself. It is respectable if a little unconventional."

Despite his claim to persuasion, Bea found this argument unconvincing and looked at the duke to gain his opinion. "I do not know," she said doubtfully. "It still sounds like stealing to me. What do you think, Kesgrave?"

"I think Mr. Garfield should empty his pockets," he replied.

"An excellent suggestion," she said, returning her gaze to their captive. "Do show us how much you chose to compensate yourself for services rendered."

"It is a reasonable amount, I can assure you," he said firmly. Nevertheless, a slight flush crept up his neck as he reluctantly drew several pound notes from his coat pocket.

"How many is that?" she asked unable to distinguish the size of the small bundle.

Mr. Garfield muttered a response.

"I am sorry, but I did not hear you," Bea said. "How much?"

"Four pounds," he repeated.

"A month's wages for a single day's work?" she asked disbelievingly.

He flinched at her doubt, but his gaze remained steady. "Mr. Huzza appreciated the value of my contribution. You have only one chance to impress investors at your debut, and he wanted to make sure he made the right impression. As I said, I possess a rare and valuable skill."

And yet his performance failed to persuade her, and she asked him to empty his other coat pocket as well.

His smile did not waver as he complied, extracting a handful of change, including two guineas, half a dozen shillings and several pence. But he was aware of how it appeared, the assortment of change, and explained that it was a gratuity. "For exceeding the obligations of the job itself. I did not have to remain until after the fires were extinguished and did so out of a wish to be helpful. It is not unheard of for such generosity to be rewarded."

"That may be true," Bea conceded, "but the decision to provide the reward is usually left to the discretion of the employer."

Garfield, looking only slightly embarrassed, observed again that he sought to spare Mr. Lynch the inconvenience of dealing with tradesmen during a difficult time. "If consulted, I am confident he would find nothing untoward in his generosity."

Bea resisted the urge to roll her eyes. "Now your trouser pocket please."

Obeying, he pulled out three—no, four—quills that were slightly mangled from the tight storage. "To cover unanticipated expenses. Because I remained so late yesterday helping out, I missed my usual scheduled shift as a clerk. Additionally, I had to pay for a hack to bring me back here, which would not have been necessary if I had been compensated yesterday, as arranged."

Although several replies to this particularly excessive display of shamelessness rose to her tongue, she refrained from comment and instructed him to reveal the contents of his last pocket.

Now his face turned sheepish as he reached into his trousers and pulled out a brass paperweight of a reclining greyhound with its front paws crossed. "You see, this one...

well, *this* one is impossible to explain, and you are right to question me. I cannot say why I took it other than my admiration for its craftsmanship overcame my judgment. But that is no justification. I shall just put that back, shall I?"

How abashed he looked, his head tilted to the side, his collar slightly raised where Kesgrave still held it, as he gestured to the back of the foundry.

Bea, who had no idea what to think about Mr. Garfield, formerly Grimes, knew she would not allow him to return to the office. She would put everything back while he remained in the duke's company.

"Everything—as in *all* of it?" Garfield asked, aghast at the notion. "But what about the four pounds for services rendered? I performed my duties in good faith and deserve to be fairly compensated. Huzza would not begrudge it to me."

Of his many unsavory behaviors, she found his willingness to exploit the dead inventor the most distasteful. "It is in Mr. Lynch's hands now, and as you have observed several times, he is not in the position to discuss the matter at present. I suggest you contact him next week to request a meeting to address your compensation. Now do hand over your ill-gotten gains so that I may put them back."

He amended this description, insisting his gains were well earned, but nevertheless surrendered them to Beatrice.

Meeting Kesgrave's eyes over their captive's, she said that she would return in a few minutes. "While I am gone, perhaps you can get Mr. Garfield's direction so we can follow up with him later if we have any additional questions."

"Yes, yes, of course," Garfield said eagerly. "I am at your service. And just so you are aware, I perform other functions in addition to spreading enthusiasm."

Bea listened to him explain how he had also served as a mourner at funerals when the collection of bereaved family members seemed thin as she made her way to the office. At the back of the foundry, it contained a very large table in the middle and several cabinets. The space was neat and orderly, with papers in a tidy stack on the table. She peered through them quickly, noting they contained mathematical equations and scribbled notations, and then turned her attention to the rosewood cabinet along the far wall. Its doors were open, indicating that it had recently been searched, and on the bottom shelf, she found a box with a couple of farthings at the bottom.

There, she thought, Garfield was not so greedy after all.

She restored the money to the box, placed the quills and paperweight next to it and examined the rest of the contents of the cabinet. She looked through a ledger that detailed expenses, noting that there was no line for a Mr. Garfield or Mr. Grimes, and flipped through more sheets detailing technical calculations.

All in all, there was very little information to be found in the office and she concluded that Huzza had done much of his work in his home. As Garfield had mentioned yesterday, the inventor was a widower with a child old enough to serve in the army, and as such would have few domestic distractions to take his focus away from his work.

Leaving the office, she found Kesgrave and Garfield near the east-facing wall, which had sustained the most damage in the accident. It contained a narrow hole, about three feet in height, through which the latter had entered.

"It was tight and I did get a tear in my coat," he explained, poking his finger through a hole in the fabric to display the damage.

"I trust you will include the cost of the repair in your accounting to Lynch," Kesgrave said.

Garfield, who had not thought to consider this expense in his original accounting, thanked the duke for his suggestion and promised to do just that. Then he took one step toward the wall and looked at Bea as if expecting her to stop him. When she made no comment, he bid her good day, turned sideways, bent his knees and twisted his body through the opening.

As he straightened his posture, Bea heard a tearing sound. "Oh, dear, I think he rent his coat again."

"I am sure he can afford to fix it, for the fabric was very fine," Kesgrave replied as they watched the intruder begin the long walk across the courtyard. "I assure you, Mr. Garfield is no clerk."

"Nor an enthusiasm peddler or whatever nonsensical description he wants to apply to his trade," she said in agreement. "What I cannot decide is if he was here to steal money, as four pounds is not an inconsiderable sum, or to recover a piece of evidence that could connect him to the crime. Do you think he heard our conversation?"

"Most likely, yes," the duke said as they strode toward the front door to keep Garfield in view. "I would say he was in the office when we arrived and was drawing closer to hear us better when he bumped into a canister. Given the state of the wreckage, I cannot imagine what he could be here to recover. It is not like Tilly's drawing room, where a sleeve button in the wrong place indicated guilt."

Bea, conceding this was true, observed, "So he could just be a thief."

"An opportunist," Kesgrave replied, noting Garfield's progress across the courtyard. "If we are going to follow him to his next destination—and I assume we are—we should be prepared to run in about forty-five seconds."

She confirmed the plan by saying that he would indeed run while she hobbled behind in her satin booties. "Given your advantage, you are sure to keep pace with him. If I fall behind, do not worry about me. It is more important that you discover where he goes. I shall return to Kesgrave House with

Jenkins to await your return," she added, punctuating her remarks with a pitiful sigh.

"It will not work," the duke announced. "You may pout all you like, but it will not persuade me to risk my credit with Hoby."

Bea fluttered her lashes prettily and swore that she was just thinking of him and his outsized concern for her welfare. "So far we have only chased villains, but sooner or later, a villain will chase us."

Shaking his head, he marveled at her perverse determination to remind him of the dangers of her unusual pursuit. "Do you *want* me to confine you to the house?"

Clearly, another tactic was in order, and deciding she would discover the extent of Nuneaton's attachment to Hoby, she said, "Oh, dear, he is at the gate. We better start running now."

On that note, she launched herself across the courtyard. The ground was dry, with gravel, and she felt the little rocks drive into her soles as her soft-bottomed shoes dropped heavily on the dirt. The track in the middle of the enclosure came up far more suddenly than she expected, and she leaped awkwardly to avoid tripping. Landing on a stone, she smothered a cry of pain and continued her race to the other side.

The duke was already at the gate by the time she reached it, which was not at all surprising given his many advantages but frustrating nonetheless. Her heart pounding from the exertion, she watched as he cautiously opened the door and gestured that it was safe to advance.

"He went right," Kesgrave said as he secured the gate behind him. "Then he turned left onto Tipton. We must hurry. It is a short street that leads to Gower, where he will be able to get a hack easily."

It was not a huge distance to the corner, and she nodded as she began running again. It was more of an effort now, as her breath was already short, and she felt her lungs burn in protest.

Nevertheless, she arrived at Tipton only a few yards behind Kesgrave, who reported that their quarry had taken another left. They hurried to the next corner in time to see Garfield climb into a hack.

As she examined passing vehicles for one she could flag down to continue their pursuit, Kesgrave stepped in front of a cart and offered two shillings in exchange for use of the conveyance.

The man, his eyes goggling in amazement, readily agreed to the arrangement and jumped down to the pavement with springy enthusiasm. "Take 'er please, for 'owever long you need. Just when yer done, return 'er to Wicklow Street."

Kesgrave, thanking the man, offered him another shilling to seek out Jenkins on Melton and instruct him to return to Berkeley Square.

His grin stretching as wide as London Bridge, the cart's owner announced that he would be delighted to perform this and any other service his lordship might require. "Anything at all, milord, anything at all! No task is too small for Gerald Smith!"

"That is all, my good man," Kesgrave said as he helped Bea climb onto the wagon's seat. The hackney carrying Garfield was moving at a steady if not remarkably fast pace, and there was no time to waste. "Thank you again, and I shall ensure the return of your vehicle as quickly as possible."

But the man, no doubt imagining a compensatory shilling or two, urged him to keep the cart and horse as long as necessary. "Don't ye rush on my account."

As the duke directed the horse into traffic, Bea said, "I really must remember to do that."

He spared her a sidelong glance as he tightened his grip on the reins. "Do what?"

"Brandish my money like a flower seller hawking daisies," she replied.

"I do not brandish; I offer," he said with a hint of defensiveness, "and it bears results."

"Yes, I know," she replied mildly. "That is why I must remember to do it. I am a Hyde-Clare, you understand, so it does not come naturally to me. We do not brandish anything."

"Except your disdain for my consequence," he pointed out.

Smothering the smile that rose to her lips, she said, "On the contrary, your grace, I am in utter awe of your consequence. Remind me, please, how many chafes-wax there are among your family tree, so that I may swoon in admiration."

Kesgrave made no reply to this particularly provoking comment, maneuvering the cart around a corner in silence after Garfield's hack made the turn. He managed to hold his peace for another full minute before clarifying, almost as if by compulsion, that none of his ancestors had ever assumed the minor sinecure. Rather, they had served as Lord Privy Seal.

For her impertinence, Bea found herself subjected to yet another lecture on the various differences between the two positions, and although she nodded at regular intervals as though she were paying attention, she was in fact listening only to the cadence of his voice.

She could not say what exactly about his pedantry appealed to her so much. It was, she supposed, the very great distinction between the man whom she had thought him to be the first time he had bored the company to flinders at Lakeview Hall and the one he turned out to be.

The chasm between the two men yawned wide enough for her to slip inside and there was something heady about the fall.

And that she had landed there—it was inconceivable still.

These thoughts occupied her for several minutes as Kesgrave directed the horse through the crowded street. The little cart did not move as quickly at the hackney cab, but the duke's skill ensured that they kept him always in view.

Finally, the conveyance stopped in front of a gracious townhouse on a leafy street in Chelsea. From the corner, where Kesgrave had halted the rickety cart before they drew too close, Bea murmured, "That is not the residence of a man who needs to a few extra shillings to pay the fishmonger."

"No, it is not," the duke agreed.

It was possible, she thought, that Garfield was employed by the owner, perhaps in the capacity of steward or solicitor, or had been hired to perform a particular function such as to recover something from the foundry. But the earliness of the hour and the assured way he strode up the stairs indicated ownership.

No underling would open the door to another man's home with such bold confidence.

The reason he had been at the foundry had nothing to do with getting paid. He had only pocketed the pounds, coins and quills to convince her otherwise. Without question, he had something to do with Huzza's death. Discovering what exactly began with learning his true identity, which would be easy enough to do with a knock on one of the neighbor's doors.

But would revealing her interest give up some tactical advantage?

Garfield believed he had successfully hoodwinked them, and until they knew more about him, it was better if he continued to think that.

How, then, to find out his real name?

Bea contemplated the question as Kesgrave helped her down from the cart, and lifting her dress to avoid a muddy puddle, she realized her hem was already filthy with ash.

She could use that to their advantage.

"I shall inquire about work," she announced, straightening her shoulders as she turned to open the door.

"Excuse me?" Kesgrave asked.

Amused by the haughtiness in his tone, she explained that she would present herself to the servants' entrance as a woman seeking employment as a maid. "So we can find out who Mr. Garfield really is. My dress is humble and convincingly stained with ash, as if I have already cleaned cinders from a fireplace this morning."

"Madam Bélanger would disagree to that description, for the fabric alone costs more than a maid earns in a month and that is not accounting for the expense of expert sewing," he said.

Bea dismissed these points as minor details no ordinary person would notice at first glance, let alone a harried housekeeper with a long list of chores to which she must attend. "I look enough like a maid to conduct a brief interview. I do not actually have to get the post to learn the name of the proprietor."

"That is to the good, as you lack all qualifications," he said.

"As the former ward of the Hyde-Clares, I must take issue with that sweeping generalization," she said. "I lack some qualifications, to be sure, but I did spend one miserable week changing bed linens and cleaning chamber pots after every member of the household came down with a virulent cold except me. Mind you, I do not think Russell was actually sick. He just knew better than to put himself in the line of fire. It is one of the few signs of intelligence I have seen in him."

The duke owned himself happy to hear it, and although Bea detected a hint of satire in his response, she did not call attention to it. "You wait here. I shall be back in twenty minutes."

In fact, she was back in five, for attempting to seek employment during the chaotic morning rush was a significant failure of timing on her part. She had barely explained her purpose before the housekeeper nudged her toward the door. The only reason Bea managed to discover anything at all was thanks to the cook, who called out that she would be looking for a new kitchen maid soon.

"This one," she added, looking balefully at a young girl with dark green eyes, "can't get it through her thick head that Mr. Garrow likes his bread lightly toasted, not burned."

Protesting, the maid said, "But Timothy likes his—"

But the irate cook was having none of it and asked who paid her wages: Mr. Garrow or his three children?

"Mr. Garrow," she mumbled.

"Correct!" the cook cried. "Mr. Garrow, who doesn't work long hours in an office in Cloak Hart Lane to be greeted with burned toast upon rising."

Muttering that dark-brown toast was not burned, the maid returned to her duties as the cook instructed the housekeeper to get Bea's information. "Mark my words, we will need a new kitchen maid within the week."

Although she was not in fact seeking a position, Bea felt curiously grateful to the cook for her support and thanked the busy woman for her consideration, a gesture that further annoyed the housekeeper. As a consequence, she was swept out the door before she could provide either her name or direction.

Regardless, she considered the mission a success and exhorted Kesgrave to take them to Cloak Hart Lane at once so they could search Mr. Garrow's office before he arrived for the day.

Adamantly, Kesgrave refused. "First, we will return to Berkeley Square to change our clothes and get the carriage."

Bea scoffed at the needless detour, observing that their outfits were ideally suited for skulking around an empty office. "You just do not wish to be spotted driving an inferior carriage."

"I do not, no, brat," he said with a laugh, "and I will not allow you to shame me for not wanting to be seen tooling around London in a pony cart."

"Ah, but this is your chance, Kesgrave, to prove your dominance once and for all," she said rousingly. "Let us spend the whole day in this pony cart and see if the *ton* apes your style. Personally, I find the prospect of the Earl of Bedford noodling about in an elegant wheelbarrow to be excessively diverting."

"Although I seek no higher purpose in life other than to provide you with amusement, I will not surrender my comfort to attain it," he said as he tugged on the reins. The horse plodded forward. "Furthermore, it is already too late in the morning for skulking. If Garrow is the well-set merchant he appears to be, then his clerks will be at their desks toiling away by the time we arrive. If we are to interrogate his staff or his business partners, then I think you will have better success if you are not dressed as a maid."

"But the fabric!" Bea cried mockingly. "The sewing!"

Humbly, Kesgrave admitted that he had overestimated the value of Madam Bélanger's fine handiwork.

"Or you underestimated my acting skills," she replied.

The duke insisted that was not possible.

Chapter Nine

Identifying the sham Mr. Garfield's place of business was remarkably easy because all the other buildings on the small lane were either stores selling their wares or private homes. Only one edifice purported to be an office.

And not merely an office, Bea noted as she read the sign posted in front, but the headquarters of the Tarwich Company. "Of course Mr. Garrow—formerly Mr. Garfield, previously Mr. Grimes—works for a rival steam engine firm. Tarwich's newest model utilizes low-pressure steam and the company stands to lose thousands of pounds if strong steam proves successful."

"An excellent motive," Kesgrave said, opening the door.

"Indeed," she replied as she entered the establishment, with its long narrow hallway leading to a modest room with a wood floor and plaster walls. The only ornamentation she noted as she crossed the threshold was a large landscape with smoke from a steam engine billowing in the distance. To the left of the painting was a corridor that receded into darkness and to its right was a door. In front of it was a desk, at which sat a clerk who smiled as they approached.

Brightly, he bid them good day and asked how he might assist them.

With an ease that was growing increasingly effortless, Bea introduced them as the Duke and Duchess of Kesgrave. "We are here to see Mr. Silas Garrow."

The clerk, bounding to his feet, announced that the estimable gentleman would not arrive for another fifteen or twenty minutes, but his partner, the esteemed Mr. Tarwich, was present. "He is in a meeting now," he continued, speaking rapidly as if afraid they might leave, "but I am sure it will conclude in a matter of minutes. While you are waiting, may I offer you something to drink? Tea perhaps? Or coffee? We also have a very fine claret on hand, although I usually don't offer it to visitors. But I am sure Mr. Tarwich would want me to make you as comfortable as possible, your graces."

Briefly, Bea inspected the room and, deciding that the clerk would most likely have to leave them alone to procure refreshments, replied that a cup of tea would be lovely, thank you.

Detecting nothing suspicious about their interest, the clerk nodded firmly and invited them to take a seat while he prepared the tray. "This won't take a minute," he said as he strode toward the door.

As soon as his back was turned, Bea rushed to the door and pressed her ear against it. She closed her eyes to focus, but all she could hear was the low rumble of voices.

Fleetingly, she considered dropping to her knees to see if the sound was clearer through the open strip at the bottom, but she knew being caught in that position would do irreparable damage to her investigation.

It was hard to be taken seriously when one was lying on the floor, even for a duchess.

Or, rather, especially for a duchess.

Instead, she contented herself with moving her ear around

the wood in hopes of finding a thinner area more suited to eavesdropping.

"Anything interesting?" Kesgrave asked, a smile hovering around his lips as he watched her shift her head yet again.

"Nothing," she said, lamenting the insufferable quality of the door as she tried yet another spot. "It must be two inches thick."

Its exact depth was made immediately known to her as the door opened at that very minute to reveal the room's occupants: a plump man with deep-set gray eyes and a dark-haired man with spectacles.

Startled to find themselves alarmingly close to an unknown young woman, they stared at her in confusion while Bea grappled for an explanation that would make a modicum of sense and settled on an insect.

"A fly!" she cried with more enthusiasm than she had intended. But she was just as disconcerted as the men and appeared incapable of restraining herself. "Yes, a large and hungry fly was stalking the perimeter of the door, but do not worry. I swatted the impertinent little beast."

Although this account hardly clarified matters, the round man swiveled his head abruptly, as if freeing himself from a trance, and said he was grateful for her service. "I do not think I am being indiscreet to admit that flies find me particularly delectable. My legs will be covered with bites while my wife's bear none. It is deuced unfair."

The other man, the one with glasses, made no reply, but his dismayed expression indicated that he thought mention of a woman's limbs was a highly unsuitable topic for mixed company.

Noting this unease, Bea decided the gregarious man must be Tarwich, for only someone who was comfortable in his surroundings would make such an indelicate comment.

"That sounds frightful," she replied with a dramatic shiver as she glanced again at the other man.

His face was vaguely familiar, she thought, focusing on his spectacles.

Without question, she had seen him before.

Where, however, remained a mystery.

Was it at the foundry during the demonstration?

She resisted the urge to close her eyes and picture the crowd.

Instead, she sought an introduction, hoping a name would help nudge her memory, but Tarwich was too distracted by the fly, asking how big it was and from which direction it had flown. As he looked balefully at the fireplace, as if that might be the point of entry, his dark-haired caller took the opportunity to excuse himself.

On the verge of calling him back, Bea found her attention waylaid by Tarwich, who asked in a flurry of anxiety. "Was it the only one or are there others lurking in dark corners?"

"He acted alone. I am certain of it," she replied, turning to see if she could still catch the man but he had already disappeared from sight.

Tarwich, his expression doubtful, did not press her to explain her certainty and merely thanked her for disposing of the threat. "Usually, my clerk can be relied upon, but he is not here at the moment, presumably with good cause, as Mr. Heath is very dependable."

Now that the uproar caused by the fictitious bug had passed, she could see that he was considerably younger than his partner. Scarcely thirty, he could not be the original Tarwich.

A son, perhaps?

She recalled Uncle Horace's observation that Tarwich's new model featured only minor improvements and wondered if that was because of a change in leadership. If the elder Mr.

Tarwich had recently retired or died, then the company could be in the hands of a new owner who did not possess the same mechanical abilities or inventive tendency.

He might at best be a tinkerer.

It was interesting to consider, she decided, as she explained that his clerk dashed off to fetch tea so they may talk. "Do let us sit down," she added, gesturing toward his office, as if inviting him in for a coze.

Tarwich furrowed his brow in confusion, and before he could refuse her request, she added that she wished to discuss Mr. Huzza's death.

His demeanor changed at once, his expression taking on a sad cast as he shook his head. "Yes, of course. It is such a horrible tragedy. It is always worse, I think, when it could have easily been averted. But some men will never learn. Do let us sit and I shall tell you all about the accident and why it occurred and how we can ensure that it never happens again."

Bea, who could not believe the warm welcome was intended for her and the duke, wondered who Tarwich thought they were. "Yes, let's, because I am curious to hear what a man of your knowledge and experience thinks about the accident. What is most striking is the fact that only half of the boiler was destroyed. As you know, a boiler explosion should destroy the entire water tank, not just a portion. Given that that is not what happened, what do you think of the possibility—or, rather, probability—that the blast was caused by an incendiary device planted in the firebox?"

Tarwich stared at her blankly for several seconds, his brows drawing together again as he opened his mouth to speak. Then he closed it and lifted a finger, seemingly intending to chastise her. At that moment, his clerk appeared on the threshold with a silver tray in his grip.

"Here you go, your graces, freshly brewed and still hot," he said.

"Your graces!" Tarwich exclaimed.

The clerk smiled placidly. "The Duke and Duchess of Kesgrave. They have business to discuss with you, and I assured them that you would be happy to meet with them as soon as your last appointment concluded. And I see that it has."

"Oh, dear! This is dreadful," Tarwich said, appearing to speak with astonishing honesty, as if unable to smother the thoughts as they popped into his head. "I cannot talk to you."

Assuredly, his clerk said that he could. "Your next appointment is not until eleven."

Tarwich blanched at this bit of information and darted a baleful look at his unhelpful clerk. "You are forgetting my ten o'clock appointment."

"I am?" the other man asked, startled.

Tarwich's head bobbed frantically up as he sought to remind his assistant of the remarkably busy day ahead of him. Appointments every hour!

"Recall, Mr. Heath, that I have Mr.... Mr...." Unprepared to supply a name, he trailed off and darted his eyes around the room looking for inspiration. Finding it on the floor, he added with gratifying confidence, "Mr. Carpeton. Yes, Mr. Carpeton is set to arrive at nine, so he should be here any minute now. After that I am meeting with Mr."—again, that frantic search—"Chair...erm, Chater. And following Mr. Chater is Mr. Jones. I could go on, but I won't because your time is much too valuable. But I am sure we can schedule something that is more convenient for you. Mr. Heath will arrange it with your steward. In the interim, do not let me keep you. Your day must be especially busy if you felt the need to start it so early. Thank you for your visit and I look forward to speaking with you again at a later date. All right, then, good-bye!"

Tarwich accompanied this speech with increasingly

pointed gestures at his clerk, as if directing his subordinate to personally eject the Duke and Duchess of Kesgrave from the premises. As this could not be what his employer actually desired, Heath stood there, at the entrance to the room, the tray of tea in his grip, utterly baffled. His brows knit tightly, he looked at Bea, as if expecting her to explain why his employer was acting so strangely, and possessing no idea herself, Bea stared back at him.

If she had to speculate—and, to be honest, that was precisely why she was there—she would say Tarwich had something to hide. Whether it had something to do with Huzza's murder, she could not say, but in general, innocent men did not invent meetings with articles of furniture.

Ignoring her host's antics, Bea asked Heath to bring the tea into the office and put it on Mr. Tarwich's desk. Then she followed him into the room, which was large and commodious with its two wide desks of deep, rich mahogany.

The clerk placed the tray on the desk to the left, which was surmounted by a portrait of a blunt-faced gentleman staring directly ahead. Although he bore a faint resemblance to Tarwich, most notably in the thick arch of the nose, his aggressive expression diverged widely from their host's agitated one.

Heath finished laying out the service, and Bea thanked him for his efforts. Then she instructed him to alert them the moment Mr. Carpeton arrived.

"We do not want to keep you from more important business," she explained to Tarwich, whose frenzied disposition had given way to a resigned languidness.

No, not resigned, for he insisted that he would be able to give them only a few minutes—and distracted ones at that. "I have to prepare for my meeting with Mr. Carpeton. He is... um...he runs a manufactory in Surrey and is interested in acquiring a Tarwich engine. Several, actually. So you see it is a very important meeting, and while I would like to spend all afternoon answering your questions, I cannot offend a customer. Business is business, your grace. If you do not understand its importance, I am sure your husband does."

Bea replied that she understood him perfectly, and her tone contained just enough arch knowingness to make him flinch. Nevertheless, he invited them to sit down and took the seat across from them at his lumbering desk.

"Are there many Mr. Carpetons?" she asked once they were settled.

As there were in fact no Mr. Carpetons, Tarwich was momentarily at a loss for how to respond. Anxiously, he picked up the quill on his desk and began to rotate it between his fingers. Then he said he could not pretend to know the extent of a client's family. "He might have several brothers, sons and uncles, or he might have none."

Bea apologized for posing the question so ambiguously and explained that she meant customers like Mr. Carpeton. "I know you debuted a new model last month, and I was seeking to ascertain its success to get a sense of how well your business is doing. Instead, I will put the question to you plainly: What are the Tarwich Company's long-term prospects?"

The hands clutching the quill tightened so quickly, the implement snapped in half. "Oh, dear," he murmured, "I must talk to Mr. Heath about the quality of our plumes." Then, as if fearing the comment reflected poorly on him and the firm, he quickly added that they purchased only the finest supplies and if there was something inferior about the current batch of quills, it was an issue of production standards, not economy. "Tarwich does not scrimp on anything. We do not have to, for the company is doing exceedingly well. Our newest model has been very warmly received because it is safe and efficient and customers value safety and efficiency above all else."

As true as this statement was, it was not the whole truth, Bea thought, for low-pressure steam would never be as efficient as the high-pressure variety. The engines were too large to power a road vehicle like the *Puffing Devil,* and road vehicles were the future.

Of that, Bea was certain.

Sooner or later, the problems with strong steam would be resolved.

Indeed, for all she knew, they already had been. The *Bright Benny*'s true potential remained unknown.

As if aware of her thoughts, Tarwich launched into a detailed description of the firm's recent successes and bright future. "This week alone, we have installed three new machines in Woolsington and secured a contract for a colliery in Birtley," he said, picking up the broken pieces of the quill and toying with the halves before impatiently brushing them aside. Then he balled his hands. "And we are in discussions with a tide mill along the Severn in Shelton to provide pumping engines. I am attending to that matter myself. You see, I am not quite the inventor my father was. He spent all his time in his workshop, fiddling with cylinders and piping, but for me it is more important to meet with our customers and court new ones personally. I consider myself something of an emissary for the company. I know it better than anyone."

Although he strove to appear at ease, keeping his voice even as he explained his role, he could not control the restless movements of his fingers and they grasped a slim knife suitable for opening letters.

"We have this office in London, of course, but our manufactory is near Sheffield," he continued, turning the narrow blade over and over in his hands, "and we employ the finest machinists, engineers and instrument makers in the country."

Adding that he personally ensured that every engine they

produced aligned with his own strict standard of quality, he flipped the knife lengthwise. Its repoussé handle, decorated with green stones, struck a chord with Bea, who stared at the blade as the image of Lord Fazeley dead at her feet flashed through her mind.

To some extent it made sense, yes, for the dagger that had ended the earl's life was also ornate, but that was where the similarity ended. The Singh dagger was delicately carved jade fashioned into the shape of a horse's head. It bore no resemblance to the opener Tarwich held.

Held, she thought, the picture in her head widening as she saw the whole scene: Fazeley falling, the knife protruding, the newspapermen swarming.

At once, she knew where she had seen him before, the dark-haired man with spectacles, and why their host had welcomed them so warmly.

Glancing again at the picture of the elder Mr. Tarwich, she made a few quick calculations and said, "That is all very well, but the truth is, your business is in decline, your patents are about to expire, and you cannot compete with strong steam."

The hand holding the knife clenched, but Tarwich managed to keep his expression blank as he assured her that was not the case. "As I said, we installed three new engines this week alone and next week—"

"That is why you sabotaged the *Bright Benny,*" Bea continued as if he had not spoken. "Powerless to stop progress, you decided to stall it by employing the strategy that worked so well for James Watt and Matthew Boulton in the wake of the Greenwich explosion in 1803. The difference is, in their case, they had an actual incident to exploit. You did not, so you created one."

Tarwich's eyes flashed furiously as he drove the knife into

his desk so deeply it stood for several seconds before wobbling to the side and clattering onto the wood.

"How dare you!" he shouted, rising to his feet and planting his hands squarely on the desk so he could tower over her.

Ignoring his display of outrage, she said, "Given that you were bracketed in this office with a reporter from the *London Daily Gazette* when we arrived, I think the question is, how dare *you*?"

Flustered by her recognition of the journalist, something he had clearly not anticipated, Tarwich flushed hotly as his jaw clenched. Then he said, "Oh, I *dare* to protect my fellow citizens from perils they can barely begin to understand. As an emissary of the Tarwich Company it is my moral obligation. The public has a right to know that high-pressure steam is deadly. The explosion yesterday was a shocking tragedy, to be sure, but a predictable one. The more you tamper with strong steam, the more likely it will tamper with you. I know it, my father knew it, and, yes, Watt and Boulton knew it. It falls to men of science to tell the truth, whatever the cost, and I will always do my duty. To imply that I would overstep the bounds of morality and decency to cause harm to anyone is ludicrous, and I cannot conceive why you decided to seek me out to lodge your accusations. I am very disappointed, your grace. I would expect better from someone of your standing in society."

Clearly, he was not an aficionado of Mr. Twaddle-Thum's work.

"In fact, we did not seek you out," she said. "An interest in your partner, Mr. Garrow, brought us here. It is only by chance that I recognized the reporter from the *Gazette.* Tell me, Mr. Tarwich, how many other reporters have you met with?"

"Two," he said defiantly. "Mr. Arnold of the *Tribune* and

Mr. O'Keefe of the *Beacon*. That was last night. I have more appointments scheduled for later today, including the *Herald* and the *Times*. And you cannot stop me, for I have the right to share my concerns. *You* have no right to harass me or my associate."

"How did you and Mr. Garrow come to be partners?" Bea asked. "As he is several decades older than you, I can only conclude that you assumed your position relatively recently."

"I am young but not inexperienced," Tarwich said stiffly. "My father made sure I knew every aspect of the business before he retired. He is too infirm now to oversee the day-to-day business, but he knows it is in capable hands. Mr. Garrow feels the same and trusts me to discharge my duties expertly."

It was, Bea thought, a revealingly defensive response, for she had asked the query only to establish the facts, not to question his competence. "Is helping your associate misrepresent himself among your duties?"

Tilting his head in confusion, Tarwich insisted he had no idea what she was talking about.

Clarifying, she explained that Mr. Garrow had been at the demonstration yesterday under false pretenses. "And we"—here she looked at the duke to include him—"are trying to find out why."

Tarwich vigorously shook his head. "You are misinformed. Mr. Garrow was nowhere near Bloomsbury yesterday. He was touring a warehouse in Stockwell."

"He was at the demonstration in the employ of Mr. Huzza, pretending to be a man named Mr. Grimes," she said, examining him for signs of additional anxiety but he had managed finally to still his fingers. It was possible he knew nothing about his partner's illicit pursuit, but given how nicely his own activities dovetailed with them, it struck her as highly unlikely. "And then this morning we encountered him at the foundry, where he was rummaging through the firm's private office, this time posing as a Mr. Garfield."

But Tarwich, shaking his head before she finished her sentence, insisted she was mistaken as he rose, walked over to the other desk in the room and shuffled through an assortment of papers. He pulled out a square sheet and held it up. "No, you see, he was in Stockwell. Here is the sketch he made of the warehouse's many rooms."

As there was nothing conclusive about a drawing chosen at random, Bea did little more than glance at it and insisted he was the one who was wrong. "But there is no reason to argue about it. We will put the question to Mr. Garrow as soon as he arrives."

"Of course, yes, an excellent proposal," he said, his expression brightening for the first time since they had entered the office. "Mr. Garrow typically arrives around noon. If you could return at that time, then I am sure we can settle this matter to all our satisfaction."

"That is all right," Bea said, leaning back comfortably in her chair. She had no intention of leaving and allowing the two men to compare their stories and arrive at a shared narrative. Furthermore, she would not surrender the element of surprise. Garfield née Grimes believed he had tricked them with his heavily laden pockets, and she wanted to see how he reacted when he discovered they had not been fooled by his facile attempt. "We'll wait. Do not mind us."

Oh, but that was impossible for Tarwich, for their presence deeply unnerved him, and he immediately began to fuss with the teapot, removing the lid and sliding it back on again. Fretfully, he warned them that it could be the *entire* day. "One never knows with Mr. Garrow. He has so many commitments."

"Then, yes, thank you, I would love a cup of tea," she said, as if he had offered.

Tarwich jumped, as if prodded in the side by a stick, dropping the lid, which fell onto the desk with a dull thud. He returned it to its place with awkward fingers and poured.

The brew was strong and reviving, and sipping deeply, Bea felt no compulsion to speak. Despite his claim that his partner would not arrive for hours, if at all, she knew he would be there soon.

It was nine forty-eight now.

Tarwich, visibly unnerved by the silence, toyed with the handle of the teapot for several long minutes, alternately tracing its curve with his fingers and tapping it to produce a simple rhythm.

Then, as if he could not help himself, he said, "The tea is souchong."

Having recognized the flavor, Bea said, "Yes."

"It's from a store near Spitalfields," he explained.

"Lovely," Bea said.

Tarwich acknowledged the accuracy of her assessment with an abrupt nod and then looked down into his cup as if fascinated by its pattern. A moment later, he continued, "On Groat Street, next to a milliner. I found it quite by accident one day. I was walking home from church, and it began to drizzle and I stepped inside to get out of the rain and I discovered I was in a charming little shop. Naturally, I felt inclined to buy something after taking advantage of its warmth and dryness."

Intrigued by his compulsion to chatter, which seemed to rival Aunt Vera's, Bea responded with another one-word answer.

Satisfied, Tarwich took a deep sip of his own tea and managed to sit without fussing for a good thirty seconds. Then he said, "I find the area actually has several fine stores. It is also where we buy our ink, at Compton's, which has an excellent formulation. Mr. Compton soaks his oak galls for a full two weeks before boiling down the liquid. It makes the ink more suitable for paper, I think, lessening the amount of disintegration over time. At least, that is what I have observed. I have not made a formal study of both. It is merely that whenever I notice that a document is particularly difficult to read because of damage to the sheet, I check my records and see that it was from a stationer other than Compton."

Having made this pronouncement, he paused, as if expecting Bea or Kesgrave to share a similar experience. When neither ventured a comment, he volunteered that the word *records* rather overstated the case, as it was really just a book in which he made haphazard notations. "It is nothing liked the detailed records a former military man like Mr. Heath keeps for the company. He is an excellent clerk, quite the most capable one I have employed during my tenure. I cannot tell you what a pleasure it is to have one's files in order. To be able to locate what you are looking for is a revelation. I do not know what I would do without him. It is so difficult to find reliable workers."

Once again, he gave Bea and the duke an opportunity to respond, perhaps with a sympathetic tale of their own difficulties in retaining good help, and continued to detail the value of competent filing when his remark was met with silence. He was describing how much easier it was to negotiate a new colliery contract with the current agreement in one's grasp when a movement in the doorway caught his attention.

"My goodness, well, look who is here two hours early!" he said, rising to his feet as Garrow entered the room. "A good thing, too, because we have visitors who are eager to meet you. They are the Duke and Duchess of Kesgrave, and although they are under the impression they have already met you at Mr. Huzza's foundry in Bloomsbury, I have assured them that is not possible because you were in Stockwell yesterday."

It was, Bea thought, a rather heavy-handed attempt to convey secret information publicly, a judgment with which Garrow agreed for he told his partner not to say another word.

"They are trying to lay the blame for Huzza's accident at our feet," the new arrival added sharply. "They have convinced themselves it was an elaborate murder plot, and we are their favorite suspects. Reveal nothing!"

Bea, turning to Kesgrave, said, "You are correct. He did hear our whole conversation."

Tarwich's eyes flew wide as he gasped, "You *were* there!"

"Of course I was," Garrow snapped impatiently, "and if you cared anything about our company, you would have been, too. Huzza's engine posed a direct threat to our business. I cannot overstate what terrible things it would have portended for us if it had been a success."

His partner laughed awkwardly at this dire prediction, then darted a glance at Bea and said his partner's gloomy outlook was needlessly alarmist. "He started the Tarwich Company with my father more than twenty years ago and remembers the struggle to establish themselves. Moreover, he has always been on the numbers end of the business, keeping the ledgers to make sure the firm had enough money to settle its debts and pay its staff. That is why he tends to look at everything as if it is a problem that needs to be solved. But that is not the case here, I promise you, your grace. Even if Mr. Huzza's steam engine had turned out to be viable, we would have no cause to fear it because we are a trusted firm with a history of manufacturing a reliable product. In twenty-three years of business, never once has a Tarwich machine exploded. But Mr. Huzza's invention was not viable because strong steam is not viable. It is too precarious, as yesterday's tragic events demonstrated. I know Mr. Garrow did not interfere because he had no reason to interfere."

Now it was Garrow's gaze that flitted toward Bea as he defiantly contradicted his partner. "I did interfere! I hinted away as many investors as possible. I did not want them sinking their money into that deadly contraption and making us all less safe. You may object to my methods but even in my deception I behaved honorably. If Huzza had examined Mr. Garfield's credentials, he would have immediately discovered that he did not exist. But he did not do even that minor amount of diligence to confirm my identity. I can only assume he brought that same level of inattention to his work. If he had been more thorough, then he would still be alive."

"No, he would not," Bea replied succinctly, "because his death was not a fault of engineering or construction. The *Bright Benny* was intentionally made to explode. It was sabotage."

Flinching at this reassertion, Tarwich begged the duchess to please stop saying the word *sabotage*. "It sounds so brutal, and I am sure neither I nor Mr. Garrow would ever do anything so ghastly. You judge me harshly for talking to reporters so soon after the explosion, but what would you have me do? Hold my tongue when I know how many lives are at stake? I cannot believe that is the proper Christian response. I must speak honestly about the dangers of strong steam even if it opens me to censure and charges of exploitation."

Garrow, lauding his partner's valiant stand against the duchess's efforts to silence him, dismissed her claim as patently silly. "Yes, I heard you and the duke talking to each other with authority as if either one of you had any idea what steam power actually entails. I was embarrassed for you then, and I am embarrassed for you now. Please do me and Mr. Tarwich the courtesy of leaving so that we may return to our work. I am sure you have consumed enough of my time today."

Accustomed to the outrage, either sincere or false, of her suspects, Bea ignored his comment and asked Tarwich if anyone could vouch for his movements the day before. "Or were you at the demonstration as well?"

"I was here!" Tarwich insisted, his voice rising as he began to cite people who could attest to his presence in the office: Mr. Heath, Mrs. Tarwich, the solicitor Mr. Kittson. Then, as Garrow's glare deepened, he laughed awkwardly and said witnesses (Oh, and Henry, who brought around the *London Tribune* every day at eleven!) were beside the point. "My partner is an honest man and as such was performing the only service an honest man could in the circumstance, which was warning investors away from high-pressure steam."

"That sounds very high-minded, Mr. Tarwich, but these are more lies. I was present at the demonstration myself and observed his behavior firsthand," Bea said. "He was wooing investors, not dissuading them."

"Ah, but was I?" Garrow asked with an intolerable air of superiority. "Because I distinctly remember telling you as bluntly as possible not to invest."

That was true, yes, he had insisted that the Duke of Kesgrave would take too large of a stake and would do better to start his own steam engine manufacture.

But Uncle Horace—he had definitely encouraged him to invest.

Well, no, she realized.

Rather, he praised the enterprise with such soaring rhetoric, her uncle physically recoiled. At the time it seemed as though he simply lacked the ability to decipher the thoughts of his listener, but in retrospect she could see that he had intentionally reinforced every one of her uncle's concerns.

"What I lied to you about was my reason for being at the foundry this morning, which was to find the designs for the *Bright Benny* to show to reporters," Garrow said with a hint of contempt. "I am sure you can appreciate why I would rather have you think I was a greedy opportunist than a business competitor seeking an advantage. I knew how it would look when I heard you and the duke speculating about the cause of Huzza's death, so I ran back to the office and stuffed my pockets with anything I could find."

"Not the office!" Tarwich said reproachfully, further dismayed by the depths of his partner's subterfuge. "I said they would never be—"

Abruptly, he broke off as a fit of coughing overtook him. He waved his hand apologetically for several seconds before continuing. "I cannot believe you pretended to be a greedy opportunist. I must apologize, your grace, for I see now why you distrust my partner. I'm sure we can attribute his shameful behavior to anxiety of being caught where he did not belong and being blamed for something he did not do."

Bea, however, was not fooled by this display. Clearly, the partners had been working together in their scheme to undermine Huzza & Company's future. The scope of that endeavor eluded her, but at the very least they were determined to exploit Huzza's death to the greatest extent possible.

"At the very least!" Tarwich repeated sharply. "Your grace, it is the very *most.* I promise you, we had nothing to do with the accident—and I am sure it is an accident regardless of what you think the boiler should or should not look like. But as men of experience and knowledge, it falls to us to secure the safety of thousands. We will not be cowed by your disapproval."

But he was, slightly, and slunk back in his chair.

"The real question you should be asking, your grace, is why I could not find the drawings," Garrow said snidely.

"That is what you should be investigating, not me and my partner, whose only crime is trying to save lives."

"All right," she said mildly. "I will bite. Why, Mr. Garrow, could you not find the drawings?"

"Because that scoundrel Lynch already took them," he replied. "They're probably ash by now."

Bea very much doubted that. The man who had stood in the middle of the courtyard yesterday and relayed the exact dimensions of the steam carriage had a reverence for technical specifications. He would not burn them. Furthermore, she could not imagine what would be gained by their destruction. Either the owner of the firm was responsible for the explosion or he had nothing to do with it. In both cases, he would be eager to rebuild the engine to recoup his investment.

Nevertheless, she duly asked why Lynch would burn the designs.

"To destroy evidence, obviously," he replied with barely concealed derision. "Careful inspection of the drawings by a man such as myself or Mr. Tarwich or a half dozen other experts would reveal that the *Bright Benny* was inherently flawed and he and Huzza blatantly ignored the danger. Mark my words, you will hear lots of talk about a valve, as if the problem is only a minor issue that can be easily fixed. That was Trevithick's ploy after the Greenwich explosion, and where is he now? Banished to the hinterlands of South America. Without the original plans, no one can prove otherwise, and all Lynch has to say is the papers were destroyed in the fire. This will allow him to start his next enterprise without the stain of this egregious failure hanging over him. I would not be surprised if he found a fresh batch of half-wits to gull into investing in a new and improved model."

"That is precisely what he will do," Tarwich inserted. "Any

man who would seek to further the cause of high-pressure steam is already without conscience."

"Only the model will never materialize," Garrow added. "Lynch will spend the next year making a great show of fixing these so-called minor flaws while in reality he is pocketing their money. It is an age-old swindle."

"Well, not quite age-old," Bea corrected, "given the relative newness of high-pressure steam."

"You misunderstand me," Garrow said. "It is Lynch with the long history of cheating investors. Every one of his businesses has ended in failure. If you are so determined to find a culprit for this awful tragedy, your grace, then I suggest you look there. Lynch is the one who is trying to exploit Huzza's death, not us. We are merely doing our part to ensure that the public knows the truth about the dangers of strong steam."

Having conducted several investigations, Bea was familiar with the habit of suspects to cast doubt in other people's direction, and she took Garrow's comments with a grain of salt. By any measure, Garrow made an excellent focus: He was partner in a firm that was likely to suffer if the rival technology succeeded, and his assumption of a false identity provided him with the access necessary to tamper with the engine. She could not know the true state of the company's finances, but she did not need to have the ledgers in hand to know that the success of the *Bright Benny* would have been fatal to its long-term prospects.

Garrow and Tarwich both had a motive for killing Huzza, but only the former had an opportunity to carry it out.

Even so, she knew she could not rule out Lynch.

If Garrow had one opportunity to sabotage the *Bright Benny*, then Lynch had had dozens. Furthermore, it was not unheard of for partners to nurse ardent dislikes of one another. Perhaps a disagreement about the direction of the business got out of hand or a personal matter erupted in violence. If Garrow's claim about Lynch's history of business failures was true, it could be a combination of the two.

Huzza might have tried to thwart Lynch's attempt to defraud their investors and therefore needed to be removed.

Bea allowed it was outlandish, but wild supposition was part of her investigative process and she had learned months ago not to dismiss a thought just because it seemed implausible.

Nevertheless, Garrow and his partner still struck her as the more viable culprits, and she spent another fifteen minutes interrogating them on their movements for the previous four and twenty hours.

Chapter Ten

It was quite disconcerting for the former Beatrice Hyde-Clare to discover that she could still be cowed by the intimidating stare of a London butler even after inhabiting the role of the Duchess of Kesgrave for several weeks and overcoming the contempt (mostly) of the formidable Marlow.

Lynch's servant possessed none of Marlow's unsettling physical traits—his brows, for example, were benign brown strips that dipped gently even as his jaw hardened with impatience—and yet she felt the familiar desire to apologize and slink away when he repeated for the third time that his employer was not at home.

He was not even scowling.

No, his visage bore an almost pleasant expression as he blocked the entrance to the elegant home in Sutherland Street.

It was absurd, she thought, for Kesgrave was right beside her, lending his consequence, and she towered over the other man by a good five inches.

He should never have been able to daunt her, and she

wondered if it was possible to add lessons on "overcoming Mayfair butlers" to her training schedule. It seemed at least as useful a skill as planting a facer and, in both cases, height could be used to advantage.

The duke felt none of her timidity, and after failing to ascertain if the owner of the establishment was not at home or just not at home to visitors, stated that it made no difference. "We shall wait on Mr. Lynch's convenience."

Startled by the announcement, the butler took a half step back, intending, Bea decided, to close the door in their faces, but Kesgrave considered it an invitation and confidently strode across the threshold.

Now the servant's eyebrows shot up and he stammered that he could not allow them to wait because their time was much too valuable. "As soon as Mr. Lynch returns, I will relay your interest and urge him to pay a call on you at your home immediately."

The answer to the duke's original query, however, was delivered with just a little too much zeal, and convinced now that the target of their investigation was already in residence, he said they would wait upon Lynch's pleasure in the drawing room. "Do inform him that there is no rush," he added, not unkindly. "We understand this is a difficult time for him and have no wish to add to his suffering. We merely seek to learn information that only he has."

Scampering to keep up with Kesgrave's long strides, the butler made another, less dignified attempt to dissuade him. "No, no, you mustn't intrude...difficult time, yes, it is very difficult. Mr. Lynch is not...he has not.... At least wait in the study. It contains Mr. Lynch's prized collection of...of...of..."

He trailed off as Kesgrave unerringly located the door to the drawing room and opened it to find the master of the house sprawled on the floor surrounded by technical drawings and empty bottles of wine.

On a strangled note, the butler said, "Books! Mr. Lynch's prized collection of books. He has one from every decade. Please let me show it to you. It is just down the corridor a little way."

Lynch, who presumably lay where he fell, his cheek missing the gentle pile of the rug by half an inch to press instead against the cold surface of the wood planks, moaned in greeting. Without opening his eyes, he flipped onto his back and insisted that he was able to receive visitors.

"Let them come, Woolley," he muttered. "Let them come and pick at my bones like the vultures they are."

The butler, unable to comply comfortably with this directive, darted farther into the room, as if to block the callers' view of his employer and pleaded with him to rise. "Sir, do let me help you to—"

Indifferent to his efforts, Lynch announced that the clock on the mantelpiece was worth ten guineas. Flinching, the butler made a second attempt to draw the sotted man to his feet and was rebuffed again—this time with the price of the candlesticks on the side table, which were made by Hester Bateman.

"Example of her in-elf-able...in-af-idle...unique style," Lynch added, stumbling over the word. "Simple, classic, graceful, simple. Won't accept a shilling less than thirteen pounds. And don't try to sharp me on the price. I know the value of a good Bateman. The vase is awful. Terribly inferior. I was sharped on that one. But let's keep that as our secret. Don't tell anyone it is not worth the eight guineas I paid for it."

The prospect of having a secret delighted Lynch, and he began to giggle, quietly at first and then uproariously, as if he were incapable of stopping.

But then he did stop abruptly, perhaps confused by the silence or alarmed by it, and he opened his eyes. Blandly, he blinked up at Kesgrave and Bea, his expression entirely blank, then the elegance of their appearance penetrated his wine-soaked mind and he scrambled to his feet. He rose suddenly, unsteadily, his arms shooting out to the side as if to seek purchase. Finding nothing within reach, he teetered slightly, first to the left, then to the right, before finding his balance.

"I must apologize," he said, his tone oddly formal for the picture he presented. Now that he was standing, Bea could see that he was still dressed in the same clothes as yesterday, the white of his shirt marred by ash, its cuffs frayed by fire itself. "I thought you were someone else."

"A creditor?" Bea asked.

Lynch, his eyes level, revealed no discomfort as he confirmed her supposition. "Many creditors. All the creditors. A veritable horde of creditors. Yesterday's incident ruined me. I have nothing left. Huzza and all that he would create are gone, taken in a flash, and I am left but an ember of my former self. But do not let my misery get in the way of your comfort. Please sit down. Woolley, do fetch the Duchess of Kesgrave—" He broke off his request and looked at her questioningly. "It is the Duchess of Kesgrave, correct? I recognize you from the demonstration yesterday. You were pointed out to me by one of our employees as among the most illustrious potential investors."

"Was that employee Mr. Garfield?" she asked.

"Oh, my," he said on an awkward laugh. "The fact that you know his real name is not Mr. Grimes tells me you have already discovered quite a bit about yesterday's event. Even so, there is no point in having an unhappy conversation whilst standing in the middle of the drawing room. I know I should dash upstairs and make myself more presentable, but there is really no point in that now, is there? It would make *me* feel a bit better about hosting you, but your time is valuable and you already know the worst. I am feeling a bit wobbly after last night's debauch and would enjoy a strong cup of coffee. May I offer you the same or would you prefer tea?"

Bea, accepting both the seat and refreshment on behalf of herself and Kesgrave, sat down as she observed that Lynch seemed surprisingly coherent for a man who had polished off four bottles of wine.

As if to disprove her point, he stared at her uncomprehendingly for several moments before looking down at the floor and examining the evidence. He let out another self-conscious chuckle before explaining that he had not drunk alone. "Mr. Rhodes—you recall him from yesterday as well?—returned here with me to drown our grief. He can dip much deeper than I. My upper limit is usually three glasses before my head starts to spin, but this was the finest my cellar has to offer and I did not allow a little dizziness to stop me. The cellar, you see, will be sold off with the house, and I saw no reason to allow the best vintage to slip away unappreciated. I must confess I am not so confident in the wisdom of that decision now."

As Woolley left the room, Lynch lowered himself into an armchair, at first gingerly to protect its light-colored silk from his charred clothes, then with indifference as he remembered it was no longer his. "Not really. Or, more accurately, not for long. It is only a matter of time before everything is gone. I have already had a note from the bank, and Waugh called at a punishingly early hour with papers for me to sign," he said with a morose grimace as he tilted his eyes down. He seemed permanently engrossed in his own sadness, but just when Bea through she would have to prod him to speak, he shrugged and raised his head. "As you can see, I have made some poor financial decisions based on my expectation of success, and I fear it has made me somewhat facile this morning. Presumably, that is why I cannot fathom the reason for this call. It cannot be to berate me for employing Mr. Garfield, for it seems like a poor use of your time. But if it is, please berate me quietly because my head is pounding from the ill effects of too much drink."

Bea could see the pain on his face, almost feel the ache in his bones, but she could not say if it was from alcohol or financial ruin. Both came at a hefty price. "Why did you feel the need to employ a man like Mr. Garfield? The *Bright Benny,* had it not exploded, would have easily garnered investors."

"Had it not exploded!" Lynch repeated with a scathing laugh. "That is perhaps the largest caveat in the history of invention. Yes, your grace, *had it not exploded,* the *Bright Benny* would have easily garnered investors, but we wanted to leave nothing to chance. I was resistant to the idea of someone like Mr. Garfield when Peter proposed hiding him in the crowd. It felt so unseemly and dishonest. But that was why it was so perfect, Peter argued. Mr. Garfield could petition openly for investments, allowing me to remain decorously quiet on the subject."

His explanation rang true, for she recalled Huzza's amused contempt for his partner's squeamishness, and was only surprised now that the inventor did not identify Garfield as being in his employ during his brief speech. "How did Mr. Huzza find him?"

Lynch pursed his lips and said he had met him in a tavern or his club. "Maybe during a stroll in Hyde Park? I should have a more definitive answer, but you have to understand how hectic everything was in the final days before the demonstration. So much to do, so much to finish, and Peter laid low with some horrid stomach ailment. He said it was something he ate—potatoes, a kipper that had turned—but I know it was anxiety. The pressure was unbearable after so many years of failure and hard work. He needed the *Bright Benny* to succeed. It was his whole life, everything he had. And his nerves could not stand it. When he introduced me to

Mr. Garfield, he said having someone in the audience brimming with enthusiasm would calm my nerves, but I think it was really for him," he explained, then tilted his head curiously, as if confounded by the conversation. "Is this truly why you are here?"

"It is related," Bea replied.

"Related to what?" Lynch asked, still bewildered by her interest.

"To the condition the *Bright Benny* was in after the explosion," she explained, raising what she considered to be the most salient aspect of his response. If she had noticed something strange in the charred husk of the steam carriage, why had he not? Intimately acquainted with strong steam and the dangers it posed, he should have spotted the discrepancy immediately.

The fact that he appeared oblivious to it argued for his complicity.

If he had destroyed the machine to remove his partner, then calling attention to the partially intact remnant was the last thing he would do.

Raising questions would be disastrous to his plan.

It was also possible that he had simply been too distraught to pay any attention to the smoldering engine. Presumably, seeing one's partner disintegrate in a ball of fire and steel had a debilitating effect on one's observational powers—especially when it was accompanied by total financial ruination. If Lynch's situation was as dire as he claimed, then his agitation over Huzza would have been mingled with apprehension for himself.

"I do not understand, and I'm sure that is my fault, your grace. On top of everything else, I am exhausted from lack of sleep. Rhodes and I were up half the night staring at those cursed plans to make sense of the disaster," Lynch said bitterly, pointing to the drawings on the floor. "The poor boy, he is crushed by Huzza's death. He is convinced he is to blame. The fusible plug. The damned fusible plug! It seems so unfair. His dedication has been invaluable and as soon as we turned a profit, I promised to reward him hugely. We were so close!" He raised his fist as if to strike something with all his might, and then let it drop ineffectually into his lap. "But please, before I go off on another tangent, tell me why you are here."

Complying with his request and the exhaustion she heard in his voice, Bea said, "It struck me as odd that the entire boiler had not been destroyed in the explosion, as would be expected if a blast was caused by an excess of pressure, so the duke and I visited the foundry this morning to investigate. That is where we found the man you know as Mr. Garfield, who was rummaging through your office in search of *Bright Benny*'s designs to prove that it was fatally flawed. He works for a rival firm and seeks to publicize the dangers of strong steam to permanently undermine the public's trust in it."

As precise and coherent as the explanation was, it utterly confounded Lynch, who gaped at her as if she had just introduced him to her pet giraffe.

Familiar with the expression, she waited patiently for him to turn to Kesgrave and make a derogatory comment about her ability to reason or her investigative pretension.

Ah, yes, I had read in one of Mr. Twaddle-Thum's amusing accounts that the duchess fancied herself something of a Lady Runner. How charming!

But he did not.

Instead, he nodded his head violently and said, "Yes, yes, yes, I see what you are saying. Yes, it is exactly that. I knew the *Bright Benny* was too well made to explode like that, whatever Rhodes said about the fusible plug being made from an alloy instead of pure lead. A rival firm sabotaged it! Was it

Watt & Boulton? Of course it was Watt & Boulton! They are evil-minded men. Look what they did in Greenwich!"

Having settled on the august firm, he immediately presented another possibility and suggested that Phillips was responsible, for everyone knew Watt was an old man now and Phillips had never quite achieved the success of his largest competitor.

"Or maybe it was Waugh," he said excitedly, rising to his feet to pace the room. "Have you considered that, your grace? He could have hired Garfield to pretend to work for Watt to ensure my ruin. I would not put it past him. The man is a sharp. The terms of our agreement were criminally harsh and excessively unfair to me. I would never have agreed if the situation had not been so dire. But I knew the *Bright Benny* would triumph. It was a wonder, and we were going to build things. Great things. Things the world has never seen before."

On this note, he sighed deeply, his excitement leaving him, and he sunk to the floor in despair. "Such great things," he repeated mournfully.

True enough, Bea thought, for nobody had ever conceived of anything like a tramroad to the seaside.

"How did your situation grow so dire?" she asked.

Resentfully, he raised his head and spat, "Rice!"

Knowing herself to be reasonably well informed on financial matters, thanks to several weighty tomes on banking and the London broadsheets, she was at a loss to make sense of this enigmatic reply.

Kesgrave, however, had an inkling and suggested Lynch was referring to the famine in the Vijayapura region of the subcontinent that was caused by the failure of the rice crop and poor management by the Dominion Trading Company. Land revenue shortfalls ensued, and Dominion was unable to discharge its debts or pay the taxes it owed. When this information became public, several banks in London collapsed. "Did you hold much stock in the company?"

Lynch shook his head vehemently and brought his hand hard on the floorboard. "None. I had no stock at all. But that is the event that set in motion all my financial troubles. Every failure I have suffered since then can be traced back to that single moment. The bank I borrowed money from to expand my business immediately called in my loans and I had to scramble to find funding at inhospitable terms. Saddled with even more debt, my business eventually failed."

In close proximity to the wine, he reached for one of the bottles and drew it to his lips, forgetting it was empty, then sputtered angrily when no liquid emerged. He bellowed for his butler, who presented himself promptly bearing the tray.

Noting its contents, which had been specifically requested by him barely ten minutes before, Lynch growled angrily and said, "Coffee? Who can stomach coffee on a day like this! Bring me another bottle of the Château de Goulaine."

Woolley replied that the cellar was empty of that vintage.

A glint of satisfaction entered Lynch's eye as he digested this information. "Is it indeed? Well done, Woolley!" he said as if the butler himself had consumed the stock. "Very well done! In that case, let us have my second-finest wine. It is a port, I believe. Kopke."

The servant murmured agreeably as he placed the tray on the table next to Bea, at whom he darted an apologetic glance.

Or perhaps it was contemptuous.

It was so difficult to tell with these impassive London butlers, she thought, and just because she had done nothing in the past minute to secure his disapproval did not mean she had not earned it.

In most cases, her mere existence was enough.

Lynch, his mood vastly improved by the prospect of more

wine, returned himself to the chair and noted the inferiority of the teapot. "It is plate silver, made by a metalworker in Brinsworth. It does not even have a mark and is worth very little. Most of the serving pieces are of the same low quality. Only the silver on the mantelpiece is pure. I am a man of business and know the usefulness of judiciously displaying items of value. Left to my own devices, I do not need to cut my turbot with sterling."

Imagining the disappointment of his creditors cheered him further, and he rattled off a list of his least valuable possessions. "The pianoforte. It is by Zumpe and very unimpressive, the type of instrument the vicar's daughter plays. The sound is bland and muddy. And my pair of bays are quite plodding. Like the teapot, they look good from afar, feisty and even, but they are high-steppers. Their stride is short, and they tire easily."

Hoping to return the conversation to more useful footing, Bea asked him what he did after his business failed.

"Started another one, of course," he replied. "An ironworks. But it was built on a millstream that could not provide enough power, especially in the summer, when its flow was diminished. I bought a Phillips steam engine to pump the water back up to the pond. It was a good machine but not powerful enough to solve my problem. I thought surely something better existed and that is how I found Peter. He had just finished building the model before *Benny,* a clever thing that turned out to be too heavy for its own tracks—it crushed them—and had to start again. He required money to do that, and the timing was opportune because the ironworks was failing after a dry spring further diminished the flow. I sold the building, borrowed money from the bank and founded Huzza & Company. We were set for a while, but we needed more money and the banks refused to extend more credit because I was already overdrawn and my house mortgaged.

We were so close. Peter just had to finish the prototype and then we would be set, so I struck a deal with Waugh. The terms were terrible, but I did not think twice because I knew the *Bright Benny* would exceed my wildest dreams."

Lynch closed his eyes and rested his head against the back of the chair. He stayed like that—peaceful, silent—for so long, Bea began to wonder if he had fallen asleep even as she watched his fingers stroke the wood armrest.

"And it did, I suppose," he mumbled, "for never in all my imaginings did I conceive a scene like yesterday."

Woolley returned then with the port, which Lynch took from his grasp with greedy fingers. As the butler had failed to deliver a wineglass and drinking out of the bottle in front of the Duke and Duchess of Kesgrave was a little too outré for the gentleman, even in his state of sorrow and fury, Lynch poured the port into a teacup. He emptied it quickly and promptly supplied a refill.

Bea waited patiently for him to remove his nose from the cup. "Why do you think Waugh was so eager to get his hand on your shares that he would sabotage the *Bright Benny*?"

"Because he is a ruthless land developer famous for his avarice and cunning," he replied, "the devil of Darby Lane, the fiend at number fifteen. If he decided he wanted to take control of Huzza & Company, that is precisely how he would do it. All of the firm's value is in its patents for the *Bright Benny.* They are worth ten times what I owe him, even sharing ownership with a parcel of unruly orphans."

"A parcel of orphans?" she asked, uncertain how parentless children had entered the conversation.

Perhaps Lynch was not as sober as he appeared.

"Peter's heirs," he explained, the slight sneer in his voice indicating what he thought of the behest. "A parcel of orphans and an assortment of widows. That is whom Waugh is partners with now."

"I think he means a charity organization," Kesgrave ventured.

"Yes, the Kindly Home for Sad Widows and Miserable Children Suffering Horribly Because of the War," he said with a cackle that turned into a cough.

"I suspect that is not the proper name," Bea said to the duke.

"No," he agreed with a hint of a smile. "It is too long to fit on the stationery."

Lynch, gulping down another cup, laughed as he imagined the challenges Waugh would face trying to conduct his business in concert with a bunch of kindhearted reformers who understood nothing about steam power.

"Ah, but Waugh comprehends little himself," he added with a giggle, "for he wildly overplayed his hand this time. Blowing up the *Bright Benny* might have gotten him the patents, but it also ruined their value. It might as well be the day after the Greenwich explosion for all the faith the public has in strong steam. Huzza & Company is worthless."

The notion so delighted him, he forgot niceties such as teacups and drank directly from the bottle. Bea, watching as he swallowed gulp after gulp in rapid succession, decided they would most likely not get much more useful information from him.

Nevertheless, she made another attempt to learn the correct name of the charity organization. For her efforts, she was subjected to increasingly juvenile titles, such as the Sad Home for Sniveling Widows and Snotty Brats Whose Fathers Were Too Stupid to Survive the War. Lynch, laughing uproariously at his own witticism, held out the bottle so that his visitors may partake as well.

Kesgrave, declining politely, said to Bea, "I find as a general rule that when the person to whom you are speaking begins offering you swigs directly from his own bottle, the conversation is at an end."

"Ah, so that is what happens at White's and Brooks's. I have always wondered why men spend so much time at their clubs. Now I know they are too addled to find the door," she said as Lynch belched—a loud, strong, pungent gust that caused his hand to tremble—and he chortled gaily as wine slopped onto the chair. "We should leave."

In complete agreement, Kesgrave rose.

Chapter Eleven

Having failed to explain what she meant by the word *leave,* Bea was only mildly surprised when the duke turned right toward the front door, instead of the left toward the staircase.

Naturally, he thought they were exiting the house, not merely the room.

Bea, however, believed a quick inspection of the upstairs was in order to make sure Mr. Rhodes was not still in residence, sleeping off the effects of the evening's indulgence. Given how much claret had been consumed during his and Lynch's late-night lamentation, she thought it was reasonable to conclude Rhodes had succumbed to the effects of alcohol long before he made it to the pavement. As his unconscious form was not sprawled languidly behind the settee—she had checked, of course, upon standing—the only logical conclusion was that the servants carried him up the steps.

"Presumably, he is still slumbering," she added with a hint of disapproval. The hour, after all, was quite late.

Kesgrave, lauding the efficiency of her proposal, suggested they put the question to the butler. "It seems simpler and far more civil than wandering around a man's home poking our noses into various rooms."

Amused by his squeamishness, she reminded him that he had literally shouldered his way into the house. "Poor Woolley asked you to leave your card, and you marched into the entryway as if it was your private domain. I think it is a little late in the day to be worried about civility."

"All the more reason to consult the staff, to demonstrate that we do not hold all social customs in contempt," he replied before calling for the butler, who appeared in the corridor so swiftly he could only have been in an adjacent room listening to their exchange.

Even so, the servant kept his expression impassive and volunteered no information until after the duke put the question to him—at which point he promptly said no, Rhodes was not occupying one of the bedchambers upstairs.

Kesgrave, who had anticipated this exact response, glanced at Bea with an air of complacency, a look with which she was quite familiar from early in her stay in the Lake District. It was usually followed by a lecture on an arcane topic such as varieties of waterfowl found in northern Scotland.

Before the duke could begin listing species of grebes, the butler added, "He is on the landing."

Startled by the addendum, Kesgrave said, "Excuse me?"

"Mr. Rhodes is occupying the second-floor landing, not one of the bedchambers," Woolley explained. "He was unsteady on his feet last evening, and Mr. Lynch insisted he spend the night. Mr. Rhodes made it only to the top of the staircase before dropping to his knees and laying his head down on the rug. I asked Mr. Lynch what we should do with him, and he said to leave him alone. He was a guest and free to avail himself of our hospitality in whatever fashion he desired. So as not to disturb his rest, the staff and I have been stepping over and around him all morning."

As this cautious behavior made the engineer available to her for an interview, Bea praised his good sense. "Clearly, Mr. Rhodes was exhausted from yesterday's tragic events and needed the restorative benefits of sleep. That being said, it is noon now, and at some point, recuperation becomes indulgence. Woolley, do be so kind as to fetch a glass of water."

Perceiving at once her intention, the butler opened his mouth as if to protest the rough treatment, then swiftly closed it as he left the hallway to fulfill her request.

Not as hesitant to speak his mind, Kesgrave remarked that it seemed needlessly cruel to awaken a sleeping man with a spray of cold water—especially one who would be suffering the disagreeable effects of too much wine.

Bea, who bristled at the charge of callousness, claimed that dousing Mr. Rhodes with water was not her primary recourse. Obviously, she would try to nudge him awake first. Nevertheless, it was good to have options, and there was, she added, no reason to assume the water would be anything but tepid. "Lynch keeps a lovely home, but it is not extravagant, and if he had installed an icehouse beneath the cellar, I feel certain he would have included its value in his catalogue of the residence's worth."

Kesgrave looked inclined to argue but held his peace and conceded a few minutes later that more extreme measures were necessary, as Rhodes proved impervious to Bea's various pokes and prods.

The butler, called to his duty, clutched the glass nervously and asked how he should proceed: emptying the whole thing at once or in sprinkling bursts.

Bea thanked him for his willingness to serve and assured him she would do the honors. Taking possession of the water, she drizzled a tentative stream on her victim's forehead, then leaned back to wait for a reaction—a wince, perhaps, or a scowl. When none was forthcoming, she decided there was no point in being overly delicate and dumped the remaining contents on his face.

Rhodes woke with a gasp, his eyes flying open and blinking wildly as water trickled over his brows. He spluttered into a sitting position as he shook his head back and forth, like a dog emerging from a pond, scattering droplets in every direction. His mouth gaping slightly as if in the middle of a sentence, he stared blankly at the duke for several long seconds before glancing all around, his gaze darting upward at the ceiling and then downward toward the floor before coming to rest on Kesgrave.

His expression equal parts wonder and confusion, he said that he had had a dream exactly like this once. "Except we were all in a wardroom together and you"—he gestured to the butler—"were a cat who kept telling me to eat my parsnips."

Woolley started at the information, his face suffusing with color as he swore he would never tell the engineer what to do or try to impose his dietary preferences on him. "And if I did forget myself enough, I would not recommend parsnips. They can be so bitter if prepared incorrectly. If anything, I would advise potatoes, but as I said, I would never dare the presumption."

As benign as this statement appeared to Bea, it thoroughly undermined Rhodes's composure and thick tears began to slide down his face, mingling with the droplets of water. He wiped at them with his sleeve as he said, "Mr. Huzza loved potatoes. He would eat them every afternoon. No matter what we were doing, he would insist that we take a break and have a light meal at two."

The flush in Woolley's cheeks deepened at this sentimental display, and he suddenly recalled that he had left the silver out in the pantry. "Just lying there on the table where anyone can see it and be tempted. I was polishing the spoons when Mr. Lynch's summons interrupted me. Do excuse me, your graces, but I must return belowstairs at once, lest something disappears before the creditors can make a proper accounting."

At the mention of creditors, Rhodes cried harder, adding a keening wail, and Woolley, his eyes resolutely down, scurried away.

Bea could not blame him, for comforting inconsolable engineers was not among the obligations of his job—a job, by all appearances, he would not have for long.

Although she was impatient to discover what Rhodes knew about the explosion and the relationship between the partners, she did not interrupt his bout of tears or advise him to compose himself. She was fully sympathetic to his plight, for she could only imagine the turmoil that roiled his emotions. As Lynch had said, the engineer believed the explosion was caused by the faulty fusible plug he had made from the wrong material.

Huzza's death was his fault, doubly so because he had yielded his position on the platform. If he had held firm in his refusal to allow the other man to feed the firebox, then it would have been his body the blast tore asunder.

The relief he must feel at being alive combined with the guilt that relief engendered could only be an agonizing blend of emotions.

Bearing that in mind, Bea decided Rhodes was doing remarkably well.

He was inconsolable, yes, but conscious.

She wondered what impact her information would have on his fragile state. Knowing that the explosion was not caused by a valve he incorrectly fabricated would inevitably provide some relief.

And yet the truth was undeniable: A man died in his stead.

A pernicious bomb rather than a faulty plug did not alter the fact that Rhodes was alive only because Huzza was not.

Oh, yes, that was a thought designed to undermine any man's sanity.

Contemplating how close Rhodes had come to obliteration, Bea realized that Huzza could not have been the intended victim. No one had expected him to feed the firebox.

Dressed entirely in white, he was supposed to move among the crowd, accepting their compliments and absorbing their praise.

Presumably, the real target was Rhodes.

Feeding the firebox was his responsibility.

If anyone was sure to be killed by a bomb placed within its confines, then it was he.

And yet it was difficult to imagine a villain going to such a lavish extreme to murder a lowly engineer.

Or anyone, for that matter.

There were dozens of ways to eliminate an enemy that were easier than blowing up a steam carriage in front of scores of witnesses.

Not witnesses, she thought now, but spectators.

Spectators of a spectacle.

That was it, surely, the reason the victim himself did not matter: The aim of the explosion was to create an extravagant display—to destroy the *Bright Benny* in front of as many people as possible, to make sure reports of the tragedy traveled far and wide.

It was the best way to ensure that strong steam never overtook low-pressure steam.

Naturally, that pointed her back to Garrow and his less cunning associate, Tarwich.

She had little doubt he would devise a scheme to undermine the success of strong steam and preserve the market for the low-pressure variety upon which he had built his fortune.

But did he devise *this* scheme?

Rhodes, his sobs intensifying, wound his arms tightly around his legs and rested his chin on his knees. His trousers grew damp as he muttered incoherent phrases under his breath.

Quietly, Bea leaned closer to Kesgrave and said, "Is he praying?"

"Possibly," he allowed, "for it has that cadence, but I have not heard a single *our Father* or *hail Mary*."

"Nor have I," she replied as she drew closer to Rhodes. She had no desire to intrude upon his grief, at least not until the hulking sobs subsided, but she also could not contain her curiosity.

Cautiously, she took another step toward him.

A small improvement but not yet sufficient.

She shuffled forward until she was mere inches from his shoulder. Then she tilted her head to the left.

Ah, that was better, she decided, as she detected the word *fawn*.

Well, no, that did not make sense. Why would he mumble about baby deer?

Something similar to *fawn,* then.

Fault, she thought.

Rhodes was mumbling, "It's my fault. All my fault."

As sensitive as Bea was to his suffering, her patience was not without limits. They could not spend the rest of the day on the landing listening to the young man wail. Their options were either to return at a later time in hopes that the worst of his grief had passed or recall him to his senses to discover whatever information they could during a brief spate of coherence.

Deciding on the latter, she said with bracing sternness, "Come now, Mr. Rhodes, do collect yourself. By all accounts Mr. Huzza was a sensible man and would not appreciate your being so sentimental over a few potatoes."

At these words, the engineer raised his head from his knees and peered at her with bloodshot eyes, wet hair plastered to his forehead. The tears continued to fall but the moaning stopped, which she considered progress, and he said on a shaky inhalation of breath, "Then you must seek a better source of information because Mr. Huzza was impractical. Very clever. Always able to come up with a solution to even the most confounding problem. But so very impractical. He wanted to build a tramroad from London to the sea."

Although his words carried the weight of censure, his tone was fond, and it was apparent to Bea how much he liked and respected his employer.

Rising to his feet as a hiccup escaped him, Rhodes sought to apologize for his immoderate display, but Bea interrupted him to say it was not necessary.

"But it is, your grace," he said adamantly. "You are right. Mr. Huzza would never approve of my behaving like this, and I owe it to him to comport myself with the decorum he would expect. I am afraid I overindulged last night, which I rarely do. I cannot recall much of the evening, not even when I decided to go to bed. It would appear from my location that I did not make the decision at all and simply dropped where I stood. That is deeply mortifying to me."

"You are suffering under a great deal of strain and sought relief in a bottle," Bea said generously. "You are hardly the first. Mr. Lynch is in much of the same condition. The events of yesterday were deeply upsetting. Do not judge yourself too harshly."

Her kindness further unsettled him, and he looked down at his hands and then up at the duke, to whom he also apologized. "I do not know why I made that comment because obviously it is not true. I would never have the temerity to incorporate a duke into my dreams and, if I did, I would never be so rag-mannered as to discuss it with a lady present. I was just so startled and confused. You must know it is a very strange thing for a man of my experience to wake up on an unfamiliar floor to find the Duke and Duchess of Kesgrave staring down at him while a disapproving butler glowers over their shoulders."

"That sounds highly disturbing indeed," Bea said agreeably, then contemplated how best to conduct the conversation now that the engineer had been returned to his senses. Ordinarily, they would remove to the drawing room, but Lynch was there and she thought it was better to keep the two men apart. Debilitating sadness had a way of leaping from one person to the other.

Another room, then, she thought, and immediately perceived the difficulties in either seeking out Woolley to show them to a space or sticking her head into various rooms until she found one herself.

Given the options, she decided the second-floor landing was the best she was going to do and turned her attention to learning more about his relationship with Huzza.

To start, Bea explained why she and the duke were there.

Slowly, cautiously, she relayed their theory regarding the explosion.

Rhodes recoiled at her words, physically jumping back a step at what he called an ill-advised attempt to absolve him from responsibility. "You must think you are being kind, but it is in fact cruel. I fashioned the fusible plug, which failed, and I must accept that, not allow myself to grasp onto a wild tale about deliberate interference to ease my conscience. I must face the truth. It is my fault Mr. Huzza is dead."

"It is not a wild tale," she said gently. "The explosion *was* caused by sabotage. Someone made sure the engine would blow up by placing a bomb designed to look like a lump of coal in the basket. Nothing you could have done would have stopped the explosion."

The engineer stared at her blankly for several long seconds, struck, seemingly almost against his will, by the certainty of her tone. Finally, he said, "How...how can you know that?"

"An examination of the steam engine," she replied, before asking if he had inspected the wreckage himself.

He flinched, turning his head to the side as if looking away from it even now. "Inspect that monstrosity that I helped build and see the remains of a man who treated me as a son? No, I did not!"

Taken aback by the description, Bea asked how long he had worked for Huzza.

"More than four years, almost five," he said. "We met while I was working in my cousin's workshop in Lavenham, making and repairing scientifical instruments. It was a good wage, but the work was dull. Most of the time I was just fixing parts for telescopes and barometers. Huzza hired me to work in his foundry for a few hours every morning before my cousin needed me. He had the general design for the *Bright Benny* even then but could not figure out how to seal the cylinder to ensure a vacuum. Eventually, he solved the problem, and we built a prototype. It was very exciting. I thought for sure it would be a success and resigned my position at the workshop. And then it failed because the carriage was too heavy. It crushed the track it was supposed to travel along. We were both gutted. I had to beg my cousin for my old job back and Mr. Huzza pleaded with me not to give up, but he had no money left to pay me. Indeed, he was deeply in debt. I wanted to accept, but I owed money for my lodgings and how would I buy food? And my cousin would not let me come back a second time if it failed again and just when it all seemed like an impossible mess, Mr. Lynch appeared like an angel from heaven. His pockets were overflowing with guineas, and he provided us with everything we needed to fix the problems of the earlier model and build the *Bright Benny.* We would be nothing without him."

Although recalling his history with the inventor had calmed Rhodes down, tears welled again as he contemplated how little remained. "We *are* nothing."

Wiping tears from his cheeks with the palm of his hand, he explained that knowing the *Bright Benny* has been deliberately destroyed made it immeasurably worse. "When I thought it was a design problem with the plug, it was almost something beyond my control. But to know that all I had to do was hold my ground and Mr. Huzza would still be alive—that is torture. He wanted to steer, you see. Rather than mingle with potential investors, he wanted to steer the *Bright Benny* along its track into the courtyard. He said Lynch could talk to investors as well as the man they had hired to stir up interest. He wanted to show his brilliant machine to the crowd, and I let him. I just stepped back and let him."

Although his sadness threatened to overwhelm him again, Rhodes managed to restrain it enough to apologize for not being able to restrain it better. "I'm sorry, your grace. I do not mean to be soggy. I got very little sleep last night and what I did get was fitful, haunted by dreams, and of course I had too much to drink."

"I am sure you will sleep much better in your own bed," she said.

"Rather than on the landing?" he asked derisively. "Yes, I am sure too."

"Can you tell us a little bit about Mr. Lynch's relationship with Mr. Huzza?" she asked.

A ghost of a smile appeared on his lips as he replied that

Lynch was often exasperated with the inventor, who always asked the other man for money as if he were a bank with a vault full of cash at the ready. "Mr. Lynch gave him whatever he required, but I think he wished Mr. Huzza understood how expensive everything was. He thought nothing of renting a foundry in London, for example, and overrode Mr. Lynch's argument that they could find space at a more reasonable price in a surrounding town. But he never truly minded because he knew Mr. Huzza was clever and the *Bright Benny* would be a resounding success."

As swiftly as Rhodes's expression lightened, it darkened again, and tears began to well in his eyes. He stammered, begging her pardon and insisting it was all his fault. "We might have built it again, fixed the fusible plug, but now...it's over, and I shall have to return to my cousin's workshop. He probably won't even make me plead because he will happy to gloat over my failure every day for the rest of my life."

Bea contemplated the value in reminding him that the explosion was the result of sabotage, not an imprecise alloy, but realized the distinction was too literal to make sense. In all the ways that mattered, it felt to him as though it was something he had done.

Instead, she asked what he knew about Waugh.

At the mention of Lynch's creditor, a fierce frown swept across the engineer's face, and he said bitterly, "I know nothing about Willis Waugh. I had never heard of him before last night. We were at the site for hours, putting out fires and making sure the building was stable, and when it was all over, Lynch insisted I come here for dinner. I don't think he wanted to be alone, and he did not want me to be alone. So we ate and drank and stared at the designs for the engine until our eyes crossed, and just as the clock struck ten, he said, 'I am ruined, Rhodes. All of this will be gone in the morning, including the company.' Then he cursed Waugh's name and started to cry. It took some effort to find out what he was talking about."

Rhodes, wiping furiously at the tears that fell from his own eyes, said he could not bear the thought of the company passing out of Lynch's hands. "He is such a kind and meticulous employer. Working on the *Bright Benny* has been the best experience of my life."

Losing his struggle, the engineer dissolved into convulsive sobs. He waved a hand in front of him, as if swatting a fly, as he struggled to take hold of his emotions, but he sank inexorably to his knees.

Bea darted a glance at Kesgrave, as if to indicate it was his turn to soothe the anguished young man, but he adamantly refused on the grounds that it was beneath his dignity.

"Is it?" she murmured curiously. "My cousin would not consider it so."

Kesgrave smiled faintly at the obvious ploy and said it was above Flora's touch. "Her frenzied ministrations would leave him permanently curled in a ball on the floor."

Bea thought this description of her cousin's skills was unfair, but before she could protest, Rhodes unfurled himself and rose to his feet. Bright pink with mortification, he promised to contain his self-pity long enough to be useful to her. "It is the least I can do for Mr. Huzza, who was always so generous with me. Please, your grace, ask me what you would like to know."

Aware that his control was tenuous, she said promptly, "Mr. Lynch mentioned that Mr. Huzza left his portion of the company to a charity organization. Do you know the name of it?"

"The Benevolent Society for Indigent Widows and Orphans of the War," he said. "The matrons often bring the children to the foundry so they can see the *Bright Benny*. Mr. Huzza would allow them to climb all over it as he told them about the amazing things it would do. It made them happy. How fortunate that none of them were there yesterday. It would have made an unspeakable tragedy even more horrible."

"So the charity was aware of his interest," she said with a thoughtful nod, warming to the notion of a greedy overseer. If Huzza had made the value of his bequest known to the organization that stood to inherit it, then perhaps one of its members decided to murder him to speed up the process. It could take decades for the inventor to die, and he could change his mind several times during that long interval.

Better to kill him now and eliminate the threat.

"I should think so," Rhodes replied, quickly adding that he could not know for sure, as Huzza had never confided in him. "But the way the matrons spoke about the *Bright Benny,* it was always with a faint air of possessiveness. They called it our engine."

Adding the governors of the Benevolent Society for Indigent Widows and Orphans of the War to her list of suspects, Bea thanked Rhodes for his assistance.

Although the blush in his cheeks had lessened, he professed himself still ashamed of his behavior and insisted on escorting them to the door. "Then I really should take my leave of Mr. Lynch. Technically, he may not be my employer any more—to be perfectly candid, I am not sure where the matter stands—but I would like to retain his good opinion. I fear my behavior stepped outside the bounds last night, and I am determined to make a dignified exit."

Alas, the dignified exit was not to be, for as soon as he reached the ground floor, Rhodes collided—literally—with Lynch, who was wandering the halls in search of Woolley. The butler, apparently, was now hiding from both the master of the house and his morose guest.

Momentarily taken aback, Lynch cried out as if discovering a long-lost friend and enveloped the young man in an embrace. "It was sabotage, Rhodes! It was not your fault. Someone did this to me intentionally."

Stricken anew, the engineer insisted that it was still his fault, for it should have been he feeding the firebox. "I let him do it in my stead. It's my fault. All my fault."

The refrain undermined Lynch's composure, and his entire frame seemed to crumble as if under a great weight. His grip on Rhodes tightened as he relied on the other man to hold him up. Rhodes barely had enough strength to keep himself erect and the two of them slid to the floor in a puddle of tears.

Bea and the duke left the two men in the hallway calling for Woolley to bring them a bottle of port. As soon as they stepped onto the pavement, she inhaled deeply, grateful to be out of the house, with its stifling atmosphere and cloying sorrow.

"Where is Woolley?" she asked with exaggerated surprise. "I thought for sure we'd find him hiding outside on the step."

"I think it is safe to say he is in the wine cellar finishing off the Kopke," Kesgrave replied. "No doubt he hopes to be acquired by the creditors, like the pianoforte and the bays."

Reminded of Lynch's debt, Bea noted that it put him well toward the bottom of their list. "If he wanted to sabotage the *Bright Benny* for whatever reason, it seems like he could have done it in a way that did not simultaneously impoverish himself. I am equally at a loss to ascribe a motive to Rhodes. The fact that he could just as easily have been the one to put the coal bomb into the firebox convinces me neither man was the target. This is about the *Bright Benny* and the spectacle of its destruction."

"Which means it is about Tarwich and Garrow," Kesgrave added.

"So it would seem," Bea agreed. "They have certainly

presented themselves as opportunists with few scruples, which makes it rather easy to imagine them committing murder to further their ends. But of course we must investigate all the suspects and not focus on them too readily."

"Very well," Kesgrave said. "Where to next? Waugh's residence or the Benevolent Society for Indigent Widows and Orphans of the War?"

Although Bea believed momentum and speed were vital elements of a successful investigation, she had passed a sleepless night and felt drained by the lugubriousness of the interviews. She craved the comforting calm of a quiet room.

A cup of tea, she thought, and a dozen or so pages of *The Life and Death of Cardinal Wolsey*.

The investigation could wait another day without detriment. Huzza's killer was not likely to flee the city, for leaving London would be tantamount to an admission of guilt.

Having devised an ingeniously diabolical plan for disposing of his victim, the villain's only recourse was to hold still and allow the investigation to run its course. Any defensive move on his part would run the risk of drawing unwanted scrutiny.

At the moment, all the Duchess of Kesgrave had were wildly implausible theories to which no self-respecting magistrate would give any credence.

The murder weapon itself was outlandish speculation.

A bomb made to look like a piece of coal.

Oh, yes, try proving *that* one to the constable!

Bea imagined the look of disdain she would receive—impatience mixed with superiority laced with irritation—if she dared to present a tidy pile of ash as evidence.

She smiled faintly at the thought of the constable's scorn and noted that she did not feel quite so fatigued as before. The eagerness in Kesgrave's tone, the genuine enthusiasm for the task at hand, she decided, had revived her.

No one would blame him, least of all she, if he chose to assume an air of stoic resignation at her larkish adventures or adopt a pose of amused tolerance. As a man of wealth and status he had every right to desire comfort and convenience in a wife, not the perpetually narrowed glare of suspicion, and the fact that he engaged in her investigations sincerely and with intellectual vigor indicated that they satisfied an unfathomable need within him.

And that was utterly baffling, for how was it possible that the drab Beatrice Hyde-Clare and the dazzling Duke of Kesgrave had the same strangely shaped hole inside them?

It simply did not align with her understanding of the universe.

The lack of comprehension did not preclude her enjoyment of it, and invigorated by the suggestion, she said they would call on Mr. Waugh, since they had his address. Firmly, she asked Jenkins to take them to fifteen Darby Street.

Ten minutes later the carriage stopped in front of a modest three-story residence with an unassuming white facade. Its interior was just as restrained, with a drawing room that eschewed elaborate design for simple comforts, such as generously cushioned armchairs.

Gratefully, Bea accepted an offer of tea from the housekeeper, and it arrived only a few minutes later, carried in by the home's owner himself.

Placing the tray on a table next to the window, Waugh explained that he had just been about to have a fresh pot while looking over some accounts. "So your arrival is perfectly timed. Doubly so, in truth, for I am quite curmudgeonly when I am interrupted in the middle of my work. If you had come a few minutes later, I would have growled angrily at Mrs. Smith and sent you away."

Waugh's voice was mellifluous, soothing and warm, as if it were accustomed to lulling babies or small animals to sleep, and it suited the room, with its shards of sunlight brightening the dark-colored wood floor and its cheerful fire crackling in the grate.

After the heavy emotionality of their previous visit, Bea relished the room's gracious tranquility.

"Now what is the reason for this call?" he asked, settling his frame into a mahogany chair with saber legs. He was an amiable-looking man of medium height and broad cheekbones, with neatly trimmed brown hair. "We do not have any business dealings that I am aware of, your grace, although I do have a venture that I know to be particularly well suited to you. It is a gracious square that carries none of the stigma of trade."

Although the comment was addressed to Kesgrave, Bea responded with a curt thank you but no. Then she explained that they were there to discuss his involvement with Lynch and Huzza. "It is our understanding that, as a consequence of yesterday's tragic explosion, you are now in possession of Mr. Lynch's shares in the company."

Waugh, stirring sugar into his tea, replied, "Yes and no."

At the intentionally inscrutable answer, Bea felt some of her pleasure in the room's warmth drain away. Clearly, their host meant to be difficult.

Before she could seek clarification, however, Waugh added that he had already sold his shares to an associate who owned an ironworks near Cardiff.

Taken aback by the information, Bea could only see something nefarious in the swiftness of his actions. In order for Waugh to finalize the deal so quickly, it had to have already been in the works, and for it to have been in the works, he had to have known what was about to happen.

A man could not sell shares he did not own.

Bea, noting the impressiveness of the speed, asked how he

accomplished the sale so quickly. "It has not even been a full day since the shares became yours."

"I am a man of conviction and singular focus," he said, raising the cup to his lips and taking a sip. "When I decide to do something, I do it and it is done. I knew Eugene Richards could be induced to buy my shares and so I induced him. Having made that decision there was no reason to quibble over details. It was merely a matter of money exchanging hands. Richards was present at the Penydarren wager, in which Trevithick proved it was possible for a steam engine to pull heavy carriages along a plate road, and I convinced him that he could build his own with Huzza's invention. All the parts are there. He just needs to reassemble them with a few minor changes. It was fate, I said, that he happened to be in London meeting with his bankers just as this once-in-a-lifetime opportunity arose. It sounds very mundane in the retelling, but I am a persuasive salesman, which is why I have developed five squares in London and am working on the sixth. He will, of course, have to negotiate with the organization Huzza left his half of the firm to, but as it is a charity that helps widows and orphans, I am confident he will have no trouble undercutting them. They will be grateful for whatever crumbs they can get for a worthless firm. Thus reassured, he accepted my offer with alacrity. It was, you see, a very good price."

Bea, eyeing him doubtfully, announced that it all sounded a little too easy. "You expect me to believe you were able to bring these various elements together at a moment's notice? On the day Lynch's company imploded you just happened to know at which hotel the ideal buyer for it was staying? And by the time you paid your call, you had already discovered the identity of Huzza's heirs? That is a tremendous amount of groundwork to do in an afternoon."

"At a moment's notice, your grace?" he said with a

chuckle. "It was a great many moments, and I assigned three of my best clerks to the project. By the time I arrived at Richard's hotel at eight forty-five last night, I had spent several hours refining the deal. And as I said, it was a very good price. I charged him four shillings on the pound. It was a huge loss for me. I recouped only a fraction of what I had advanced to Lynch."

"Then why sell them?" Bea asked, not at all appeased by this explanation. Even if someone *could* move that quickly, it still struck her as unlikely that they *would*. "As I noted earlier, you had them for scarcely a day."

Amused by the query, Waugh smiled faintly and shook his head. "What do you think might have changed with the passage of time? In a few weeks, the *Bright Benny* would be no less rubble, its inventor no more alive. The only thing that would have been different if I waited even a single day was Richards's willingness to be convinced. In the heightened aftermath of the explosion, he was able to allow himself to believe my offer was an act of Providence. The hand of fate finding him in his hotel in Bond Street."

The rich melodiousness of Waugh's cadence took on a slightly sinister cast as he explained how he had manipulated the ironworks owner. "So you have no compunction about selling shares that you know to be worthless?" Bea said.

"Not worthless, your grace, never that," he corrected with a glint of mischief in his eye. "Four shillings' worth, as I have just explained to you, and I believe Richards got good value in the exchange. If it strikes you as unethical, your grace, is it because you have no understanding of how ordinary business is transacted. Deals such as this one are struck every day by men like me, men who oversee businesses, not workhouses. It is my obligation to attain success for myself and the workers whom I employ. I did not want to own a steam engine manufactory. I do not want *things* that must be stored and maintained. I build residential squares and immediately sell the properties. Others must see to their upkeep, not I. The moment the *Bright Benny* exploded, Huzza & Company became my problem, and I dealt with it as I do all problems: by passing it off to the first interested buyer. Do I believe Huzza's machine will change the way we live our lives and fight our wars?"

Lifting his shoulders in a shrug, Waugh said that was the wrong question. The right one was: Did he care?

And the answer to that was no.

"The company was a burden to me, worthless or not," he explained, "but thanks to Richards, I was able to salvage something. Maybe the patents will turn out to be valuable. I do not know. I am a land developer and do not deal with inventions in the regular course of plying my trade. I wish Richards luck with them and will bear him no grudge if they make him so appallingly rich that in a few years, he can buy and sell me several times over."

The generous sentiment, however, was undermined by the amused disbelief in his voice. It was inconceivable to him that the patents would ever be worth the parchment on which they were written.

It was a gross miscalculation, Bea thought, and yet also a self-fulfilling prophesy. By selling them to a man who wanted only to construct a plateway from his ironworks to town, he had all but guaranteed their value would never be realized.

For this reason, she was inclined to move him to the bottom of the list, below Lynch. If he had transferred the shares to someone else while secretly retaining ownership of them, she would wonder if it was a feint to make it appear as if he had no interest in the company going forward.

In fact, he *had* no interest in the company going forward.

"And even if I am wrong, I am still right," Waugh added, retrieving one of the several newspapers stacked in a neat pile and holding it in the air. It was the *London Tribune,* with its front-page headline condemning the hazards of strong steam. "The tide has turned against high-pressure steam. You may be too young to recall the Greenwich explosion, when Trevithick's darling blew itself to high heaven, taking several good men with it, but I remember it vividly. The public outcry was fierce, and I am certain it will be intense again. By the time it subsides, the patents will have expired."

Bea glanced at the story and was not surprised to see a quote from Tarwich jump out at her: "Strong steam is notoriously dangerous to harness, and the longer you tamper with it, the greater the odds it will tamper with you."

He had said the exact thing to her and Kesgrave during their conversation earlier.

No doubt he had repeated it verbatim to Mr. Marcus of the *Gazette* and the reporter from the *Times.*

Tarwich would be gratified by the progress of his crusade. It was still early in the campaign, and opinions were already being set.

Needing no more information from Waugh, Bea thanked him for his time and apologized for the inconvenience.

Waugh scoffed at the idea that his time had been wasted, for he was delighted to host the duke in his home. "And now that the business with Lynch is done, we can discuss Kesgrave Square—twenty residences around lush parkland in west London. The architect is Harold Kent, with whom I assume you are familiar. His work is very tasteful and modest, with classic lines and unadorned arches. Everyone has aped his style, even Nash, but he was the first, which makes him the best. As a developer, I take pride in that simplicity. I never do anything too elaborate that would call undue attention to itself, and you must not worry that Kesgrave Square will be garish. It will be as elegant as you are."

Firmly, absolutely, his tone subdued in its horror, Kesgrave said, "No."

Murmuring agreeably, Waugh professed to understand his aversion to a square named in his honor and suggested an association that was a little less conspicuous: a charming row of houses near Bond Street. "Nobody would ever know you were involved, except your steward and your banker."

The duke declined this opportunity as well, but their host had other projects in mind and as he escorted them to the door, he proposed them one after the other in rapid succession: a square in Bath, a village in Surrey, a factory in Northumberland. Although the house was quite compact, the walk to the entrance felt endless to Bea as Waugh described in exhaustive detail the cottages he was constructing in Blyth for a colliery. The lovely timber in his voice, the soothing richness with which he spoke, began to grate on her nerves, and by the time she stepped onto the pavement, she found herself pining oddly for the plaintive sobs of Mr. Rhodes.

Somehow, it was less relentless.

Chapter Twelve

Despite her anxiety about having to oversee the seemingly endless assortment of servants who attended to Kesgrave House, Bea had grown accustomed to the convenience of a large staff with alarming ease. Indeed, only a week before she had lamented the lack of a fifth footman to assist in her investigation into Lord Myles's death.

The more footmen the duke employed, the more footmen she could deploy in her pursuit of justice.

Now she sent out two: Edward to Steven's Hotel to confirm that Eugene Richards, the ironworks owner, had actually purchased Waugh's shares, and Joseph to the Benevolent Society for Indigent Widows and Orphans of the War to find out more about the charity. The former had been provided with a note introducing her as someone who bore a personal interest in the matter after witnessing the horrific tragedy, and the latter had been instructed to make a donation in her name after thoroughly inspecting the organization and meeting its governors.

Joseph, daunted by the assignment, which diverged

sharply from his prescribed duties, suggested that perhaps Mr. Marlow or Mr. Stephens would be better suited to the task of secretly gathering information.

Bea recoiled slightly, imagining the customary impassivity with which the imperious butler would greet that suggestion, and assured the footman with brusque certainty that his reconnaissance skills were highly developed. "You correctly identified suspicious aspects of Mr. Réjane's murder and coherently articulated them to me. I am positive you will demonstrate the same competence now. Here, let us use one of Mr. Stephens's cases and pack it with a few supplies so you can take notes. And you could borrow a pair of his eyeglasses to augment your disguise."

Joseph paled. "I am assuming a disguise?"

Bea, realizing her misstep, shook her head firmly, proclaimed he was right to object and complimented him on his finely honed instincts. "You will be an excellent investigative assistant."

The footman found so many things dismaying about this statement, from her assertion that he would dare to make an objection at all in her presence to the prospect of being an investigative anything, he could not form a response and meekly followed her to Stephens's office.

Recruiting reluctant footmen was difficult work, and by the time Joseph left for Radnor Street, Bea was ravenous. As her stomach rumbled, she looked at the clock and noted it was already three.

No wonder she was so hungry.

Summoning the housekeeper, she requested a small plate of bread, fruit and cheese.

"At once, your grace," Mrs. Wallace murmured.

Smothering a yawn, Bea thanked the other woman and wondered if she would be able to keep her eyes open long enough to enjoy the tray. Her sleepless night had well and truly caught up with her, and although the prospect of a quiet rest was delightful, she had no desire to perpetuate the cycle incited by yesterday's exceedingly long nap.

Determinedly, she picked up the book on the table, opened it to the marked page and skimmed until she found where she had left off.

She barely made it to the bottom before her eyelids fluttered shut.

Bea tightened her grip on the novel, straightened her shoulders with purpose and tried again.

Almost immediately, her eyelids began to droop.

Deciding the bergère was the problem, for it was far too cozy for her to stay awake, she moved to a wood chair away from the fireplace. It helped, to be sure, for she managed to keep her eyes open, but her mind wandered and required particular effort to stay the course.

Just as she was finishing the chapter, Mrs. Wallace appeared with a lovely selection of cheeses and fruit.

"Perfect," Bea said, drawing her hard seat closer to the table as she examined the tray. Her mouth watered in anticipation. "This is wonderful. Thank you."

The housekeeper left, and Bea, accepting the futility of reading, allowed her thoughts to drift freely as she spread cream cheese on a thick slice of bread. She wondered how Aunt Vera was faring in the august company of the Dowager Duchess of Kesgrave and imagined her stare of amazement as she beheld the splendor of Haverill Hall for the first time.

No, not stare, she thought.

Gawk, rather.

Maybe even swoon.

There was no way her relative's brain could comprehend the immensity of the Matlock family seat, with its capacious rooms graciously appointed with the finest Dutch paintings, Palladian furniture and Greek sculptures.

In truth, Bea could not blame her, for she could make no sense of the abundance herself.

Having marveled only a half hour before at the disconcerting swiftness with which she had grown accustomed to the luxury of Berkeley Square, she felt her belly quiver now at the thought of being mistress of such a colossal concern.

How excessive it all seemed—the hundreds of rooms, the thousands of acres, the scores of fountains, gardens, stables and pineries.

All of it in service to a single family.

Anyone who had been raised with a modicum of moderation would flinch.

Even Lady Victoria, she thought. Growing up in the shadow of Haverill Hall would have done little to inure her to its wonders, and if she had actually managed to achieve her dearly held goal of nabbing the duke, her delicate frame would have trembled in apprehension.

Bea, whose own hand shook slightly in contemplation, smiled at the ridiculous turn of events: She had begun by mocking her aunt and ended by unsettling herself.

Serves you right, she thought, placing a slice of cheddar cheese on a section of apple.

For all she knew, Aunt Vera had responded to the inexplicable extravagance of Haverill Hall with cool dignity.

It was unlikely, to be sure, but not impossible, for at some point all that gold would start to look like dross, like the stage scenery for a production of *Hamlet.*

"Yes, your grace," Bea muttered cynically under her breath, "do keep telling yourself that."

Deeply perturbed, she resolved to think of something more amiable and turned her mind with resolved focus on the matter of Huzza's tragic death.

Silas Garrow, aided by his young associate, remained firmly fixed at the top of her list, for she had yet to encounter a suspect whose actions appeared more dubious. Even Tyne, who was literally caught fleeing the scene of Lord Myles's murder, had managed to wiggle convincingly off the hook.

That was, she thought, a salutary reminder that occasionally the person who looked the guiltiest was in fact the guiltiest.

Sometimes there was no mystery to it at all.

But even as Bea allowed herself to contemplate the simple solution to Huzza's murder, she could not make it entirely convincing. Every one of Garrow's actions could be the product of the more-innocent-though-still-nefarious explanation he offered. Presenting himself as Mr. Grimes, he had in fact discouraged both her and Uncle Horace from investing, and he did not have to cause the accident to capitalize on it. Tarwich and he knew how the newspapers would respond. Watt and Boulton had shown them exactly what to do with their cynical manipulations following the Greenwich explosion.

In attempting to steal Huzza's designs, Tarwich and Garrow had merely sought to augment the original scheme by providing visual evidence.

It was, she thought, a reasonable improvement.

The problem with removing Garrow and Tarwich from contention was it left her with few other satisfying prospects. If Lynch ruined himself in the present to earn some invaluable reward in the future, then he was playing a game too deep for her to decipher. By all appearances, the destruction of the *Bright Benny* was the worst possible thing that could have happened to him. If he had simply wanted to eliminate an unwanted business partner, there were a hundred less conspicuous methods for arranging it, such as administering poison or pushing him out of a third-floor window.

Blowing up the prototype—essentially exploding the company itself—and hoping your target was killed in the process defied sense. No villain set on murder would take such a circuitous route to achieving his objective, especially not when it meant the end to his material comfort.

Despite these persuasive arguments against Lynch's culpability, Bea still tried to come up with a motive and recalled Huzza's treatment of him at the demonstration. The amused contempt with which he not only took over the platform but also dismissed his partner indicated a general scorn for his opinions. And Rhodes had mentioned how Huzza regarded Lynch like a bank vault, always reaching in to withdraw more funds.

Perhaps Lynch felt himself to be ill-used by the inventor and struck back.

It was not inconceivable, no, for many men had been goaded to murder by resentment, but she still could not believe he would destroy himself in the process.

Unless there was some missing piece that eluded her—such as Lynch and the ironworks owner conspiring together to hoodwink Waugh—she could not make a case against the surviving owner.

Very well, she thought, turning her attention to the next name on her list: Rhodes.

She had no motive for him, not even the bright glimmer of dislike. Based on his account, Huzza had provided him with an income, a purpose and a sense of family all at once.

Nevertheless, she tried to manufacture something.

Money was the greatest motivator, and she wondered how she could connect the destruction of the *Bright Benny* with great wealth.

A bribe, she supposed, was one possibility.

Tarwich and Garrow, for example, might have hired Rhodes to blow up the steam carriage on the promise of a generous reward and a job at their own foundry.

Practically speaking, Rhodes could have done it, for he

had complete access to the machine and could sabotage it at will. Holding off until the demonstration aligned with Tarwich and Garrow's goal of destroying the reputation of strong steam.

And yet as some aspects of the case grew stronger, fundamental weaknesses remained. Huzza's insistence on feeding the firebox could not have been planned for. In hiring the engineer to create the spectacles, Tarwich and Garrow could not rely on him to create the spectacle.

No, it had to have been done by someone who did not care who died.

Furthermore, the theory did not account for Garrow's presence at the demonstration. If he had hired Rhodes to sabotage the *Bright Benny,* then the last place he would be on the day of the demonstration was in the courtyard. Paying someone to ensure you were not associated with a heinous deed and then inserting yourself prominently into the heinous deed defied sense.

Having employed Rhodes, Garrow should have been miles away from the foundry.

Waugh *was* miles away from the demonstration, but she found it difficult to picture him patiently proceeding through the many steps required to cajole an engineer into murdering his boss while destroying his own life's work. A wealthy man, he could have easily hired a pitiless ruffian from Saffron Hill in the mold of Trudgeon. No doubt Hell and Fury Hawes would have been delighted to recommend someone suitable in exchange for a small referral fee.

Furthermore, Waugh lacked motive.

The problem was her list was too short, which was why she kept returning to Tarwich and Garrow.

Consolingly, she reminded herself that there was still the Benevolent Society for Indigent Widows and Orphans of the War to consider. Any one of its governors—and who knew how large a group that constituted—might have destroyed the *Bright Benny* to fill the charity's coffers or avenge a wrong.

For that matter, so could any of the one hundred or so spectators who attended the event. The barriers positioned around the steam engine had been barely enough to keep the benign curiosity of interested spectators at bay, let alone a murderer who wanted to slip a seemingly harmless lump of coal into a basket.

Very clever, your grace, she thought, picturing the crowd, now you have too many suspects.

Ah, but not *everyone* could be reasonably considered.

Her cousins, for example, would not know the first thing about constructing a bomb. She smiled, imagining Flora in an apron leaning over a fire with a pritchel in her hand and a bag of gunpowder at her feet that was slightly too close to the flames for safety.

Knowing nothing of military weaponry, her cousin would surely blow herself—

Oh, but military weaponry!

Bea recalled suddenly that her uncle had pointed to an officer in the British Army yesterday—a lieutenant-colonel. Across the yard, he had lowered himself to one knee to inspect the tracks.

What had Uncle Horace said?

And there is a lieutenant-colonel in His Majesty's Armed Forces. Such illustrious company underscores the momentousness of the occasion.

It was a leap, she allowed, to go from military man to murderer, and yet the precision of the strike forged the connection. A man who had risen through the ranks of the army would have the experience and tactical awareness to limit casualties to only his intended target. Not a single one of the spectators was seriously harmed—that indicated rigid control and a well-trained mind.

But what resentment could an illustrious member of the British Army nurse against an audacious inventor who sought to carry Londoners to the seaside via tramroad?

No, not Huzza, she reminded herself.

Against the *Bright Benny*.

Or high-pressure steam itself.

Incapable of conceiving what the connection could be, she decided no useful hypothesis could be devised without knowing the man's identity. Resigned, she rose to her feet and walked to the door to pay a call on her uncle. Then, realizing she was being hasty, she scurried back to the table to gather the food. She wrapped it all in a serviette, except the Stilton —she feared that might be too pungent to travel with—and strode into the corridor to summon a footman to ready the carriage.

She was slipping into her pelisse when Kesgrave appeared in the entry hall to ask where she was going. His presence was surprising, as he had disappeared into his study with Mr. Stephens promptly upon their return. Several important business matters had been neglected in the days since his uncle's murder, and the lull before dinner had seemed like an ideal time to catch up.

"I thought you were resting," he said with a hint of disapproval in his tone.

"And find myself once again too well rested to sleep?" She shuddered lightly at the horror. "No, I was reading in my office. Now I am going to call on my uncle."

The duke, his nose twitching as if he found something suspicious in her response, raised an eyebrow curiously. "Is that Wensleydale?"

Unaccountably, a slight blush rose in her cheeks, and she said it was not. "It is cheddar."

This answer provided little enlightenment and he asked why she was bringing cheese to Portman Square. "I know your relatives are frugal, but I did not think the situation had grown so dire you needed to deliver provisions. The turnips came in this week, and the crop was unusually abundant. Shall I have Mrs. Wallace wrap some up as well?"

Of course he knew the extent of the turnip harvest.

No doubt he could describe the length of each stem.

"You are very amusing, your grace," Bea said.

He dipped his head in acknowledgment. "But do tell me why you are visiting your family. It has already been a very long day, and you said you were going to rest."

"*You* said I was going to rest," she clarified. "*I* did not argue."

"Yes, the surest indication I know that you are tired," he replied, a smile teasing the corners of his mouth. "Which is why I am surprised you are paying a social call. I can only assume this has something to do with the investigation. What information do you seek?"

As his deductive skills had never been in question, she was not at all taken aback by this query. "The name of a lieutenant colonel who was in attendance at the demonstration."

If he understood the source of her interest in the military man, he did not reveal it as he nodded. "All right. Let me tell Mr. Stephens we are done for the day."

"But you just began," she protested. "You have been bracketed with him in your study for not even a full hour, which is barely enough time for Mr. Stephens to list all the problems on the estates, let alone present solutions. You must stay or he will blame me. The roofs will collapse, the tenants will revolt, and we will be forced to seek refuge in a wretched little cottage on the outskirts of London."

"Would that be so horrible?" he asked softly, pressing his lips against her forehead. "Banished to a quiet room with few interruptions save Mrs. Wallace with regular meals and

Marlow to complain about how the dampness is ruining the curtains."

Suspecting a ploy in the seductive warmth of his voice, she stepped back and observed that his understanding of the nature of peasant uprisings was lamentably incomplete if he thought he could take his housekeeper, butler and silk drapery with him to the hovel.

Whatever underhanded scheme he had intended to lure her to their bedchamber for a proper rest was forgotten in his compulsion to correct the inaccuracy of her statement. His family's fortunes had been forged in the fire of the Peasants' Revolt of 1381, which, he insisted, gave him a profound understanding of the repercussions of insurrections.

As delighted as Bea was with this impromptu lecture, she was keenly aware of the hour growing late and his steward's patience wearing thin. Interrupting his speech, she suggested Mr. Stephens might benefit from the history lesson as well. "I'm sure he will find it utterly fascinating. Do return to your study to enlighten him at once."

But Kesgrave remained firm in his determination to accompany her, and Bea, comprehending the source of his intransigence, swore she was only going to her uncle's house. "And then I will come right back and submit to your dissertation on Wat Tyler's rebellion. You have no cause to worry."

Mildly, he reminded her that the same condition applied the day before as well. "You were only going to your uncle's house to literally stare at a wall, and yet somehow you came within a hairsbreadth of being blown into little pieces."

"Not at all, actually, no," she said, shaking her head vigorously. Happily, she would accept responsibility for the risks she had taken but refused to be called to account for the ones she had not. "My life was never in danger because the thoughtful villain who blew up the *Bright Benny* took pains to limit the carnage to only one unavoidable victim."

It was impossible, she discovered, to describe a murderer as thoughtful without sounding at least a little facetious, and Kesgrave scowled at her. "You may find this funny, but I do not," he said sharply.

Bea was instantly contrite, for she had not meant to make light of his apprehension. It was daunting for her too, the excessiveness of emotion she felt for him, which bore no relation to the sweet affection she had imagined as a green miss embarking on her first season. She did not relish contemplating his vulnerabilities, the sundry hazards he faced every time he stepped outside.

Horses reared, carriages swerved, footpads lurked.

Poor Kesgrave did not even have the illusion that she was safe within the confines of their home, for Bentham had attacked her a few dozen yards from where they stood.

Even so, his solution was untenable. He could not escort her every time she crossed the threshold. He had to be free to follow his own pursuits.

Taking his hand and clutching it tightly, she apologized for appearing flippant. "That was not my intention. I merely wanted to accurately assess the threat posed by the explosion because overestimating the danger helps no one. I understand your concern, but you cannot be with me every minute of the day. I was teasing just now about the roofs, but you are in peril of letting whole villages fall into disrepair if you spend all your days squiring me about."

Despite this sincere display, the duke's expression remained grim, and he asked why she thought he would be so feckless in his duty to his estates that he would entrust them to a steward whom he did not believe was capable of managing them without his constant supervision. "I assure you, I am happy to leave them in Mr. Stephen's capable hands. But speaking of accurate assessments, my love, it has been only twenty-six hours since the explosion, so I have not spent *all* my days squiring you about. I have spent one."

She conceded this graciously and sought to establish how many days of squiring a steam engine explosion warranted. "Just so that we have clarity on the matter going forward."

Kesgrave, citing the novelty of the situation, admitted he did not have a precise number in mind, which provided Bea with an opportunity to propose three. "And that includes the day of the explosion as well."

The duke countered in hours—seventy-two—and then hastened to add that it applied to all explosions, not just steam engines.

Amused, she asked if he imagined she would spend much time in collieries.

He realized then the shortsightedness of his response and widened the field to include all the possible disasters she might encounter in the regular course of her day: fire, collisions, floods, avalanches.

"Avalanches," she repeated quizzically. "Am I taking tea in the Alps?"

But Kesgrave was impervious to her mockery and continued to recite calamities, however improbable, and the exhaustiveness of the list (tidal waves, shipwrecks, mine collapses) had the familiar debilitating effect on her senses. Powerless against her own compulsions, she pressed her lips against his.

He responded at once, tightening his grip on her hand and tugging her toward him so that she could feel the tautness of his body. He deepened the kiss, yes, his passion exerting a subtle pressure as her bones seemed to melt, and yet he continued his catalogue, murmuring catastrophes against her mouth like terms of affection. His hands, sliding up from her waist, encountered the delicate trim of her bodice, and she felt every muscle in her body weaken with desire.

The serviette with bread and cheese slipped from her fingers to the floor, where it remained for a strikingly long time.

Chapter Thirteen

As it was unusual for a member of the family to answer the door, Bea was startled to find herself confronted on the top step by her cousin Russell. Glaring at her with a pugnacious frown, he announced he was going to Gentleman Jackson's. "And you cannot stop me."

Given that she had no dominion over his actions, she readily agreed. Aunt Vera took a dim view of the salon and its activities, but it did not fall to her to enforce the strictures of his absent mother.

Instead, she advised him to distribute his weight evenly across both legs, keeping his knees slightly bent. It seemed like a minor thing, but during her own brief career as a boxer, she had learned the importance of mastering one's stance.

Her practical reply disconcerted Russell, and he aimed his belligerence at the duke. "You cannot stop me either."

Kesgrave, whose interest in the matter was negligible if not nonexistent, only exhorted him to convey his regards to the celebrated pugilist.

Far from being reassured by the lack of resistance to his plan, Russell tightened his lips in annoyance and brushed past them with a slight jerk of his shoulders. Then he trotted down the stairs to the pavement and turned right toward Fitzhardinge Street.

Amused by her cousin's antics, Bea entered the townhouse and found Flora in the hallway shaking her head with disgust. "He has been doing that all afternoon, announcing his intention and daring anyone to stop him—and I do mean 'anyone'. The poor servants. He has been bedeviling them, too, as if Mrs. Emerson is going to tell the young master of the house that he cannot do as he pleases. Obviously, she is not going to say a word, nor Dawson or Annie. But they do know how Mama feels about it so there is an awkward nervousness about their silence. If Russell had the capacity to think of anyone but himself, he would know better than to pester them. But come! Let us not stand in the hall discussing my brother," she said, leading them to the drawing room. "Let us do that in comfort."

True to her word, Flora continued her critique of Russell as she rang the bell and sat down on the settee. "I think he spent all morning worrying about it, girding his nerve until he had the spine to announce to Papa that he was going to Gentleman Jackson's salon. And Papa did not argue. Indeed, he lent his support. He is still impressed with the way he kept his head yesterday after the explosion. Naturally, it is easier to keep one's head when it is primarily made of cotton, but I did not begrudge him the improvement in his status. It is not easy to earn Papa's esteem and Russell has little of the facility with Latin and science that I have, so he must do what he can with his meager abilities."

Her cousin broke off when Mrs. Emerson appeared in the doorway and asked for a fresh pot of tea. Bea, her stomach rumbling, requested something to eat. Nothing elaborate, she insisted. Just a light morsel to sustain her till dinner.

The housekeeper nodded, and as soon as she disappeared

into the hallway, Flora continued, for her capacity to deride her brother was without limit.

"Paternal approval is an unprecedented experience for him, so it is not surprising it left him feeling quite bereft," she said. "Even so, that does not give him the right to torment the staff. I do not know what will horrify Mama more when she returns: the fact that Russell has taken up boxing or that he dared the servants to refuse to allow him to take up boxing. But that is neither here nor there. You will both be very distressed to know that Mr. Holcroft has not responded to my letter."

In fact, Bea was not, and she doubted that Kesgrave was particularly troubled by the news either. Her cousin's impatience to hear back from her beau was well-known by now and failed to account for his obligation to his father, whose sanguinity must have taken a heavy blow when he discovered his oldest friend had tried to murder his son.

Blandly, she reminded her that it had been less than a week since his last note. "You must allow time for the note to get to Norfolk and back."

Flora, whose tightly woven fingers indicated her anxiety, had just launched into an explanation of why this sensible course was not available to her when her father entered the room to chastise her for sending for food when dinner would be served soon.

Heatedly, he said, "You know how your mother feels about snacking. She considers it frightfully uneconomical. It is already bad enough that upon her return she will find out that her son is a brawler. Let her not also discover her daughter is a snacker."

"I am afraid it is my fault," Bea said, rising to greet her relative, whose back was turned toward her and the duke. "I was hungry and asked if I could have something simple to eat."

Startled by their presence, Uncle Horace spun on his heels as the color drained from his cheeks. No doubt he was embarrassed to realize she and the duke had overheard his speech. In general, he liked to affect indifference to his wife's harping, and it was mortifying to be caught enforcing one of her injunctions.

Bea was about to ensure him she had heard worse when he stiffly apologized to the duke for exposing the duchess to danger. "Naturally, you felt compelled to call on me personally to issue a rebuke. I visited Kesgrave House this morning for just this purpose, but you were abroad. Please be free with your criticism, for I know I deserve it. I was a terrible guardian to my brother's daughter, and now that I have been given an opportunity to make amends, I almost got her killed in a steam carriage explosion. The only defense I have is that I thought it was safe, as evidenced by the fact that I brought Flora and Russell as well. Nevertheless, I deserve every ounce of your anger."

Much like Russell earlier, Uncle Horace stood before the duke with his shoulders taut in expectation. His expression, however, was diffident, not defiant, and Bea rushed to assure him that Kesgrave had no desire to take him to task.

"He has concerns about my safety, to be sure, but he is not so irrational as to hold you responsible for events beyond your control," she explained.

"No," Kesgrave agreed amiably. "I hold Bea responsible."

Reassured by this comment, she said, "You see, you have no reason to be alarmed. We are here for an entirely different reason. We wish to know the name of the man you pointed out to me during the demonstration, a lieutenant-colonel. If you recall, he was inspecting the tracks."

Flora gasped and shot to her feet. "You think it is murder!"

Amused by this unfathomable leap in logic, Uncle

Horace apologized for his daughter's outburst. "She has been acting strangely all day, teasing her brother and pestering Dawson for messages. I believe she misses her mother."

Calmly, Flora began to pace the floor as she tried to make sense of this new information. "You think it is murder, and Kesgrave agrees. How could that be possible? I was right there beside you. I saw the exact same thing, and it was an accident. It was very clearly an accident. The pressure in the boiler grew too great, and as a result the whole engine exploded. That is the danger with high-pressure steam. It was in the paper this morning. But if you think it is murder, then something else had to have happened," she murmured, halting abruptly as an idea occurred to her. "Someone made it explode! That is it, isn't it? Someone deliberately broke the machine to make sure it would explode. How did they do it? By tampering with one of the valves? Mr. Tarwich of the Tarwich Company said in this morning's *Tribune* that no valve is a match for the destructive capabilities of high-pressure stream."

Uncle Horace shook his head indulgently and said that they had all been adversely affected by the incident. "Russell got a bee in his bonnet about Gentleman Jackson's and I nearly jumped out of my skin when David dropped a serving spoon at breakfast and Flora is imagining sinister plots. I expect it might be some time before we put the explosion firmly behind us."

"If anyone is imagining sinister plots it is Bea," Flora said defensively. "I am merely trying to follow her line of thought."

Obviously, her father could not allow this insult against the Duchess of Kesgrave to stand and he leaped to her defense, forcing Bea to admit she did in fact have some questions about the nature of the accident.

"But it is mere speculation," she quickly added. "I have no proof."

To her credit, Flora kept her features even, revealing none of the satisfaction she would have displayed had her brother been present. "And you think this lieutenant-colonel had something to do with it?"

Moved now to defend the absent military man, Uncle Horace exclaimed incredulously, "Impossible! Rupert Flexmore is one the finest men the kingdom has to offer. His reputation is gold, and you will banish that thought from your mind this minute, young lady!"

Flora pointed out that it was not *her* thought but Bea's, again compelling her father to exhort her to cease defaming the duchess.

"Yes, darling," Flora murmured soothingly, as if mollifying a man in his senility.

Bea, whose familiarity with modern warfare was one of the areas in which her education was lacking, glanced at the duke for confirmation.

"Flexmore has had a distinguished career and is quite well respected," Kesgrave replied.

"He reported directly to Wellington during the war," Uncle Horace said firmly, as if this piece of information were all the evidence one needed to affirm his superiority.

The duke, however, kindly elaborated. "As an exploring officer early in the war, Flexmore ventured into enemy territory and made a study of how the French army was coordinating its supply lines to figure out how to disrupt them. Napoleon's soldiers were particularly well fed during the Ulm campaign."

"*C'est la soupe qui fait la soldat,*" Flora said confidently, turning to direct a smug grin at her brother, which promptly faded when she recalled he was not in the room.

Even so, her father nodded approvingly and said, "Soup *does* make the soldier."

"Flexmore's reconnaissance revealed that Napoleon had devoted whole regiments to ensuring necessary supplies such as food, boots and ammunition reached the soldiers on the front lines," Kesgrave continued. "It was important information because the tactical support provided by these battalions gave the French military an advantage over the English. Flexmore applied what he learned to helping the British Army improve its own lines."

"I believe his efforts changed the course of the war," Uncle Horace added, "although it is not the sort of heroics about which newspaper reporters typically write admiring dispatches. Nevertheless, the difference it made in our soldiers' readiness to fight was significant. I have seen him once or twice at my club but would never be so impertinent as to interrupt him while he is enjoying a claret."

Bea, knowing this to be true, imagined her uncle also lacked the impertinence to interrupt the lieutenant-colonel while he was not enjoying a claret. "Why did he attend the demonstration?"

But this, too, was an imposition, for her relative would never presume to know the motivations and inclinations of a great man whom he had never met. Then, unbending enough to speculate slightly, he suggested a former campaigner of Flexmore's character would almost inevitably have an intellectual curiosity in modern machines. "I do not base that supposition on his attendance at yesterday's demonstration. He was also at the Tarwich last month."

Admittedly, there was nothing extraordinary about an interest in steam power, and yet Bea could not help but feel the lieutenant-colonel's attention was noteworthy.

Flora, her lips pressed together, leaned against the arm of the settee as she stared at her cousin. "You think either Flexmore had something to do with the explosion or knows something about it," she said softly before turning to her father to ask in what capacity the lieutenant-colonel served now, in peacetime.

It was a perceptive question, and Bea was impressed once again with her cousin's shrewdness. Flora had an airiness about her, a light-as-foam buoyancy, and yet she was substantial in a way that would horrify her mother. Young ladies, particularly those of the Hyde-Clare extraction, were meant to simper prettily while posing artfully, preferably against a flattering background, although an unbecoming one would do in a fix provided the lighting was poor.

"He works for the Board of Ordnance now," Uncle Horace replied, "reporting directly to the lieutenant-general, Sir Hildebrand. He still oversees the distribution of supplies and is in charge of making sure the army is prepared for its next military engagement."

Flora acknowledged this information with a nod, which was entirely benign, but Bea recalled her tenacity and sought to distract her. Although her cousin was more than a frivolous ball of fluff, she still possessed a giddy egoism that made her alarmingly easy to distract.

Consequently, Bea said, "And what of Mr. Holcroft? He has sent no word at all?"

Flora sighed heavily and collapsed onto the settee as if she no longer had the strength to stand. Her father, wincing visibly, groaned as she launched into a ten-minute dissertation on the resounding silence of Mr. Holcroft.

Helpless, he looked at Beatrice, as if they were both prisoners of an invulnerable jail. She pursed her lips apologetically just as Dawson arrived with the tray, which he placed on the table in front of the settee. Then he scurried out of the room, as if he, too, could not bear to hear another jeremiad about Mr. Holcroft's inconstancy.

Bea poured tea for everyone, Flora first, as the poor girl's throat must be parched from her long lament. Then she handed a cup to Kesgrave, who leaned in closely and asked what her strategy was for extracting them from their current situation.

"If we do not leave within the hour, I fear Russell will return and regale us with every last detail of his session with Jackson," he added with a theatrical shiver.

Inspecting the assortment of pastries, Bea told him not to worry, for when the moment arrived—approximated as sometime after she had eaten her third or fourth cake—she would yawn dramatically and announce that her sleep had been disturbed by thoughts of the accident, which was only the truth. "Uncle Horace will insist on escorting us out, I am certain of it."

Flora, observing this sotto voce conversation, begged Bea to share her thoughts with everyone. "For you know Mr. Caruthers almost as well as I do."

Unaware that the topic had strayed to the disgraced cousin, Bea had no idea of the correct reply and rather than say something wrong, she asked again if Flora was absolutely certain Holcroft had not responded.

It was a facile ruse, the product of fatigue and hunger, and Flora, suspecting a trick, narrowed her eyes before looking thoughtfully at her father. "Remind me, Papa. Where did you say I could find Lieutenant-Colonel Flexmore?"

But it was a strategic mistake, using the first-person pronoun rather than the comfortingly distant *one,* and Uncle Horace started in surprise. He would certainly never condone a member of his immediate family seeking out the great man, and he began to list all the honors Flexmore had won during the Peninsula campaign as proof he was too consequential for Flora, who had never earned any wartime distinctions.

He had just mentioned the Order of the Garter when

Russell entered the room, sullen and despondent at not being able to have his first lesson until the middle of next week, when his mother was sure to be in residence again. His expression brightened when he realized Kesgrave was still present, and he asked if there was something he could do to delay his grandmother's return.

"Perhaps trouble with another one of your estates," he suggested.

Flora mocked the idea of making an infirm old woman travel around Cambridgeshire rather than find the spine to defy his mother.

Russell sneered that she was jealous she could not learn the fine art of brawling.

Kesgrave, his voice low but urgent, told Bea to yawn.

Bea, who was accustomed to her cousins' bickering after almost two decades of enduring it silently, could not immediately comply because her mouth was full of seedcake.

The duke, presumably recalling that his rank precluded the need for ruses, announced they would be leaving. He thanked Horace for the information regarding Flexmore, wished Flora luck in her pursuit of Holcroft and congratulated Russell on his new diversion.

"Yes," Bea said, rising to her feet as Flora colored slightly at the description. "It has been delightful. Please do give my regards to Mrs. Emerson, for these cakes are most excellent. I hope you do not mind if I take one or two for the carriage."

Her uncle urged her to take them all and rang for a footman to package them properly for travel, a courtesy she insisted was not necessary.

"Kesgrave does not mind crumbs on the upholstery," she said, gently cradling the assortment of pastries in her arms like a litter of newborn kittens.

In fact, the duke did mind crumbs, for he was averse to vermin in a way only someone who had not been subjected to them constantly in their childhood could be, and he watched her eat in the carriage with a hint of disapproval.

"They brush off, you see," she said conversationally. "You just sweep your hand across the cushion and voilà—they're gone. It is quite miraculous."

"No, they drop to the floor," he replied. "There is nothing miraculous about gravity."

Bea conceded the point, mostly because she was too tired to formulate a response, which, had she had the vigor, would have involved brooms and dustpans. Instead, she rested her head against the back of the bench and allowed her eyes to drift closed. She felt the carriage sway lightly as Kesgrave switched positions, pressed his side against hers and lowered her head to his shoulder. Then he took her hand in his own and rubbed her palm gently with his thumb.

"Your beautiful tailcoat," she murmured. "It is going to get crumbs."

"I have been assured they brush off," he said.

She smiled faintly and apologized for failing to extricate them as promised. "I believe I am ready for that nap now, so you may cease haranguing me."

"Am I haranguing you?" he asked.

Bea did not have to open her eyes to see he was amused. "Dreadfully. Those lovely circles you are drawing have a very coercive effect."

"Perhaps I just like caressing my wife," he replied softly.

Although she laughed and admitted that his preference had been well established, Kesgrave apparently felt further proof was in order and his hands moved expertly up her body.

She was quivering by the time they arrived in Berkeley Square, and despite the earliness of the hour, the duke requested that dinner be brought to their bedchamber as soon as possible.

When it was delivered an hour later—a wonderful assortment of meats, vegetables and sauces gloriously free of pineapple in all its forms—she was more ravenous than ever. She ate quickly, efficiently, appreciating the chef's skill with even a simple repast, while Kesgrave read snippets from his grandmother's letter, which had arrived that afternoon.

"Why only snippets?" she asked curiously.

"Because I love you far too well to subject you to her complaints about various physical ailments," he replied, waving one of the several sheets in the air. "She goes on for five paragraphs about the joint in her left hip. Here, you see, she even drew a picture of it in a spastic convulsion."

Bea glanced at the page he held aloft and noted it was the letter S. "I expect the coach dipped into a hole while she was writing."

Kesgrave, his eyes narrowed as he looked at the scribble again, said with mild annoyance, "I do not understand why, if she takes so much enjoyment in grumbling about her many maladies to me, she would deny herself the pleasure of doing so in person. I am sure it would be more satisfying than writing this long missive, which caused her hand to ache. I know it caused her hand to ache because she devotes six sentences to it before asking about your lessons."

No, Bea thought, reconsidering his tone. It was not mild annoyance.

It was surliness.

Aggrieved by his grandmother's intransigence, he had adopted a sullen air, like a child thwarted in his ambition to stay up late or have ices for dinner.

His petulance amused her because it was so unwarranted. He understood precisely why the dowager preferred to grumble to him via the written word, for she had explained her aversion to his company concisely and coherently, and yet he was determined to take a pet.

Given how relentlessly rational he was about most things,

she imagined it required a great deal of exertion to maintain his sulkiness.

It was, she thought, a testament to his affection for his grandmother that he was determined to make such an effort.

"Do tell her I sympathize with her aching hand and expect my own to be in the same condition after my pistol lesson tomorrow, during which I will be required to endlessly discharge an empty weapon," she said.

Kesgrave, who had heard this lament on multiple occasions, launched into a detailed and familiar explanation on the importance of growing accustomed to the way the flintlock's trigger felt before using gunpowder. If she flinched in expectation of the flash, recoil or noise, she would jerk her grip away from her target, negating the usefulness of the firearm.

Bea, however, was unwilling to allow him to change the subject and suggested that he also include a line in his reply stating that he understood why she felt the need to make the journey without him. "To be sure, she does not need your approval, but I think she would like it."

Predictably, he drew his brows together in a heavy frown and said her name with a hint of reproach as if to warn her off from the subject.

Of course he was cross.

His grandmother had been the only person to offer the lonely dukeling affection, and as a result, he felt a protectiveness toward her that could not be assuaged.

It did not help that she was in her dotage and now perceived as frail.

But whatever fragility she had attained in her later years was merely physical. Mentally, she was just as strong as ever, and Kesgrave had no right to undermine it.

To help him overcome his temper, she gave him permission to indulge it. "Regardless of how long your sulk goes on,

I will remain placid and patient. My temperament is well suited for sullenness, and I once withstood Flora's mopes for two full weeks without snapping at her a single time. The poor dear had not been invited to Miss Silversmith's early-summer garden party and was quite cut up about the slight. I mean, even Miss Clement warranted an invitation—Miss Clement of the spots *and* spectacles."

A smile tugged at the corners of his mouth as he asked what she would do when comparing him unfavorably to Flora ceased to influence his behavior. "At some point, I will stop rising to the bait. Then what will you do?"

"Compare you to Russell," she said blandly.

"That is low, brat, even for you," he replied.

She accepted the compliment with a dignified nod and then reached across the table to take his hand in her own. "Tell her you understand, Damien. Even if you do not, respect her wishes enough to tell her you understand. It will relieve her mind greatly, and allow her to focus fully on the more pressing matter of her joints."

"Fully?" he repeated as he contemplated her over the top edge of the letter, his eyes glinting with humor. "She devotes two pages to her knees. I am not certain how much more attention her joints can bear."

Bea, heartened by his lightened expression, urged him not to underestimate the dowager. "She is sturdy, despite her ailments, and might yet compose epics to her aches."

Kesgrave shuddered dramatically and professed deep horror at the prospect of an ode to her joints written in dactylic hexameter. Then he tightened his grip on her hand, his expression turning serious again as he said, "I do not like it, not being beside her at a time such as this."

"I know," she said gently. "But it is not about you."

A simple enough comment, it somehow startled him, and Bea watched in amusement as incomprehension swept across his features. What a hugely foreign concept it must be for a man around whom whole planets circled. Even matters that were not about him were actually about him—because it was a very great privilege to be able to ignore the things one wished to ignore.

His bewilderment was fleeting, however, and a moment later the gleam returned to his eyes as he asked with exaggerated confusion, "Then who *is* it about?"

Naturally, Bea kept her own tone perfectly neutral as she replied, "Aunt Vera."

"The ideal traveling companion, according to my grandmother's report," Kesgrave replied. "Accommodating and uncomplaining if you can believe it."

Peevishly, she reported that she could not believe it. "How is it possible that my wretched relative is the ideal anything? For the whole of my life, she has been narrow-minded and miserly, withholding affection from an inconsolable orphan out of some imagined wrong done by my mother. If she has other dimensions, must I consider them? Am I obligated to review our history and examine all her behavior based on this new information? It hardly seems fair that, after her ill treatment of me, I must reevaluate my treatment of her."

"Oh, I see," Kesgrave said with a teasing lilt as he tugged her to her feet and into his arms, "this is really about you."

Bea smothered a sigh as she dropped her head onto his shoulder. It had been a long day after a wakeful night, and she was thoroughly exhausted. With very little effort, she could fall asleep right where she stood.

"It was just so very bizarre," she murmured, "her volunteering like that. Only the moment before she had been trying to disappear into the upholstery, and then suddenly she offers to escort a dowager duchess on a multiday journey. It defies sense."

"She did it for you," he replied, brushing his fingers against the nape of her neck.

Comforted by his touch, she exhaled softly and closed her eyes. "If I tell you that is precisely what Flora said, will you consider it a taunt? Because I do not mean it to be."

"Your cousin is not without her insights, even if she is capable of epic bouts of sullenness," he observed gently. "Two weeks you say?"

"Every morning, weeping silently onto her eggs, as if struggling against a great sadness," Bea said, recalling the scene.

Kesgrave shook his head in wonder, then said her aunt was trying to make amends. "She lacks your uncle's natural warmth, so it comes across as strange and stilted. Her efforts are sincere, I think, but do not require a wholesale reevaluation of her character, only a slight softening in your judgment going forward."

Bea, grateful for his excessively rational understanding of the situation, settled herself more comfortably into the crook of his neck as she thanked him for providing her with a loophole through which she could wiggle.

"My pleasure," he said, sweeping her into his arms.

She wanted to protest, for it seemed so very silly. They were only a few feet from the bed, and she was not so fatigued that she could not traverse the short distance on her own.

And yet it was such a lovely sensation—the strength of his arms, the security of his hold—and she sank into it with a satisfied moan.

Gently, he laid her on their bed, and the moment her body touched the mattress, she curled up on her side and fell asleep.

Chapter Fourteen

At eight o'clock, Bea arrived in the garden to the west of the stable, eager for her shooting lesson and hopeful she would finally be allowed to discharge a loaded pistol. The flintlock's recoil was indeed fierce, but she was familiar with it now. She knew what to expect, the way it pulled on her shoulder, and was confident she could hold her gun steady.

Her instructor begged to disagree.

"You are making excellent progress," Prosser added as he gestured to the nailhead a good distance away, on the side of the stable. "But you are not there yet. Trust me, the more accustomed you are to the movement of the gun, the more effective you will be at defending yourself with the gun, which is the point of these lessons as I understand it from the duke. I am to make sure you are capable of defending yourself. I would be remiss if I did anything less."

As Bea had heard similar defenses of their painstakingly slow methodologies from her other instructors, most recently Egan, who had been engaged to teach her boxing but would not let her strike anything, she was not surprised by it.

In fact, it made sense that a man who was meticulous in all his dealings would hire men who demonstrated the same propensity.

Nevertheless, one did grow weary of pretending to shoot nailheads.

"Anticipation is the obstacle to a steady shot," Prosser reminded her as the hammer dropped. "Holding your hand steady—that is the challenge. If you expect the drop, you respond to the drop and pull your gun off the target. You must become inured to every action the pistol makes. There is no point in shooting if you cannot hit your target."

Bea, who had eagerly complied with every demand made of her while a homicidal actor pointed a flintlock at her heart, did not necessarily agree with this assessment. Nevertheless, she followed his directions to the letter.

After the lesson, she returned to her dressing room to wash and change into a walking gown. While Dolly arranged her hair in a far more elaborate style than the day's schedule required, Bea reviewed the information Joseph had gathered on the Benevolent Society for Indigent Widows and Orphans of the War.

It was a relatively small organization run by two widows whose husbands had died on the Peninsula. Although they themselves had suffered no financial hardship, they observed that many women of their acquaintance had not been as fortunate and established the charity as a way to help them. They provided packaged meals to approximately fifty families in the area surrounding St. Anne's and ran an orphanage on the outskirts of the city, where children were taught how to farm.

New donations were assiduously courted but not desperately sought.

"Appears to be on solid financial footing," Joseph wrote in his tight scrawl.

Mr. Huzza's death, he noted as well, had put a pall over the group, with Mrs. Carson apologizing repeatedly for the general malaise of her and her colleagues.

If the governors felt any joy at inheriting the inventor's shares, the footman could find no evidence of it.

But, he hastened to add, subterfuge and uncovering secret information were not skills in which he was trained, and he hoped she would not consider his conclusions to be in any way conclusive.

"Duly noted," Bea murmured.

By the time her maid released her, it was after ten o'clock, and she returned to her office of rout cake enjoyment to compose a response to the dowager's missive. Naturally, she wanted to ask a dozen follow-up questions regarding her assessment of Aunt Vera's behavior, such as: "How do you quantify accommodating?" and "What do you think *ideal* means?"

She restrained herself, of course, keeping her reply light with amusing anecdotes from her shooting lesson. She had just finished sharing her opinion of the nailhead ("impertinent and taunting, like your worst joint of mutton") when Marlow delivered a missive from the lieutenant-colonel, who agreed to meet with the Duke and Duchess of Kesgrave at their earliest convenience.

Pleased, she called for Jenkins to bring around the carriage and informed Kesgrave of their imminent departure. They arrived at his residence less than a half hour later, and although Flexmore had claimed he was delighted to meet with them, there was no warmth in his greeting.

Curtly, he instructed them to sit down.

Slightly taken aback by his brusqueness, Bea glanced briefly at Kesgrave before thanking the military officer for consenting to see them on such short notice. "I appreciate your willingness to be of assistance."

"I cannot tell you anything," he replied as he folded his hands before him on a desk so pristine Bea wondered if it had been delivered fifteen minutes before they arrived. "That is not my personal decision, your grace. It is the stricture handed down by our commander-in-chief of the forces, Prince Frederick. As a member of the military, I have no choice but to comply."

The cool authority in his voice confounded Bea, for how could he be so certain when she had yet to explain her purpose. His standoffish pose combined with the emptiness of the room gave the exchange a peculiar theatricality, and it felt oddly as though they had been dropped into a play in the middle of the second act and his speech was in reply to someone else's comment.

But if Lieutenant-Colonel Flexmore was not Lieutenant-Colonel Flexmore, then who had gone through so much trouble to stage an elaborate ploy to mislead them?

No one, she told herself.

Obviously, he was the real lieutenant-colonel.

Old soldiers were given to their quirks.

Bea assumed an ingratiating smile and said she understood his caution. "And as a British citizen I am grateful for your forbearance. Knowing your deep respect for the rules makes me feel immeasurably safer. Thank you."

Flexmore, his shoulders as rigid as the tailoring of his uniform, announced he was only doing his duty. "Nothing more, nothing less."

Bea nodded in acknowledgment and, hoping to flatter him out of his severity, added that she would expect nothing else from a man with his storied career. "You could not have accomplished half so much if you were any less unyielding in your standards. As such, I am sure the demands on your time are many and we will keep our visit brief."

"I am at your disposal," he said, then immediately reiterated that he could not tell her anything.

Further disconcerted by his definitiveness, she replied that she had not yet asked him anything. "All I have done was sit down at your invitation and thank you for seeing us."

His face, square and lightly creased with age, did not soften. If anything, the narrow line of his lips tightened as if disapproving of her intentions. "That is correct. You have not asked me anything yet. But I wanted to make it clear from the onset that I cannot tell you anything. Communicating your objectives plainly is essential to overseeing a successful regiment. Misunderstanding leads to confusion, which leads to chaos, death and defeat."

As if to punctuate this grim picture, a crow perched on a branch outside the window cawed loudly.

Smiling amiably, Bea again extolled his caution, which, she was certain, benefited the entire country. "I feel even safer knowing the empire is in your capable hands. I can only imagine the weight of the burdens you shoulder."

This particularly determined bit of sycophancy yielded no pliancy, his demeanor remaining stiff, and she continued. "The reason I asked for this interview was to discuss the demonstration of the *Bright Benny* on Monday. You were in attendance."

"I cannot confirm that," the lieutenant-colonel replied.

It was a puzzling response to a straightforward statement of fact, and Bea, seeking to reassure him that he was not the subject of gossip, explained that she had seen him herself.

Flexmore, committed to a single course of action, stated again that he could offer no confirmation.

"I do not require you to confirm what I saw with my own two eyes," Bea said snappishly. "The matter is not up for debate. I saw you at the demonstration of the *Bright Benny* two days ago. You were across the yard, near the speaking platform, lowered to one knee to examine the tracks. Not only did I see you but also my uncle and the scores of other people in attendance. You were there."

"Bea," Kesgrave said gently, laying a hand against her own, which was now clutching the chair in frustration, "he cannot confirm that."

Already agitated by Flexmore's intransigence, she thought the duke was issuing a rebuke. She thought he was telling her to stop hounding the poor man, who was only abiding by the limits of his office.

Her temper severely frayed, it was all she could do not to growl at Kesgrave.

Instructing her on how to behave!

What an utterly predictable response from a man!

But then she heard the words again, the way he said them, and noted where he had put the emphasis: cannot.

He *cannot* confirm that.

Startled, she looked at Kesgrave and realized he had caught a subtle distinction she had missed.

"Oh, you clever, clever man," she murmured admiringly.

He acknowledged the compliment with that familiar dip of his head.

Bea looked back at Flexmore and said, "If you cannot confirm your presence at the demonstration, that means your confirmation would reveal something related to the safety of the country."

Now his demeanor changed. It was ever so slight, but a muscle in his cheek jumped.

Aha, she thought.

Nevertheless, his voice remained even as he said, "I cannot confirm that."

"No, you cannot," Bea said pensively, "because your presence at the demonstration had something to do with the security of England. Chaos, death, defeat—all that lovely stuff."

That was the crux of it, she thought, confident that the truth about his attendance correlated somehow with the military and its operations.

How could Huzza's invention help keep England safe?

"You were there on behalf of the army, that we know," she said to Flexmore in a conspiratorial tone as if they were figuring out a great mystery together. "Your work during the war involved ensuring that supplies reached the soldiers on the front line. That is a matter of public record, but I will of course pause here to allow you to not confirm it."

Flexmore pressed his lips together, as if to deny her the satisfaction of dictating his speech, but then he issued the statement, either because he could not help himself or the situation required it. "I cannot confirm that."

Bea thanked him for his contribution and resumed ordering her thoughts. "We know little about your current position, but it is reasonable to assume it is related to your previous work: ensuring the integrity of the supply line. If that is the case, then your interest in the *Bright Benny* is related to supply lines. Yes, but how?" she asked, fully aware that this was the crucial question.

The answer, she felt certain, was on the edge of her mind, just waiting to be discovered. To that end, she continued. "The most common use for steam engines is to pump water out of mines. But the *Bright Benny* was mobile, so it had another purpose. Huzza's own wish was to create a tramroad that could carry dozens of passengers at once to the seaside near Whitstable. Passengers," she said again, tilting her head at Flexmore as an idea struck her. "Soldiers are passengers."

Flexmore stared straight ahead, his eyes fixed firmly at some point behind her.

She was getting close, she thought.

Loosening her fingers on the arms of her chair, she leaned forward and sought to draw his attention. "Lieutenant-Colonel, I said, soldiers are passengers. That is your cue to say you cannot confirm it."

He remained mute, and his silence spoke volumes.

Bea had it now.

Understood it precisely.

"In your capacity for the Board of Ordnance, you are charged with figuring out how the steam carriage may be employed in military operations to transport soldiers and supplies," she announced, then immediately marveled at the ambitiousness of the project. "It is a monumental undertaking, sir, requiring an immense network of tramroads crisscrossing the countryside and the Continent as well, if it is to be of any use during another Peninsula campaign. It will take years to build."

"I should think decades," Kesgrave said as the crow outside the window cawed again. "But well worth it if it can be done."

"*If?*" the army officer repeated, his lip curling in a faint sneer at the intimation of doubt. "*When* it is done, Britain will rule the land as thoroughly as she does the sea."

Given his prior reticence, his vehemence now was shocking.

Flexmore seemed aware of it, too, unfolding his hands for the first time and laying his palms on the surface of the desk. Then he leaned back in his chair.

Bea, looking at the duke, said, "Oh, dear, I think he just confirmed it."

Despite his efforts to say as little as possible, the lieutenant-colonel did not look very troubled by the prospect and he said to Bea in a much more natural tone, "If you repeat one word of this conversation, young lady, it is treason."

'Twas a remarkable word for Beatrice Hyde-Clare to hear in relation to herself, *treason,* for it was an astronomical thing, as vast as the universe and just as absurd. It was inconceivable that anyone would include her in any category that contained Anne Boleyn, Lady Jane Gray and Charles I.

She wanted to laugh.

Oh, yes, imagining herself at a garden party surrounded by that illustrious, strange trio, complaining about the lemonade, gossiping about Prinny, she felt an unaccountable urge to giggle.

Flexmore was wide of the mark.

And yet she could not quite smother the quiver of disquiet she felt at being even that close to the executioner's blade. The road to the Tower of London was long, and it had to begin somewhere.

Why not in this commodious room, with its pristine desk and bird calls?

"You are mistaken," Kesgrave said blandly. "My wife has not engaged in a conversation with you. All her efforts to have a rational exchange were rebuffed by your refusal to make a sensible reply. If you disagree with my understanding of the events, do let me know and I shall take up the matter with Prince Frederick. It has been several years since we spoke, and I would welcome the opportunity to renew our acquaintance."

It was a show of strength, Bea thought, a hound baring its teeth at a hare, and it was difficult to tell who was more taken aback by it: she or Flexmore.

As the muscle in the officer's cheek pulsated wildly, she decided he was more flustered and wondered if the reason was he realized belatedly that he had threatened the Duke of Kesgrave as well as a drab spinster who had married above her station.

The lieutenant-colonel would have no compunction about trying to intimidate a toadying mushroom who dared to decipher the intentions of the British Army.

She bore the ancient title, too, of course, and was due the same deference as her husband, but she lacked the fanfare and presumption of someone who had been raised in its excesses. In her posture, she was still a burdensome orphan and prone to cower when presented with a threat, particularly one that carried the weight of king and country.

And yet, even with the security her position afforded her, Kesgrave had been compelled to push back, an indication that the frisson of alarm she felt had not been entirely fanciful.

Smoothly, Kesgrave continued, inviting Flexmore to have a conversation with the duchess now. "Assuming you agree to dispense with the threats, that is. It is not my wife's fault that your heavy-handed attempt to conceal your motives made them blatant. If you disagree on that point as well, we can also take that up with the prince if you like. We are happy to defer to your preference."

But it was not a deferral, no, and their host was clever enough to recognize that he had no choice.

"My preference is to be as helpful as possible on the clear understanding that any information disclosed in this room should remain between us," he said, folding his hands again and resting them on the immaculate surface of his desk. "I *must* have your word that—"

He broke off with an awkward smile that obscured the persistent twitch in his cheek and tried again. "I would be grateful if you would refrain from making any of the matters we discuss here widely known. I say that on behalf of the prince regent, the commander-in-chief of the forces and the entire military apparatus of England. The welfare of the nation rests in the balance."

It struck Bea as hyperbolic, his description of what was at stake, and yet she could not help but think if there was a glimmer of truth in what he said, then it would serve as a very good reason for murder.

"Naturally, you may rely on our discretion," she said reassuringly. "I have no desire to aid the cause of chaos, death and defeat. I simply want to discover who murdered Mr. Huzza."

To this surprising statement, Flexmore had no reaction other than to nod as if she had confirmed something he had long suspected. "Yes, I assumed you would say something to that effect when you requested this meeting. Although my life is dedicated to keeping my fellow countrymen safe, I am not above a little town gossip and as such have read Mr. Twaddle-Thum's accounts in the *Daily Gazette*. I will not try to reason you out of your fancy, for that is your husband's responsibility, and as he is here, I can only conclude that he indulges you to an inordinate degree. Behavior like that would never stand in my regiment."

"Then we are lucky we do not serve in your regiment," Kesgrave said laconically.

Flexmore's mustache jumped as he tightened his lips when the source of the problem became clear to him. "Do tell me your theory. I am curious to discover why your knowledge is superior to that of the reporter for the *Tribune*, who spoke to several men who are experts on the hazards of strong steam."

Having read the article to which he referred, Bea knew it cited only one authority, Mr. Tarwich, but she refrained from pointing that out. Asking him to acknowledge an inaccuracy would only entrench his disdain, which would make getting useful information from him even more challenging.

It was already difficult enough.

"My knowledge is the result of an examination of the wreckage itself, which neither the reporter nor his sources had an opportunity to make," she explained calmly. "Based on the behavior of exploding boilers, I can say definitively that the damage was not caused by a problem with high-pressure steam or a faulty valve, as the story reports. It was caused by a bomb—a bomb disguised as a lump of coal. As a man of war, you are familiar with such contraptions and would know how to make one."

Although she had obliquely accused him of murder, Flexmore did not take offense. His posture remained calm as his expression changed from contemptuous to curious. "A bomb disguised as a lump of coal? Well, that *is* a crafty little thing. How does it work? I suppose it would have to go into the firebox for the gunpowder to ignite," he said, his voice growing softer as he contemplated the possibilities. "But how would you get it into the firebox without anyone being the wiser? You could throw it in yourself, but that would defeat the purpose of the subterfuge. The man tending the fire has to be gulled into doing it himself, and therein lies the difficulty because the weight and appearance would not be exact."

Flexmore pursed his lips and began to tap his chin with the three middle fingers of his right hand. "A soldier might notice because he is trained to be observant, but in an environment like the demonstration? There were many distractions, so much noise and activity, and Huzza was waving at the crowd like Wellington at a victory parade. He had no idea what he was feeding the firebox. It could have been a custard pie for all the awareness he showed. But at campsite at night when a soldier standing guard throws more coals onto the fire? Could it work?" he wondered thoughtfully. "Yes, I think it might, provided a skilled blacksmith made it. Getting the shape right would be essential. But if you did, I can see its potential, yes. A great deal of potential."

The admiration was so keen, Bea expected him to thank her for bringing the idea to his attention.

He did not, of course, and instead speculated about the damage it could do: perhaps kill a few soldiers, maybe injure several members of a battalion.

Unnerved at the prospect of advancing the cause of warfare, she reminded herself that an officer of Flexmore's stamp needed no help from her. Having gleaned the potential for global military dominance in a wisp of black smoke, he possessed all the creativity required to devise dozens of wily contraptions to vanquish his enemies.

But had he devised *this* wily contraption?

"Do you possess the skills to make a lump of coal bomb?" she asked.

"It is not the manufacture of the device that is so remarkable but the conception," he said cheerfully, again displaying no defensiveness in response to the implication. Somehow, being accused of murder improved his disposition. "Who is clever enough to think of something so devious? I have to assume you are dealing with a military mind. Only someone who is intimately acquainted with war and warcraft would think to imbue a mundane necessity with the specter of death. And that is why you have come to me, is it not? You think this is my invention."

Bea said yes.

Flexmore nodded approvingly. "A rational conclusion, your grace, and one I would have drawn myself, for I do make a rather excellent suspect. Almost certainly, you are looking for someone who served during the war and is familiar with munitions. During my varied and successful career, I have deployed a great many explosives and know how to contain a blast to limit civilian casualties. I was present at the demonstration and possess the cunning to come up with the ingenious idea. Most important, I have the courage to carry out the plan. A man with less internal fortitude than I would have wavered at the sticking point, either out of fear of being caught or sniveling morality. I suffer from neither. But I am not a blacksmith, and although I think that is significant, it is not an insurmountable hurdle because I could have hired one. But what is my motive?" he asked curiously, as if intrigued by the question. "How does Huzza's death benefit me?"

Silently, he tapped his chin, his lips pressed tightly in thought. Then he shook his head, seemingly disappointed with the limits of his ingenuity. "You see, there your logic breaks down because I have no reason to murder Huzza. I am relying on his company to supply the British Army with the greatest tactical advantage since Hannibal crossed the Alps with elephants."

Having deciphered the general outlines of Flexmore's plan, Bea was nevertheless startled to discover he had settled on a particular steam carriage. She had assumed he had attended the demonstration as part of his initial investigation into various engines, not to reaffirm his choice.

"You were *relying* on him—as in the matter between you had been settled?" she asked, wondering why Lynch had not mentioned such a significant detail in the lament of his downfall.

Fear of treason, presumably.

"I cannot confirm that," Flexmore said, then immediately added that no papers had been signed so describing it as *settled* was overstating the case a little. "But I am confident an agreement will be reached. Lynch has been amenable to my requests so far and assures me there is no reason for concern."

In fact, there was one rather significant reason for concern, but Bea did not think it fell to her to inform him of Huzza & Company's new owner. She was there to find a motive for Flexmore—an endeavor that just got easier now that a contract worth several thousand pounds had entered the fray.

The existence of an agreement made his attitude toward the explosion highly suspect, she thought. If England's military superiority rested on the success of the *Bright Benny,* then why was the lieutenant-colonel so sanguine about its catastrophic failure?

The obvious answer was that he knew it had not failed catastrophically.

But why would he tamper with something in which he was preparing to invest tens of thousands of pounds?

Ah, maybe *because* he was about to invest tens of thousands of pounds.

By engineering the disaster, he reduced the value of the company. What was supposed to be Huzza & Company's finest day turned into its worst moment as the fires raged and onlookers screamed in fear. The reports of the disaster focused on the terror, and the firm's reputation suffered accordingly. If Lynch required more money to rebuild the *Bright Benny,* he would have a difficult time finding someone willing to support the seemingly doomed project. At that point, Flexmore could swoop in and buy the company cheaply on behalf of the British government. Owning the patents would save the army thousands of pounds as well as make it a small fortune from leases.

The prospect of generous profit no doubt appealed to the Board of Ordnance.

Or maybe the plan was to withhold the technology from others so that only the British government had the option of laying tramroads.

Killing a man to destroy a company's worth was unscrupulous, to be sure, but Flexmore had already declared himself to be free of sniveling morality.

And he had been full of admiration for the deviousness of the coal bomb, had he not?

Perhaps he had just been admiring himself.

But if the lieutenant-colonel orchestrated the disaster to take possession of the firm, then Lynch's shares would not have passed to Richards. An experienced exploring officer like himself would have researched every aspect of the situation before enacting a plan that forced a change in ownership. Presumably, he would have known about Lynch's debts and Huzza's orphans and devised a scheme that took both into account.

"Your enthusiasm for the *Bright Benny*'s potential seems untempered by the explosion," Bea observed. "If you are relying on Huzza & Company to supply the British Army with the greatest tactical advantage since Hannibal crossed the Alps, then why are you not more upset that your elephant just blew up?"

Flexmore waved airily and insisted it was just a valve. "All the papers say so. I am confident the Rhodes fellow can fix a valve. He struck me as a very capable young man. The explosion is only a temporary setback, and if what you say is true, then there is nothing to fix. The *Bright Benny* is the success Lynch hailed it as and we can begin laying our tramroad in a few months. Sir Hildebrand will be pleased."

Again, he spoke like a man who did not know he was in business with an ironworks in Cardiff. That being the case, she was at a loss to ascribe a motive to him.

Personal animus?

It was a perennial favorite, to be sure, especially in the absence of another, more obvious reason, but Flexmore struck her as too much of an old campaigner to allow a private dislike to get in the way of world domination.

"How did you settle on Huzza's invention?" she asked.

"Supplying our brave soldiers with the best of everything is my sacred duty, young lady," he said with pompous self-importance, "and this was no different. I researched the field of steam power methodically and identified the most auspicious contenders, then sought out the appropriate people for interviews, tours and demonstrations. As always, I was assiduous and diligent, leaving no stone unturned in my search, and the conclusion I arrived at is high-pressure steam is the future. It has its risks, but its advantages over low pressure are incalculable."

"I trust the proprietors of the Tarwich Company were very disappointed to hear you say that," she said.

His eyes flickered at the certainty in her tone as he assured her that was not the case at all. "They are working on their own high-pressure, light-weight steam carriage, which they estimate will be ready for inspection in six months. They have great hopes for it, and while I was unable to offer them encouragement because I saw no reason to wait half a year when Huzza & Company's machine was ready now, I did say that if the leading contender did not work out for any reason, I would be happy to consider it. Despite their disappointment, both Mr. Tarwich and Mr. Garrow were quite genial."

That did not sound right, Bea thought, none of it. Mr. Garrow was more pugnacious than genial, and his company was definitely not developing its own strong steam engine.

Quite the opposite, in fact, for Tarwich had spent the past twenty-four hours maligning high-pressure steam in an effort to permanently curtail its usage. They would not have done that if their own company's future depended on its widespread adoption.

Whatever the owners told Flexmore about their plans to create a strong steam engine was almost certainly a lie. If they were working on a machine utilizing an entirely different type of steam, then they would not have spent time and money on the Tarwich carriage they debuted last month.

Either they were looking to the future or holding fast to the past.

Bea, convinced which path they had chosen, thought

Flexmore's interest had left them no choice. They had to sabotage the *Bright Benny* or stand back and watch strong steam become an unstoppable force.

Once the military began building tramroads suited only for Huzza's cogged pinion wheels, then all steam carriages going forward would have to employ the same system.

Or maybe they simply wanted extra time to develop their own high-pressure steam engine.

But that would take years, not months, Bea thought.

"Has Mr. Garrow or Mr. Tarwich contacted you since the explosion to ask if you are reconsidering your decision?" she said.

They had not, according to Flexmore, but Bea did not think that signified. Even Mr. Garrow had to know how unbecomingly mercenary it would appear to propose his product so soon after the tragedy.

He would wait a few days, perhaps even a week.

The lieutenant-colonel, whose faith in the fixable valve never wavered, added that he had no expectation of hearing from Garrow. "As I said previously, I make a practice of communicating my objectives plainly. It is essential to overseeing a successful regiment. Misunderstanding leads to confusion, which leads to chaos, death and defeat."

Indeed, this time it had, Bea thought.

Given Flexmore's evidence, she crossed Lynch off her list of suspects. With the pending agreement with the British Army, the man had even less incentive to sabotage the *Bright Benny.* Securing a contract to sell its steam carriage to the military would secure Huzza & Company's success for decades to come and allow him to dispatch his debts swiftly.

By the same token, she also removed Rhodes. He simply had nothing to gain by the death of his employer, not even satisfaction, for their relationship was long-standing and cordial, and she simply could not imagine any man blowing up another without some material reward.

The case against Waugh was similarly undermined because the land developer was far too shrewd to sell a company with a pending contract worth thousands, let alone lose four shillings to the pound on the sale.

Always, there was the possibility that the widows and orphans stood to benefit in some unseen way, but more than Tarwich and Garrow?

It seemed highly unlikely.

Flexmore was convinced the culprit had served in the military because only someone who had deployed gunpowder in a combat situation would know how to exploit it so effectively.

Neither Tarwich nor Garrow fit that description.

Nevertheless, she was convinced of their guilt and decided to put aside the issue of whether they conceived the bomb to focus on how they manufactured it. Flexmore said it would require a blacksmith of some skill. That meant Garrow or Tarwich hired someone to fashion it for them, so all she had to do was find that person.

Given the duke's vast resources, an exhaustive search for the blacksmith seemed easy enough. She would start with the men in Tarwich's own manufactory.

That did not mean, of course, that she would not interrogate the owners on this new information she had discovered.

Obviously, they would be paying a call on Cloak Hart Lane posthaste.

"If Mr. Tarwich or Mr. Garrow does get in touch with you to discuss their new high-pressure steam carriage, I would be grateful if you would send me a note," Bea said.

"I am sure they will not!" Flexmore said firmly. "I could not have been any clearer in my lack of interest."

"Even so, in the unlikely event that they do contact you," she said.

Begrudgingly, he agreed and, bringing their interview to a close, reminded her that he had spoken so frankly on the understanding that every word of their exchange would be confined to the room. "We cannot have the Frenchies or Prussians learning of our plans to dominate the Continent. It would be as disastrous as the trumpets at Zama. That is, you understand, where Scipio defeated Hannibal. Elephants are an impregnable force to be reckoned with until someone sounds a trumpet and then they retreat with all the vigor of a new recruit. It is a helpful reminder of our unexpected vulnerabilities, which, you understand, is my job to anticipate."

"I do understand, yes," Bea said assumingly, "which is why I am so grateful for your cooperation. You have given me a lot of useful information."

The lieutenant-colonel scowled at this remark, as being helpful had not been his intention, and announced that he would escort them to the door.

"He wants to make sure we leave," Bea murmured quietly to the duke as they rose to their feet, "and do not double back to search his files."

"Are there files?" he asked, noting, as she had, the sparseness of the office.

Flexmore, explaining that he still had much to do that day, hurried them along and firmly shut the door behind them.

Actually, Bea thought in amusement, it was more like a slam.

Good riddance, young lady!

As they walked to the carriage, Bea mentioned the army officer's fondness for military history and observed that he clearly saw the strategic advantage gained by reading about battles. “He would, I am certain, agree that Shakespeare counts as training.”

Kesgrave stopped and spun on his heels, owning himself delighted to return to put the very question to Flexmore, and Bea, horrified at the prospect of spending more time in the lieutenant-colonel’s company, advised him to send a note instead.

Chapter Fifteen

Convinced the owners of the Tarwich Company lied to Flexmore about their forthcoming steam engine utilizing high pressure, Bea asked to see evidence of its existence.

"It does not have to be much," she added airily, after Heath had shown her and the duke to their office for the second time in two days. "Some technical drawings would be ideal, but a scrap of paper with a few calculations would do as well—just something that proves your claim to the lieutenant-colonel was more than an ill-conceived attempt to secure the lucrative contract for yourselves."

As was his habit, Tarwich simpered and picked up the first thing his hands could find on his desk—a small jar filled with black ink. Anxiously, he explained that their plan was not ill-conceived. "We are practical-minded men of science with a firm understanding of how steam power is produced and harnessed, and if we turned our mind to solving the problems of high-pressure steam, then we would solve the problems. The only reason we had not was we believed it was a disservice to the public. Lieutenant-Colonel Flexmore's visit forced us to reconsider our views, for if the British Army does not share our concern, then who are we to continue to have it?"

"I am sure your concerns underwent a radical transformation," Bea said amicably. "So please do show us your designs."

"But I cannot do that," Tarwich said, restless fingers toying with the bottle as he turned it upside down with little thought to its contents. Black ink leaked out of the vessel, staining his skin, and with a surprised shout, he dropped the bottle onto his desk. It landed with a hard thud as it fell over and dislodged the topper. Ink spilled over the documents he had been reading when they arrived.

Shaking his head with exasperation, Garrow handed his young associate a handkerchief and told him to wipe his fingers before he stained the furniture. Then he explained that the information was confidential. "The success of the company depends on our plans remaining secret. We cannot allow our competitors to discover confidential information. I am sure you understand."

Kesgrave, his lips twitching, assured the other man that he had no intention of setting himself up as a manufacturer of steam carriages.

This heartening announcement only increased Tarwich's discomfort, and he clutched at the cloth in his hands so tightly his fingers glowed red against the cream square.

Noting the subdued color of the fabric, she thought it was amusing how much more audacious Mr. Grimes's fashion choices were, with his vibrant yellow waistcoat and ridiculous walking stick with its garish golden knob. How out of place he had looked...

Oh, but wait.

Its garish golden knob.

Inhaling sharply, she looked at Garrow, perceiving suddenly the real reason he had been at the demonstration under a twice-false name. "This is about the designs. All along, you were after the designs for the *Bright Benny.* That is why you were there! You were going to steal the designs during the demonstration. Your walking stick—it is hollow, is it not?"

Garrow laughed heartily at the suggestion, complimenting Bea on her lively imagination, just as Tarwich laid his head on his desk and said, "Yes, your grace. You caught us."

But his partner refused to concede any ground, insisting that all she had caught them with was a handful of coins and a few worthless trinkets, which he promptly returned.

He dared her to prove more.

It might have worked, his obstructive approach, but Tarwich had no defiance left in him and confessed that the only reason they had maneuvered Huzza into hiring Garrow for the demonstration was to gain access to the drawings. "He was going to steal them while everyone was distracted by the demonstration, but the engine exploded before he got the chance. And then they were gone by the time he returned in the morning," he said, raising his head to reveal a black splotch at his temple. "I know it sounds bad, but stealing valuable information from one's competitors is actually a time-honored business tradition. Silas, tell them about Bavaria."

Garrow, glowering balefully at his partner while gesturing at him to wipe the ink off his forehead, explained that the government of Bavaria obtained the plans for one of Watt & Boulton's engines by sending a metalworker to the manufactory to bribe a guard into allowing him to enter.

"You see!" Tarwich cried triumphantly. "It is a common business practice and what else would you have us do? The

British Army *has* to buy our steam carriage! The arrangement would save our company and allow us to provide for our workers for years to come. If we fail, it is they who will suffer. Think of Mr. Heath!"

"Yes," Garrow said with a moue of concern. "Think of Mr. Heath and his six children. Do you really want them to starve?"

But it was exaggerated, his pout, and Bea knew he had never once considered his clerk's welfare in his entire life. All he cared about was money.

No doubt he paid his staff as little as possible to increase his own profits, and Mr. Heath struggled to put enough food on the table for his family.

It was a terrible way to treat a man who had fought for his country, and yet all too common. Officers returning to England got half pay, but noncommissioned soldiers received nothing, forcing them to fend for themselves under unfavorable conditions. The end of the war meant a glut of men looking for work, and Heath was lucky to have found anything at all. As a veteran, he could have suffered an injury—

Bea stiffened as she realized how utterly caper-witted she had been, searching high and low among blacksmith shops when the firm's clerk had been right there all along.

A former member of the army, competently filing documents in the front office!

"Summon Mr. Heath," she said.

Tarwich, who had rushed to correct his partner's understanding of Heath's domestic situation, for he had only four children—two sons and two daughters—looked at her in confusion.

"Excuse me?" he said.

Rising to her feet, Bea strode to the threshold of the

room, stuck her head into the hallway and called for Mr. Heath.

Bewildered, Tarwich turned to the duke and asked, "What is she doing?"

Bea, receiving no reply, raised her voice as she tried again.

Agitated by this behavior, the cause of which he could not fathom, Tarwich dashed to the entranceway and begged her grace to take a seat. "If you are so eager to talk to Mr. Heath, then I will of course fetch him for you."

He did not have to, however, for the clerk appeared then, his posture apologetic as he explained he had been in the cellars, looking through some boxes for a document from January of last year. "It should have been in the section marked 1815, but it was not, so I had to search all the boxes from the past months and...that...meant..."

The clerk trailed off as he seemed to realize he was rambling. "Regardless, I am sorry to have kept you waiting. How may I help you?"

Although he posed the question to Beatrice, he looked at Tarwich, as if expecting his employer to respond.

Presumably, that was why he jumped slightly when she answered.

"As you may know, I have been investigating the explosion of the *Bright Benny* because it was sabotaged by a small bomb made to look like a lump of coal," she said.

Heath professed to know nothing of sabotage. "I thought it was an accident with one of the valves, which is a risk of high-pressure steam. Why would anyone want to tamper with it?"

It was, Bea thought, an impressive display, for he revealed no apprehension at the prospect of being confronted with his own perfidy. Taking a few extra seconds to respond to her summons had caused him more anxiety.

"Money," she replied succinctly before elaborating. "A

great deal of it, in fact, as I am sure you know. And to secure it, you had to make sure the British Army bought steam carriages from your company, not Huzza's. That is why you devised the coal bomb—to destroy the competition."

The effect of these words was immediate, with every inch of his body revealing the depth of his shock.

Clearly, he never expected anyone to figure it out.

His eyes as wide as saucers, he shrieked, "What?"

Then he looked at his employer.

No, Bea thought. He glared at Tarwich, fury lighting his eyes with the brightness of a dozen candles.

"It cannot be true," Heath said hotly. "I refuse to believe it is true. After all that I have been through with the war, all the terrible things I have suffered, I cannot believe that the company for which I work would consider for even one moment allowing the British Army to use its remarkable invention to spread death and destruction. I do not care how much money you would make from the bargain, it is a corruption of something pure and good. If that is the immoral end to which this firm is working, then I must give my notice immediately."

Tarwich sighed heavily and looked across the room at his partner. "You see? I told you he would not like it."

"And I agreed," Garrow replied smoothly, "which is why we did not tell him."

Heath's anger deepened at this exchange. "It is clear to me that I cannot continue to work here after this blatant display of disrespect. I shall pack up my things and leave at once."

Shifting to block his progress out of the room, Tarwich urged him not to be hasty, for there was no deal to take a pet over. "They were just preliminary conversations. Nothing had been decided."

Garrow, raising his voice to be heard over his partner's attempts at placation, took the opposite approach, jeering at the notion that they required their clerk's approval for business decisions. "He works for us."

Heath reminded him that he did not.

"No, please, you must reconsider," Tarwich said plaintively. "You are the best clerk we have ever employed. If you resign we will be forced to endure chaos again. Why do you think the document you were looking for was in the wrong box? Because your predecessor was an incompetent fool. They were all horrible and incompetent. In twenty months, I have employed and fired five clerks."

"Then perhaps you should have considered that before you allowed your invention to be corrupted," Heath said icily. "Now please permit me to leave."

"But there is no agreement," Tarwich whined as he stepped aside to allow his former clerk to exit the room.

"Excuse me," Bea called before the clerk could disappear into the corridor.

Startled, Heath halted in his steps and turned to look at her with an almost confused expression. Tarwich appeared equally disconcerted.

"If you recall, Mr. Heath, I was talking to you," she said.

He did recall, yes, but only at this reminder, and his whole face reddened as he hurried back into the room to stand before her. "Your grace! I most humbly submit to your censure. I let myself become distracted by personal concerns. I am truly sorry. You have my full attention now. How may I assist you?"

Bea, who had watched the scene unfold with a jaundiced eye, wondered if it had been performed for her benefit. It seemed improbable to her that the clerk had actually resigned his position on a whim.

There were still those children to support—two sons, two daughters.

The income could not be insignificant to their welfare.

"Let us sit down," Bea said, inviting the clerk to take the chair next to hers at Tarwich's desk. When he was settled, his hands folded loosely in his lap, she continued. "Before you angrily stormed out of the room, I accused you of conspiring to murder Mr. Huzza."

Heath stared at her, his eyes blinking owlishly for several seconds, before he laughed awkwardly and said, "Oh, you are serious."

"Yes, Mr. Heath, I am serious," Bea said flatly. "The case against your employers is unassailable. They have already confessed to trying to steal the *Bright Benny*'s technical drawings so they could make their own high-pressure steam carriage. But that is only half a plan. The drawings would be worthless to them if the army went ahead with its agreement to buy steam engines from Huzza & Company. That deal had to be scotched as well, and the best way to do that was by destroying the machine in a spectacular display during its triumphant debut. The only problem with this theory is neither Mr. Tarwich nor Mr. Garrow possesses the technical abilities to devise or create a clever little bomb like the one that killed Mr. Huzza and blow up his steam carriage. But you do. Lieutenant-Colonel Flexmore told us to look for a man with military experience—experience you have."

Now he gasped sharply, his hold slipping as he stammered in surprise. "I cannot believe....it is inconceivable to me....You must understand, your grace, that it was a horrific experience for me, the army, the war, all of it. I would never do anything to.... And I knew nothing of the lieutenant-colonel—neither of his visit nor his interest in our engines. It was kept from me. You heard them. They deliberately withheld the information from me because they are selfish and amoral men."

Garrow, either genuinely offended by the underling's judgment or determined to intercede before he revealed too much, opened his mouth as he stepped forward.

Kesgrave silenced him with a look.

Unconvinced of Heath's ignorance, Bea knew he was the weakest link in the plot. A lowly clerk with several mouths to feed, he could not afford to hang for another man's crime.

Softly, then, cajolingly, she promised to help save him from the noose if he would just tell her the truth. "Confess everything now and I will use my influence to ensure you do not swing for Huzza's murder."

Heath lost all color in his face as he gaped at her, and panic overtaking him, he shot to his feet. The chair teetered and then toppled. "Swing? Swing! I do not understand what you are saying."

His fear was convincing, Bea thought, and yet she could not decide if it was induced by the anxiety of wrongful accusation or the dread of being caught. "Oh, but you do. You know the penalty for murder is death. And if you do not realize it, then I promise you, your employers do. Do you really think, Mr. Heath, that they would sacrifice themselves for you? Mr. Tarwich and Mr. Garrow, who have already shown themselves to be without morals or scruples, infiltrating Mr. Huzza's firm under false pretenses to steal its designs and arranging half a dozen interviews with newspaper reporters to blame Huzza for his own death before his corpse had even cooled. Do these seem like men who would stand up for you if the situations were reversed?"

Tarwich grumbled that he was the victim of an unfair character assassination, for if the inventor's body had been torn asunder, then what was left to cool? "How long would you have me wait, your grace?"

Bea, her eyes trained on the clerk's pale face, said with harsh disdain, "*That* is the man you are protecting with your silence. Is that really what you want to do, Mr. Heath? Think carefully because this offer of help is fleeting. In a moment I will extend the exact same one to Mr. Tarwich. Do you think he will refuse it?"

Heath's jaw flapped in the air, as he began and abandoned different defenses. Before he could settle on one, Garrow ordered him to stay quiet. "Do not say a word, man, for she is trying to trick you. We have done nothing wrong, so there is nothing she can prove. She is merely an irrational female who nurses a grudge against us—why, I have no idea. Probably because she is an irrational female."

"I have Flexmore's testimony," Bea said smoothly, unbothered by his charge, "in which he states that the bomb was devised by a man who served time in the army. I have the two dozen quotes Mr. Tarwich supplied to the various newspaper reporters he summoned in the wake of the tragedy to advance his own agenda. I have Mr. Garrow's admission that he tried to steal the designs for the *Bright Benny.* I have a contract with the British Army worth many thousands of pounds to the company that can manufacture the most efficient high-pressure steam carriage. And that is just the beginning. I will get more, Mr. Heath, you may depend on it. Now you can choose to stay silent, as your employer demands, and hope that I will just go away, or you can tell me everything now and save your life. Think of your children, Mr. Heath, and what it will mean to have a father executed for murder. What kind of future will they have?"

As the clerk stood in the middle of the room, ashen and dazed, Tarwich asked in a plaintive whine why the duchess was so determined to persecute them. "What have we ever done to deserve such ill treatment?"

Bea ignored them, her gaze focused on Heath, whose eyes were filling now with water. Silently, drops began to spill onto his cheeks, which he wiped frantically with tightened fists as he swore he had no idea what she was talking about.

"I did not kill anyone. I could never hurt anyone, not after what I saw in the war," he cried, his voice tight with apprehension or frustration, his body shuddering with horror or fear. "Violence is repugnant to me. All that death and destruction! I had my fill of it on the Continent and cannot endure any more. Just the very idea of bloodshed turns my stomach! I find it sickening, your grace. All I wanted when I returned to England was to live a peaceful and productive life. That is what I thought I had found here, at the Tarwich Company. Steam power does no harm, I thought. It makes things possible. Discovering that the army seeks to pervert that goodness by turning it into an engine of war is repellent to me. Mr. Tarwich and Mr. Garrow knew how I would feel. That is why they hid it from me."

The tears were streaming down his face now and he brushed them away with the palms of his hands, pressing them against his eyes as if to fix the problem at the source.

It made no difference.

Struggling to regain control of himself, he tried to take a step back and crashed into the upset chair. He cried out in alarm, as if a small animal such as a dog or a raccoon had attacked his legs, and wobbled precariously.

Rather than fall over, Bea thought he might just sink to the floor.

Instead, he recovered his balance by grabbing onto the desk, then leaned down to return the seat to its upright position.

None of this helped his composure, and he only sobbed harder as he stared at Bea, his hands shaking. "I would never do something so despicable as make a bomb, and hearing you accuse me of it is a nightmare, a terrible nightmare, and it feels as though I am back in the army, back in that lobsterbox, and my sergeant is sneering at me for not having the spine to shoot my rifle."

It was a strange thing to be struck by—the term "lobster-box"—but something about it resonated with her. Bea felt an odd sort of tickling at the base of her spine.

What did it mean?

The phrase itself was army cant.

That was easy enough to recognize: soldiers in their bright red uniforms mucking about in a confined space.

A barrack, presumably.

Yes, but why was that significant?

Desperately, she closed her eyes and let the words echo in her head: lobster-box, lobster-box.

Nothing about it seemed to matter.

The use of army slang was hardly novel. Many former soldiers and sailors incorporated the everyday language of the military in their civilian lives. All it revealed was that Heath had served his country, and that was information she already possessed.

It was the reason she believed he had a hand in the plot to destroy the *Bright Benny*.

But if he had a hand in Huzza's murder, then when had he adamantly refused to betray his employers? Surely, he was calculating enough to comprehend the value of aligning with the Duke and Duchess of Kesgrave against a pair of steam merchants? With the investigation at an impasse, it was her word against theirs, and given her clout, recent history of success and the evidence already cited, every magistrate in London would gladly take her side.

And yet the clerk refused to admit to wrongdoing.

His sobs increased, and Bea opened her eyes in time to see him drop to his knees. As he collapsed on the floor, Bea allowed for the possibility that he was innocent. His opposition to warfare seemed sincere, for it was not unheard of for men to return from battle scarred by the atrocities they were forced to endure. If he was among that number, then he would be horrified by Flexmore's plan to increase England's efficacy in killing its enemies by employing a network of tramroads.

He would never do anything to aid the lieutenant-colonel.

Indeed, he was so ardently opposed, he had resigned his position rather than continue with a company that would even consider it.

Ardently opposed, she thought.

Good God!

Turning abruptly on her heels, she strode across the room to Garrow, who, perceiving something unnerving in her intensity, took a step backward.

"The *Bright Benny*," she said briskly. "At the demonstration, you claimed Huzza named it for his son."

Stung into defensiveness, Garrow insisted that it was not *his* claim but Huzza's. "He said it was a way to honor his sons."

"Sons?" she noted sharply. "Plural?"

"Well, yes, I suppose," he said hesitantly, unnerved, it seemed, by the force of her interest. "I believe he had two sons, whom he sought to honor with the naming of his engines. The *Bright Benny* was the most recent model, and the *Brilliant Bert* came before it."

"Because they both died in the war?" Bea said.

Garrow nodded. "Victims of Napoleon's tyranny."

Taken aback by the phrasing, Bea asked if that was how Huzza put it.

"Well, no," he replied cautiously. "He made some rather harsh condemnations about the imbecility of allowing second sons to purchase captaincies, but it amounts to the same thing."

But it did not.

No, it bore no relation at all, and she looked at Kesgrave across the room and knew he was thinking the same thing.

"He was opposed to war," she said.

"Or the British military at the very least," he replied.

Heath, sensing that the duchess's focus had shifted elsewhere, rose to his feet and said, "Any rational person would."

Huzza, supremely rational and mourning his dead children, had turned down the deal. He refused to sell his steam carriage to the British Army.

Of course he had.

He wanted to use his wondrous invention to bring people to the beach.

Bright and brilliant.

Yet Flexmore remained convinced the agreement had been settled.

Lynch had told him so.

But why was Lynch so confident?

He knew precisely why the inventor was opposed and could have little hope of overcoming an anguished father's grief.

The only way to remove Huzza's objections was to remove Huzza.

Oh, yes, she thought, that made sense.

Lynch would have had the means to make the bomb, Bea thought, as he had overseen the fabrication of the *Bright Benny*.

And that resigned look on the platform.

He had known his partner would usurp the attention, gobbling up every last bit for himself. It had been a reasonable gamble, betting that Huzza would insist on feeding the firebox.

Lynch was such a perfect suspect, and yet the lone argument against his culpability was implacable: his debts to Mr. Waugh. Every time and from every angle, she ran into the clutch fist of Willis Waugh. Whatever extravagant hopes Lynch might have nurtured for the future, he had one modest goal for the present and that was to ward off disaster. Destroying the *Bright Benny* to remove Huzza made no sense.

'Twas like stabbing himself with a knife.

Lynch would have never done it.

No, all he wanted was to get through the demonstration without incident and then scoop up giddy investors.

Ward off disaster, she thought again.

This time, however, the word lodged in her mind, reverberating like *lobster-box,* and then suddenly and with stunning clarity she knew why Heath's use of military cant had struck her so ominously.

Rhodes had said *wardroom.*

Yesterday afternoon, after she roused him from his drunken slumber by pouring water in his face, he had used the term. Describing the strangeness of being woken by the Duke and Duchess of Kesgrave while prostrate on an unfamiliar floor and shrinking under the penetrating gaze of a butler's disgust, he said that it bore a resemblance to a dream he once had.

Except we were in a wardroom, and you were a cat who kept telling me to eat my parsnips.

Yes, there it was—navy slang for the room where officers took their meals.

Mr. Rhodes, who possessed no conceivable motive, had served in the military.

Except he did have a motive.

His dedication has been invaluable and as soon as we turned a profit, I promised to reward him hugely. We were so close.

It made sense, she thought, the case against Rhodes.

Unlike every other suspect, he had full control over the use of the bomb and reserved the right not to deploy it if events did not take the turn he expected.

But he knew they would.

The inventor loved being the center of attention so much

that he refused to allow his partner to begin his speech, let alone finish it. If Lynch had known Huzza's tendencies well enough to shrug resignedly when the other man pushed him aside, then Rhodes, who had worked alongside the inventor for twice as long, would have relied on them.

And yet she could not quite reconcile the extravagant destructiveness of the act with its goal. If all Rhodes had wanted to do was remove his employer, there were far simpler ways to arrange it.

Again, she listed the easiest: poison, firm shove out of a window, carriage accident.

Why demolish the machine you had spent years building if it was not absolutely necessary?

Oh, but maybe it was, she thought, recalling the stomach ailment that had bedeviled Huzza in the week leading up to demonstration. Lynch had attributed it to anxiety, and Rhodes mentioned breaking every afternoon to eat potatoes with Huzza. In that case, as with the steam engine, the engineer had the means to administer the poison and the opportunity.

Possibly, if she examined Huzza's final days, she would find other instances where he narrowly escaped an accident or suffered a mishap.

Exploding the *Bright Benny* might have been an act of desperation.

Or perhaps Rhodes had grown impatient.

Or maybe he decided the spectacle of destruction befitted a man so committed to peace.

Either way, he must have found his employer's obstinacy maddening.

She recalled his description of the tramroad to Whitstable as "very impractical," which she had thought at the time conveyed as much fondness as censure.

Now she realized it was all censure.

Thinking he was removing the lone obstacle to immense wealth, Rhodes must have been gutted to discover the extent of Lynch's debt.

All that devastation!

And for what?

Huzza dead, *Bright Benny* destroyed, and he remained as far away from a great fortune as ever.

In the wake of that disappointment, it was not extraordinary that Rhodes finished two bottles of wine on the night of the explosion.

Rather, it was outstanding that he had not consumed three.

How zealously he must have sought oblivion.

And yet he could not escape the truth, for it was all that he could say: It's my fault. All my fault.

She had assumed it was a drunk and despondent mind grappling to comprehend the utterly random nature of the universe.

But for Huzza's vanity, it could have been him.

In truth, it was a confession.

Perceiving how grossly she had misjudged the situation, Bea apologized to Mr. Heath. "I see now that you have done nothing wrong and are to be commended for your morals. I cannot say the same for your employers, but I hope there is some consolation in knowing you work for men who are rapacious, not murderous."

Tarwich, noting something in her reply that reflected well on him, nodded vigorously in gratitude, while Garrow frowned and demanded she explain why she had changed her mind.

Somehow being released from suspicion only made him more churlish.

Although Heath's tears had yet to abate, he was in greater control of himself, and he was able to reply calmly. "I am very relieved to hear it, your grace. Thank you. I appreciate your perspective, but the exact nature of Mr. Tarwich's and Mr. Garrow's depravity does not concern me, as I have already resigned. It is a matter for their next clerk to resolve in his heart. If you would be so kind as to excuse me, I will gather my things and go."

"I do not excuse you," Tarwich said, deeply troubled by the prospect of the clerk leaving. Clearly, it unsettled him in a way that being suspected of murder had not. "You must stay and allow me to change your mind."

"I am sure that is not possible," Heath said, sighing deeply, visibly exhausted from his ordeal.

Tarwich fervently disagreed, insisting they could come to some arrangement. "I value you far too much to lose you. Tell me how to put this to rights. I will say anything you like. You are the most capable person to ever hold the position and you simply must stay. There is no alternative."

When blandishments failed, Tarwich switched tactics, promising to increase his salary by five shillings per week. This offer was refused as well, and the owner, not understanding the constraints imposed by the possession of a conscience, held out greater and greater sums until Garrow was forced to step in and retract the offer. He refused to pay the clerk more money than he himself earned.

Chafing against the rationality of this position, Tarwich argued that a competent clerk was worth his weight in gold. Garrow agreed this was true in a figurative sense, not a literal one, and while the partners squabbled, Heath slipped out of the room to collect his things from his office.

When Tarwich noticed his absence, he scurried after him and resumed his persuasion. Lacking the ability to secure his loyalty for a price, he reluctantly accepted the futility of his pleas and sighing in defeat, asked Heath if there was a family member he could recommend with the same set of skills.

A brother, perhaps, or a cousin.

Alas, there was not, and as Bea and Kesgrave left the premises, Tarwich was quizzing the clerk on the ages of his sons and their familiarity with the principles that governed the filing of documents.

Chapter Sixteen

Finding neither Rhodes nor evidence of his culpability in the engineer's lodgings, despite an extensive search that included checking the floorboards for secret compartments in light of Flora's recent successes, Bea suggested they pay a call to Sutherland Street. "I expect he is still there. Given the state he and Lynch were in when we left them yesterday, they probably drank through several expensive vintages of port and passed out on the second-floor landing together."

Kesgrave, agreeing with her assessment of the situation, asked how she would convince Rhodes to confess.

A very reasonable question, Bea thought as they climbed into the carriage, and one to which she had no satisfying answer.

One method that had proved fruitful in the past was provoking a murderer into trying to kill her to either suppress evidence or evade punishment. It had worked particularly well with Bentham, whose guilt she had barely begun to ponder when he attacked her in the quiet of her own sitting room. Contemplating how to find proof to support her suspicion, she had envisioned an expensive, drawn-out search of blacksmiths in London and perhaps the surrounding villages.

With his homicidal attack, the earl had saved her a good deal of trouble and possibly weeks of frustration.

Could Rhodes be persuaded to act with the same impetuosity? If he believed she had uncovered a piece of evidence that tied him conclusively to the murder, then he might try to silence her before she could reveal it.

It had potential, yes, but also presented several insurmountable obstacles, most notably, the wreckage of the crime scene itself, which allowed for very few opportunities for a discovery like Bentham's sleeve button, and Kesgrave's refusal to allow his wife to intentionally position herself as a target.

It was remarkable enough that he let her do it unintentionally.

"Perhaps we can exploit his guilt," she said, the carriage swaying as it pulled into the road. "The fact that he kept saying, 'It's my fault. All my fault,' indicates that he is troubled by his conscience. Perhaps we can compel him to confess by deepening his sense of remorse."

Kesgrave, his expression doubtful, allowed it might work if Rhodes was still deep in his cups. "Which, as you observed, is possible. But I think it has little chance of succeeding if he is sober. A man who would trick his employer into destroying himself does not possess a surfeit of scruples."

"True," she said, "and yet he kept repeating the refrain. Perhaps the reality of tricking one's employer into destroying himself—and for nothing—is worse than the imagining of it. If that is true, then we need to figure out how to use that against him. Huzza is not survived by children, so we cannot use their orphanhood against him. His wife is likewise deceased. That leaves us with few options other than Lynch. I suppose he will have to do."

The duke remained skeptical, but Bea insisted Rhodes

might feel some sort of kinship toward him, for they had both been thwarted by Huzza's opposition to war.

"And now Lynch's life is in ruins," she continued. "He has nothing left. Rhodes is responsible for that. If he is already remorseful, knowing he ruined two lives might push him over the edge. To apply pressure, we have to make Lynch's suffering more acute."

Bea recalled Mr. Heath's reaction to being unfairly accused of murder. Highly upset, he had collapsed to the floor in grief, anxiety, frustration and fear.

For a man already grappling with regret, that would be a terrible scene to witness.

Dubious, Kesgrave suggested she would have better luck with the Cheltenham tragedy she was staging if she ensured Rhodes's inebriation before attempting the scene. "Or you could try to convince him you discovered a particularly damning piece of evidence that tied him inextricably to the crime."

Bea smiled faintly at the proposal. "You say that now, your grace, so nonchalant and matter-of-fact, and yet later, when I am driving my jeweled magnifying glass into his eye to repel his attack, you will be all curmudgeonly and out of sorts because I take too many risks."

"If you think I need to wait until you are repelling a murderer with a piece of jewelry to be curmudgeonly and out of sorts with the risks you take, Bea, then you have not been paying attention," he replied coolly as he rapped on the door and waited for Woolley to answer.

When neither the butler nor another servant responded, Kesgrave tried the handle and found that the door was unlocked. Entering, they called out for Lynch, whom they discovered in his drawing room, sitting on the floor surrounded by empty bottles of wine. Unlike the previous day, there were no other seating options, as the settee and chairs had been removed, and the vintage of claret was considerably less elegant. From the smell, Bea gathered it was only one step up from vinegar.

The sparsity of the room was unsettling to her.

Having never incurred debt, she did not know that it could be discharged so swiftly. Less than four and twenty hours had passed since their last visit and already the house had been stripped of its valuables.

Lynch, perhaps mindful of the desolate tableau they presented, glared angrily at Bea as she and the duke crossed the threshold. Rhodes, sprawled on his back, stared up at the chandelier, seemingly unaware of their presence.

He looked worse for wear, Bea thought, noting his pale skin and drawn features. His eyes, darkened with shadows, had an unnatural puffiness about them.

Their host, failing to offer any greeting, glowered pugnaciously, as if daring them to draw farther into the room.

"Good afternoon," Bea said, stepping forward.

At this mild remark, Lynch's scowl deepened, and he curled his lip balefully, as if annoyed by their persistence.

Apparently, he had expected them to slowly back out of the room and leave.

In derisive homage to his welcome the day before, he announced that the curtains were worth fifteen shillings. "And that is for the whole set, not each panel. Take it or leave it, your grace, for that is all I have left."

Bea's eyes tilted upward to the ceiling, from which a lovely cut-crystal light fixture still dangled.

Lynch barked out a bitter laugh as he explained that the men from the bank would be back for that in a few hours. "There are still some items upstairs they have yet to remove. As efficient as they are, there is only so much they can do at a time."

Having no reply to that, for what consolation could she

offer, Bea nodded in acknowledgment and then said, "Hello, Mr. Rhodes."

The engineer did not respond immediately, but slowly, inexorably, his head lolled in her general direction. "Your grace," he said, then repeated it to Kesgrave before falling silent.

Apparently, the condition of intoxication had been met, she thought, noting the slackness of his muscles and the blank expression on his face. It was strange, addressing two grown men who were occupying the floor, especially when one was flat on his back, but she figured the relaxed pose would work in her favor.

Neither man appeared to be on his guard.

She turned to Lynch to accuse him of murder and realized she was curiously at a loss for how to say it. Previously, she had made her allegations with confidence, convinced she understood the motives and actions of the suspect. Several times she had been erroneous in her assessment, but those inaccurate claims, arrived at through sincere miscalculation, had been delivered with the same certainty as the correct ones.

Now she wanted to lodge an accusation that she knew to be wrong. She could not just make the Rhodes case against Lynch, for the facts would not bear out.

She had to make the Lynch case.

Alas, there was no Lynch case to make.

Untroubled by the growing silence, Lynch raised the nearest bottle to his lips and drank deeply. She watched his Adam's apple bob as he took several large gulps.

It was a salutary reminder, Bea thought, of his reduced capacity to reason, and she realized the facts did not have to align perfectly. Lynch was in no state to counter her charge cogently, and regardless, he was not the audience for it.

Only Rhodes had to find it persuasive.

He had to believe Lynch would be hanged for his crime, and given how worn thin by guilt he already was, it would require very little to elicit a confession.

"Mr. Lynch, I have spoken with Lieutenant-Colonel Flexmore and I know everything," she said firmly. "I know that Mr. Huzza was an insurmountable impediment to the immeasurable success of your company and as such had to be removed."

Slowly, Lynch lowered the bottle to the bare wood floor as he stared at her and murmured, "An insurmountable impediment?"

"An insurmountable impediment, yes," she replied firmly, "for he would never have come around."

Seemingly baffled by the statement, he said, "He would not?"

"He would not," she said, noting what a strange sensation it was to accuse one man of murder while looking at another. "That is why you came up with a diabolical scheme to remove him."

As straightforward as this allegation was, Lynch's wine-soaked mind failed to grasp it and he gaped at her in confusion. "I did?"

Worried that Lynch might be too drunk for her ploy to work, Bea was gratified when Rhodes darted suddenly into a sitting position to goggle in surprise. "*What?*"

At least one of them was sober enough to understand what was happening.

Ignoring Rhodes, she kept her eyes focused on Lynch, whose expression had yet to clear with comprehension.

Nevertheless, she pressed on. "The money was too great to resist, especially for a man in a situation like yours, in debt up to the eyeballs. You needed the lucrative deal Flexmore was offering. The British military buying your steam carriages and creating a network of tramroads on which to operate them would mean thousands of pounds, possibly tens of thousands as collieries and mills followed suit, trusting the army's endorsement. You had no choice. You had to kill him."

Something flickered in the depths of Lynch's eyes, an understanding, she thought, as he began to shake his head. Now he would shriek in denial, his anxiety mounting as the vileness of the accusation fully struck him.

But he did not.

Calmly, he insisted that Huzza would have come around. "Peter was not unreasonable."

Appreciating that his denial was the product of an innocent conscience did little to help Bea shame Rhodes into a confession and she tried again, this time citing his resentment at the way Huzza treated him—as if he were a bank vault.

Unruffled, he asserted again that he was certain Huzza would have changed his mind. "He understood the value of money and knew the funds provided by the deal with Flexmore could pay for the other inventions he had in mind. He had so many ideas!"

She darted a glance to Rhodes to see how he was receiving this exchange and was encouraged by the astonished expression he wore.

That was good, she thought. It meant he could not believe his employer was being blamed for his sin.

Bea pushed harder, then, insisting she had proof of Lynch's guilt.

Rhodes, hearing that, patted the other man consolingly on the back and said, "A dreadful turn and a surprising one, but I am sure you had your reasons."

Lynch recoiled from the understanding in the engineer's voice as he realized the other man believed it. It was one thing for the Duchess of Kesgrave to point a finger, for that was what she did, randomly accuse people of murder until she stumbled onto the actual culprit, but for his friend and associate to think it was deeply unsettling.

"You must not believe her. Please, you must not," he said to Rhodes, his manner suddenly agitated. "She has no idea what she is talking about. I harm Peter? I would never! Huzza & Company is nothing without him. I swear, Mr. Rhodes, I would never do anything so despicable to advance our business. Killing to achieve success would make all your hard work meaningless."

Mr. Rhodes laughed.

It was a slight thing, barely a chortle, not even a chuckle, but it revealed his true frame of mind, and hearing it, Bea realized that he was too sober to indulge his emotions freely. Judging by the revealing slip, she could not believe he would be compelled by guilt to confess.

On a heavy sigh, she turned to Kesgrave and said, "I still think it was worth a try."

Graciously, he admitted that he had thought it might actually succeed when he saw all the bottles on the floor.

"It seems the thing I failed to comprehend was the source of his remorse," she said.

"The fortune slipping through his fingers," Kesgrave agreed, "not the murder."

"If only he had stuck to more mundane methods like poisoning the potatoes," she added with a pitiful shake of her head.

As they conducted this exchange, the color faded from Rhodes's cheeks. Lynch, whose head had been swiveling back and forth, from Bea to Rhodes and back again, settled his astonished gaze on the engineer.

"Yes, Mr. Rhodes, we know you did it," Bea said in the same conversational tone with which she had conducted the tête-à-tête with the duke. "I thought I could shame you into confessing. The duke thought it was possible only if you were drunk. It appears we were both wrong."

The engineer remained silent as Lynch said, "I do not understand. You don't think I did it?"

"Lacking your confidence in Mr. Huzza's willingness to be persuaded, Mr. Rhodes killed him to secure the contract with the army. But he knew nothing of your debts and was inconsolable to discover the company would pass out of your hands. He assumed you would rebuild the *Bright Benny* and make a fortune from selling steam carriages to the military," she explained. "You promised him a portion of the profits, and he was impatient to claim it."

Rhodes owned himself deeply amused by her theorizing, but his chortle now was awkward and forced. He was anxious—that was clear—even if he still believed he could brazen it out.

"You may be as entertained by my antics as you wish, Mr. Rhodes, but it will make no difference. The constable, who is on his way, will nonetheless take you into his custody."

Fear sparked in his eyes and immediately disappeared. "Take me into custody based on what? The Duchess of Kesgrave's very strong feeling?"

It was said mockingly, satirically, with disdain for her arrogance and self-importance, and Bea marveled at how quickly it had come to this. She had occupied the position for less than two months. Scarcely six weeks before she could not have imagined being addressed as "your grace" without flinching and now she was consigning men to the gallows based on her title alone.

But no, it was not on her title alone.

In the past six months, she had apprehended half a dozen murderers and proven her aptitude. Although he might grumble about her sex and presumption, the magistrate would listen when she presented her evidence, which was, she acknowledged, mostly based on circumstance.

She had yet to discover anything that connected Rhodes definitively with the crime—*yet* being the operative word.

It was, she believed, only a matter of time before she found proof.

A confession would simplify the process, she said to Rhodes now, pausing just long enough to allow him to laugh again, but she was happy to do it the complicated way if necessary. "You see, I have unlimited resources and I will expend them to gather evidence. Somewhere in your various attempts to kill Mr. Huzza, you encountered other people. I will interview your shipmates, schoolmates, bedmates, roommates—anyone with whom you have had contact in the past ten years—and find at least one person who knows of your scheme. I will find the man who sold you the gunpowder or the apothecary from whom you bought the poison. No crime is committed without leaving some sort of trail, however minor, and I will uncover it. And while I am looking, you will sit in your cell in Newgate awaiting trial."

Bea, who thought this was an unsettling little speech, full of menace and determination, was surprised to note that Rhodes's expression remained unchanged. Bearing that same look of mild good humor, he stretched to his left to pick up the bottle of wine from which Lynch had recently imbibed.

He would enjoy his last moments of freedom in a drunken haze—a far from revelatory choice, she thought, given how he had passed so many recent hours.

Rhodes shrugged, as if submitting to the inevitability of fate, and gripped the bottle more tightly. Blithely, he said, "Oh, I see. In that case—"

It was startling, the sound of shattering glass, the way it echoed off the barren walls of the nearly empty room, the way the shards darted and skimmed across the floor.

Briefly, Bea thought the bottle had slipped.

In the first second after the resounding crash, she assumed it slid from his grasp.

Of course she did.

Off to Newgate to stand trial for murder.

It was enough to make the toughest man's bones turn to jelly.

But then her brain processed the movements: the lifting of the bottle, its deliberate smash against the floor. Clenched in his hand, the jagged glass glinted with sharp edges, and before she or Kesgrave could respond, Lynch was held captive in the other man's embrace, the broken neck of the bottle pressed against his jugular.

It happened so quickly, Lynch did not have a chance to cry out in alarm.

"—I better leave before he arrives," Rhodes continued easily, his smooth tone revealing none of the exertion of the past few seconds.

He had done it again, she thought, fashioned a weapon out of something harmless, and was not even breathing hard.

Rhodes rose to his knees, tugging his captive into the same position. Lynch grunted and twisted his shoulders, as if to get away from the makeshift blade, but the measure only brought it closer. The glass cut his skin, drawing a narrow scratch on the thin column of his neck.

"Oh, dear," Rhodes murmured. "I fear that might hurt."

He sounded a little mad, Bea thought, as she watched him jerk Lynch to his feet. Despite his demeanor, he was not entirely composed.

She had no idea what that meant for Lynch.

"I am not worried about what you will find," Rhodes said as Lynch steadied himself. "I took meticulous care and left nothing behind that could point to anything untoward in my behavior. But I do know that among your boundless resources is your husband's influence, and that I cannot risk. Now Mr. Lynch and I will be on our way. If you follow me, I will slice him through. Do you understand, your grace?"

What she understood was that Lynch's life was in peril, thanks to her interference, and she could not rely on Rhodes to make a reasonable assessment of his situation. Having a hostage benefitted him now, but as soon as he fled the house, the calculus would change.

Lynch would become a burden.

At that point, Rhodes had two choices: Fling Lynch to the ground and start running or slice Lynch's throat and start running.

The running part was assured.

Less certain was how he would treat his captive once he no longer needed him to guarantee his own survival.

Logically, slowing his progress for even the few moments it would take to kill Lynch was an ill-advised waste of time. Every second counted in a narrow escape.

Rhodes was too smart not to know that.

And yet how satisfying it must be to hold in his hands the life of the man whose unknown financial obligations had literally cost him a fortune.

Revenge would be sweet.

Fearing the lure of vengeance would be impossible to resist, Bea knew she could not allow Rhodes to leave the room.

Once he was gone from their sight, it would all be over.

Ultimately, Rhodes would not get far.

He had proved wily, yes, but he could not return to his lodgings and would be forced to fend with whatever money he had on him.

It was difficult to flee London without resources.

But his eventual apprehension meant little if Lynch was dead.

No, he must be detained, then disarmed.

How?

She needed time to come up with a plan.

Grappling for a distraction, she recalled his question, then decided to ignore it entirely. That would at least force him to repeat himself.

"Thank you," Bea said.

Rhodes frowned darkly as he adjusted his grip on the bottle, raising it a fraction of an inch so that she could see the red mark on Lynch's neck. It was long but not deep. "Do not play games with me. I asked if you understand what will happen to Lynch if you follow me. I will slit his throat and he will die where he stands and that will be on *your* conscience. Do you understand that?"

Lynch whimpered at the ghastly description, and Bea swept her gaze around the room, carefully taking note of everything in it. Admittedly, there was very little to work with. Even so, she took stock: curtains, chandelier, broken glass, candelabra, Kesgrave.

Rhodes ordered his captive to shut up and told Bea he was waiting for a reply.

"What I understand, Mr. Rhodes, is that your confession will make convicting you easier, and for that I am grateful," she said. "Thank you."

"I confessed nothing!" he exclaimed.

"Technically, no, not in so many words," she allowed, her eyes seeking out the duke's as she spoke. He had taken several steps to the left, putting himself at once in her line of sight and in closer proximity to Rhodes, who did not notice. That obliviousness, she felt certain, could be attributed to the wine. He could focus on only one thing, and at the moment it was she. "But your denial is de facto confirmation because one cannot take meticulous care with something one did not do. *Modus tollens*, my friend, the 'mood that denies.' Read your Stoics."

Rhodes sneered at her reasoning, which Bea took as an invitation to continue.

"And of course there is this whole thing," she said, gesturing to the dramatic scene before her: the broken bottle, the exposed jugular, Lynch's terrified stance. Even as she drew Rhodes's attention to his hostage, she kept hers focused on Kesgrave. His expression, as intent as her own, indicated he knew what she was doing. He would wait for the distraction and then pounce. "Taking a man prisoner reveals your hand. You might as well have stood in the middle of Bond Street and yelled, 'I am guilty, do please arrest me,' for all the subtlety it has." She shook her head, deeply unimpressed. "Not very clever, I am afraid. The lump of coal bomb—now *that* was clever. But a little too clever, I think."

Goaded by her smugness and the smirk of a grin she gave him, Rhodes swore angrily as he stepped forward. Lynch lurched, driving the glass deeper into his skin, and he cried out as blood dripped from the cut. Rhodes yanked his victim's arm to still him and growled that Bea was not nearly as clever as she thought either. "I know what you are doing, trying to get me to remain until the constable arrives. It won't work. You"—he positively spat the word as he tilted toward her—"stay here or he dies."

He took a step back, pulling an ashen-faced Lynch with him, and Bea, with a meaningful look at Kesgrave, said with a hint of her cousin Flora's airiness, "You mean here, right here? Or may I stay over there?"

She motioned with her right arm, her finger pointing to some unspecified spot nearby, and Rhodes's head turned, seemingly of its own volition, like eyes squinting at the sun.

The duke lunged, thrusting Rhodes forward while wrenching his arm right back, and Bea heaved the stunned hostage to the side. Lynch inhaled sharply, as if gasping for air after being submerged in water, just as Rhodes, his balance restored, swung the deadly glass at Kesgrave. He missed, just barely grazing the duke's shoulder, and bellowed with impotent rage as his head snapped back from the power of Kesgrave's fist.

Snarling as the duke reared up to tackle him, Rhodes flung the broken bottle at Kesgrave's face, slicing his cheek, and hurled himself into the air to grasp the bottom tier of the chandelier. He swung back and then forth, his wildly flailing legs plunging into the duke's stomach. The momentum propelled Kesgrave backward just as the pain pitched him over. Rhodes cackled as he arched his back and dropped down from his perch. He darted for the door, and Bea, knowing she could never run as fast as he, not with her skirts, not in her booties, leaped as far as she could and then slid on the floor, sweeping her legs under his.

Rhodes fell with a thud.

Bea scampered to her knees to immobilize him as she had Taunton a few months ago on the balcony during the Leland ball, which was by sitting on his chest, but Kesgrave was already there, tugging him to his feet.

Jenkins, entering the room with the constable in tow, shook his head at the picture they presented—the duchess's hitched skirts, the duke's bloody cheek—but otherwise refrained from comment.

"Ah, there, you see," Bea said with a nod of satisfaction as she stood up and straightened her dress. "My delaying tactic did work. Thank you, constable, for your timely arrival. This is Mr. Rhodes. You will be escorting him to the magistrate's office. He has confessed to the murder of Mr. Huzza, whom you might have read about in the paper. He died in a steam carriage explosion that was wrongly attributed to the general unreliability of strong steam. It was actually the handiwork of Mr. Rhodes."

Snapping with fury, Rhodes said he did not confess.

"*Modus tollens*, my friend," she said chidingly. "*Modus tollens*."

The constable took possession of the culprit, and Kesgrave accepted a handkerchief from Jenkins. Dabbing his cheek, he said, "Flora would be impressed with your Latin."

Bea bowed her head modestly and insisted she would not. "I know only scattered phrases. My cousin knows aphorisms and commonly cited quotations."

Something about this exchange further disgusted the groom—its lack of respect for the urgency of the situation or her cousin's fluency, she did not know—and he announced that he would wait with the horses.

As Jenkins left the room, shaking his head, Kesgrave conferred with the constable and Bea asked Lynch if there was anything she could do to make him more comfortable.

It was a sincere question, for he appeared so forlorn there, in the middle of the floor, clutching his neck where a thin stream of blood trickled, but in the empty room, with its bare walls and dearth of furniture, it sounded vaguely satirical. Helplessly, she looked around, wondering what she could do and noted only the same elements as before: curtains, chandelier, broken glass, candelabra, Kesgrave.

At the very least, she decided, she could clean up the glass.

In fact, she could not, for she was the Duchess of Kesgrave, and Lynch found the prospect of a personage of her rank and influence picking up shards from his own drawing room floor intolerable.

He insisted on doing it himself, his hands still shaking from the ordeal he had undergone, and he cut himself on the sharp edge of the very first piece he touched.

Wonderful, Bea thought, now his situation was even worse.

Lynch refused to use his clothes to stem the bleeding, and the suggestion that he allow her to employ her own gown caused him to recoil in horror. Compromising, he agreed to use the curtain, which was already a wine-dark red, but only the hem at the very bottom.

Consequently, he sank to the floor, leaned his back against the windowpane and thanked Bea for her kindness in rescuing Huzza's reputation from the trash heap. "That is an invaluable service. He deserves to be remembered as a great man. I am sure Mr. Waugh will have huge success with the patents from the *Bright Benny*. It is a marvelous carriage."

Across the room, an irate Rhodes, who was now struggling against restraints around his wrists, swore viciously and consigned Lynch to every circle of hell. He was still issuing profanities at the top of his lungs as the constable led him from the house, and Lynch murmured anxiously, "Oh, dear, the neighbors."

Bea, who had thought the situation could not become any more pitiful, felt a fresh pang of sympathy for Lynch. As he was about to be evicted from the property, worrying about the ardent disapproval of his neighbors was a luxury he no longer had.

Fortunately, this did not occur to him, and she thought it was better that he fret over their displeasure than the bleak future stretching before him.

There was something appropriately macabre about Rhodes's machinations ensuring his own destruction, but it struck her as unfair that Lynch was also destroyed in the wreckage.

It was a shame Waugh had failed to grasp the value of his new possession. If he had held on to it rather than selling it within hours of acquisition, he might have employed Lynch to oversee the construction of Huzza's tramroad network. Acting as a supervisor was not the same as owning the company, but it was certainly an improvement on impoverishment.

Instead, he had pawned it off on an unsuspecting ironworks owner.

Eugene Richards was equally oblivious to what he possessed.

As she lamented the depths of their ignorance, a wild idea—oh, indeed, a very wild and outlandish idea—struck her, and her heart began to race painfully as the thought lodged itself into her mind.

Was it possible?

Of course it is possible, you dunderhead, she thought derisively. You mention giving pin money to a street urchin and Kesgrave counters with founding a hospital.

And then there was the Particular. The duke invested great sums in the theater simply to gain them access to its company for her investigation.

Hundreds of pounds handed over on a whim!

Without question, she could purchase patents for a revolutionary steam engine with no more consideration.

Well, a *little* more consideration.

Obviously, she would have Stephens thoroughly examine the documents before making an offer to Richards—a very fair offer in which he would make a tidy sum after holding the company for only a few days.

And the widows and orphans.

They, too, would be appropriately compensated.

But money was merely a technical detail.

It was never about the expense.

Always, it was a question of audacity and how much of it she had. Was her strange investigative habit not enough of an eccentricity for the new Duchess of Kesgrave? Must she really have another? And one that made her Lady Runner affectation seem quaint by comparison.

That would teach them to gasp in dismay at her ingenuity.

Poor Kesgrave!

Only an hour ago, he had sworn to Tarwich that he had no intention of setting himself as a manufacturer of steam engines.

How confident he had been!

And now here she was, not only contemplating the prospect but also delighting in every tut of horror Mrs. Ralston would emit, every salacious sentence Mr. Twaddle-Thum would write. She felt an unbearable pressure in her chest at the thought of indulging so recklessly in the thing her mother loved. She recalled the breathless paragraphs Clara had devoted to Mr. Phillips's invention all those years ago and felt so close to her.

We are going to build steam engines, Mama.

If Kesgrave refused, she would of course respect his decision.

Even the most open-minded of dukes had a breaking point, and a wife plying an industrial trade was a very strong swing of a hammer.

Nevertheless, she hoped he would not object.

Because she wanted to dash giddily from the house, Bea made herself linger.

Lynch, however, was discomfited by their presence, insisting that they had already done enough for him. "Please do be on your way. My housekeeper should be back any minute, and she will help me clean up."

Bea, finding this claim unlikely, knew better than to question it and bid Lynch good-bye as he clutched his bleeding hand in the hem of the curtain. As soon as they returned home, she would send Marlow with a basket of provisions and a proper bandage to secure his wound.

Once in the carriage, she restrained her enthusiasm further by complimenting Kesgrave on his deft handling of Rhodes.

It was not, she told herself, an attempt to soften him with flattery.

Nonetheless, she did add, perhaps gratuitously, that the cut under his eye—which, she could see now, was not deep enough to leave a blemish—gave him an appealingly rakish appearance.

"It is nothing so dashing as to rival Mr. Davies's lavish mark of valor," he said with a grin, "but it is early days yet and I expect it will not be long before I am sporting a scar that complies with your romantical ideal."

"Miss Otley's ideal," she corrected gently. "I made him up to align with Miss Otley's romantical ideal to induce her to confess to her father's murder. My ideal has long been tyrannical pomposity and withering condescension."

Such extravagant praise was more than the duke could withstand, and although Bea had intended to discuss her plan to build dozens, possibly scores, of *Bright Bennies,* she found herself suddenly perched on his lap, his lips pressing soft, seductive kisses against her own as his hands skimmed her body.

It was almost enough to make her forget her intention.

Almost.

The notion niggled in her mind, a flickering flare of light, and just as she was about to pull away, Kesgrave raised his head and brushed a strand of hair behind her ear. His touch was gentle, possibly reverent, but his eyes glittered with mischief as he said, "Out with it, brat."

Genuinely baffled, she wondered if she had missed something.

She found his kisses intoxicating, yes, but she rarely lost track of a conversation.

Shaking his head, the duke laughed at her expression and said, "You only have that gleam in your eyes when you are about to ask me something outrageous. I have already provided you with the daily schedule of the stable boys at Haverill Hall so that you can sabotage the pinery, and I have agreed to shave an hour off your lessons each week to include the complete works of Shakespeare as training."

"There is as much strategic value in Bottom's schemes as Macbeth's," she interjected. "I am certain Flexmore would say the same."

"I have accepted full blame for the removal of pineapple from the menu," he continued as if she had not spoken. "So out with it. Tell me what preposterous thing you would have me do next. I am prepared to be horrified."

But he was not prepared, Bea thought, grinning widely as she launched into an explanation of her scheme.

Not nearly enough, no.

My Gracious Thanks

Pen a letter to the editor!

Dearest Reader,

A writer's fortune has ever been wracked with peril - and wholly dependent on the benevolence of the reading public.

My endless gratitude to the gracious reader for rewarding an intrepid author's ceaseless toil.

Keep reading for an excerpt of the next Bea installment: An Extravagant Duplicity

An Extravagant Duplicity

If compelled to give the reasons she refused to allow her son to take lessons with Gentleman Jackson, Vera Hyde-Clare would have listed expense first. Engaging in the art of pugilism required not only tutelage, which came at a premium, but also equipment and rigging. By the time Russell had acquired all the necessary accoutrement, the financial investment would be double the estimate he had provided.

She knew this to be fact because she had seen it happen time and again with her friends. A child developed an interest in a sport or leisure activity, and then a few months or years later the household would be overwhelmed by debt.

Poor Mrs. Potter—she could barely afford new hair ribbons since her son had taken up yachting. Wilfred's determination to win the regatta in Barton had necessitated an ever-increasing fleet of boats, and the family lived under the constant strain of looming penury. (Could their anxiety also have a little something to do with the series of bad investments Mr. Potter made in a minerals company? Well, yes, that was almost certainly a factor. But everyone knew a sailing habit doubled the precarity of any circumstance.)

After cost, however, Vera would have cited brutality.

Boxing was such a savage diversion. All those clenched fists smashing into all those chins; all those cheeks bruised like apples at the bottom of a barrel. All that blood!

It chilled her to the core of her being, and she found it incomprehensible that an occupation as uncouth as bare-knuckle brawling could be perceived as an elegant pastime of gentlemen.

John Jackson had much to answer for, imbuing the sport with scientifical principles! As if the mathematical analysis of how to land a blow magically divested the action of its barbarity.

And yet, if the loathsome pursuit was indulged in by a personage no less exalted and refined as the Duke of Kesgrave, was it not incumbent upon her to temper her judgment? Was she not obligated to concede it might have a redeeming quality or two?

Unequivocally, yes.

Nobody would dare imply that the duke's taste was anything but impeccable.

That being the case, he *had* recently aligned himself with Vera's own drab, spinsterish niece, so it was possible his infallibility was not quite as inviolate as one would—

With an abrupt shake of her head, Beatrice, Duchess of Kesgrave, halted the thought in the middle of the sentence. She had resolved to stop assuming she knew every idea and notion that passed through her relative's mind, and the only way to do that was to actually stop assuming she knew every idea and notion that passed through her relative's mind.

It was a challenge.

Having spent twenty years in the other woman's care, Bea could not conceive of her as anything other than a villainess —a comedic one, to be sure, with elements of absurdity, but a villainess nonetheless. Aunt Vera, possessing a breathtaking lack of generosity, always formed the meanest opinion about a subject and met every situation with a miserly understanding. Vaguely aware of these limitations, she often sought to soften her position with clarifying statements that inevitably rambled with clumsy imprecision, further obfuscating her stance.

Although these attempts at coherence frequently caused Bea to smile with perverse enjoyment, they did not outweigh the cruelty to which the woman had subjected her for much of her life. Consequently, she had a difficult time seeing her relative as a fully formed human being capable of complexity and growth.

Aunt Vera struck her as more closely resembling a fish—able to perform a small assortment of basic tasks over and over. Not even the revelation that her harsh treatment of the orphan entrusted to her care was based on a gross misunderstanding of the girl's parents could significantly alter her behavior.

She was simply too much of a turbot or a mackerel to overcome the pettiness that lived in her heart.

Or so Bea believed.

And then, two weeks ago, Vera offered to accompany the Dowager Duchess of Kesgrave to Cambridgeshire to attend the funeral of the septuagenarian's son. The peeress roundly refused to accept her grandson's escort and an argument was brewing, possibly a heated one—definitely a protracted one—and into this fray stepped the inordinately timid Mrs. Hyde-Clare with a helpful suggestion.

It was an unfathomable turn for a variety of reasons, not the least of which was that Bea's aunt was not renowned for solving problems. She was more famous for wringing her hands over the slightest awkwardness and lamenting the lack of decorum. For her to offer gallantly to take the two-day journey was an astonishing act of generosity, for it would expose her to an intolerable amount of discomfort.

Traveling by itself was always an unpleasant enterprise, what with the confined space of the carriage and the lamentable condition of the roads and the harrowing threat of highwaymen, but to undertake it in the presence of an elderly noblewoman was a form of torture for Aunt Vera. She found everything about the British peerage overwhelming, from its noble bearing to its family crests. (It was appalling to her, all that excess—to be so magnificent as to warrant *three* lions!)

Given how breathless finely veined marble made her, she was likely to suffocate before they left London.

Never in a million years could Bea have imagined her relative making such an audacious proposal, and she found it remarkably difficult to reconcile the generous act with the woman she knew. Even as Aunt Vera opened her mouth to suggest it, Bea had braced herself for yet another harsh critique of her hoydenish conduct. (In this case, running after a suspected murderer in the middle of a bustling street with her skirts raised to reveal her ankles.) No matter what she did, her relative always had a complaint.

Except this time.

This time she had a solution.

Confounded, Bea was forced to consider the possibility that she might not in fact have privileged access to her relative's mind.

Perhaps she did not know what Aunt Vera was thinking at all.

Well, no, that was going too far in the opposite direction.

After two decades of exposure, she had *some* idea and could reasonably conclude that her offer to the dowager was an anomaly. The fact that the two women happened to rub together well made the event's singularity more pronounced, and Bea was convinced nothing like it would ever happen again.

Even so, she nevertheless found herself determined to be fair and resolved to withhold judgment. Going forward, she would give her aunt the benefit of the doubt.

Alas, it was more easily said than done, and Bea found herself often falling into the old habit, ascribing thoughts to her relative based on the tilt of the other woman's chin and the rigidity of her shoulders.

Like now, for instance.

The harsh line of Aunt Vera's lips grew thinner and thinner the longer her son talked—a clear indication that she disapproved of his words. Rarely could she hold her tongue for more than a few minutes, and it had already been a full ten.

They were gathered in the drawing room at 19 Portman Square, convened there at the request of Russell, who had issued an invitation to Bea and the duke asking them to participate in a family conversation.

That was the way he described it in his note: a *conversation*.

'Twas a curious thing to receive, a formally worded missive from her cousin, and Bea promptly rearranged her schedule to comply with the request. Kesgrave, who had had a more interesting afternoon of riding in the park with Nuneaton planned, was likewise too intrigued to decline.

After attending thoughtfully to his guests, including his parents, who he made sure had tea prepared specifically to their liking, Russell had launched into an extensive description of his experience at Gentleman Jackson's. Most surprising to him was the genial company he had found at the salon. When petitioning for the right to take lessons, he had not considered the camaraderie of like-minded fellows.

"All I wanted when I began my training was to perfect my uppercut," he said.

At this statement, Aunt Vera compressed her mouth so tightly her lips disappeared, and Bea felt a disconcerting itchiness between her shoulder blades as she struggled to hold fast to her resolution.

Without question, Vera Hyde-Clare's patience was at an end. She had indulged her son with painstaking tolerance—accepting the invitation affably, receiving the cup of tea thankfully, listening to his speech silently—and all she had gotten in exchange for this extraordinary act of child-rearing was a dissertation on the benefits of violence. Whatever pact she had made with her husband to allow the training, it certainly did not include submitting to the provocation of juvenile taunts.

Did Russell really think she would endure such an incitement without summarily rescinding her approval and demanding he withdraw at once from—

No, Bea thought, shaking her head again.

Aunt Vera's pinched look could mean any number of things, such as dissatisfaction with the room's temperature or irritation with the state of the curtains. Both were decidedly imperfect, with the latter possessing a rather large U-shaped stain along the edge about halfway up and the former subject to the unusually chilly weather. Given that such conditions exposed her to charges of lax housekeeping by the august Duke of Kesgrave, she could be composing a sternly worded lecture to the housekeeper, Mrs. Emerson.

It was possible, Bea thought fairly.

Yes, but not likely.

With his speech, Russell was waving a red flag at a bull, and it struck Bea as a particularly ill-advised decision. The last thing he should do was draw more attention to his new hobby. The much better way to serve his goal was by pretending not to take lessons at all. Every time he left the house for 13 Bond Street, he should act as though he were visiting the tobacconist or calling on a friend.

Seemingly oblivious to the damage he was doing his cause, Russell described a strike he had dealt Ripley—that was, Viscount Ripley, second cousin to the Marquess of Eastleigh—that knocked his lordship's nose so hard, blood seeped from it.

"For a moment he claimed to see double," Russell added giddily. "He said there were two of everything—two sparring partners, two Jacksons, two clocks, *four* of his own fists."

If he thought the potential to befriend young peers through the sport of boxing would endear the occupation to his mother, then he was even more buffle-headed than Bea had supposed. As Vera Hyde-Clare could not bear the presumption of her son sharing a tailor with men of noble rank, she was hardly more likely to welcome the prospect of his assaulting them physically.

Planting a facer on a viscount!

Had Russell abandoned every notion of modesty?

Did he not recall his place at all?

Unable to stand it one second more, Aunt Vera leaped to her feet, her hands clenched tightly at her side, her eyes flashing with anger, as she wailed that she would not permit it.

She would never permit it!

How dare he sully them all by even having the temerity even to suggest it!

"You ungrateful child!" she cried with unrestrained agitation. "I knew this would happen. You've had a small taste of the power and now you want more. That is what violence does: It spreads and destroys until everything has been devoured. I held firm against your boxing for years, and then I go away for one measly week and come back to find my son so drunk on the glory of bare-knuckle brawling, he wants to participate in a public fight. I will not have it! I am sure your father feels the same way, and he will say so as soon as he is given the opportunity. And the duke! What is he to think of us? We have always striven to be an unassuming family, to stay beneath the notice of our betters, and then Beatrice began poking her nose into other people's affairs, as if it is any business of ours whom Lady Skeffington decides to attack in the library—in the privacy of her own home, no less. Is no place safe anymore from the glare of interest?"

It was an incredible speech.

Even for a woman who had made a career of nonsensical blathering, it was an extraordinary outburst, and no one in the room was immune from its effects. Kesgrave's lips quirked as he sought to hide his amusement in a cup of tea, and Uncle Horace's face turned bright red at the inexplicable assumption his wife had made. Flora, who had been curiously out of sorts for the past week or so, stared at her mother blankly, while Russell goggled in astonishment.

Bea smothered her own smile while she waited for someone to address Aunt Vera's concern. From the grimace on her uncle's face, she assumed he had something to say, and Russell would surely be impatient to correct his mother's egregious misconception.

Neither spoke.

Aunt Vera continued to breathe heavily, further unsettled by their silence, which seemed to confirm her worst fears.

Then Flora said calmly, "The law."

Swiveling her head to glare at her daughter, Vera squawked, "What?"

"Given that murder is illegal, even for peeresses with whom you went to school, the law gave Bea the right to poke her nose into Lady Skeffington's affairs," Flora replied waspishly. "You are the one who just said violence spreads if not checked. Well, Bea held her ladyship's violence in check. I would think you would laud her for that, not continue to berate her all these months later."

Aunt Vera gasped and waved her arm behind her back as if to locate the chair nearby before she collapsed to the floor in disbelief. Gently, she lowered herself to the seat and pressed her hand against her chest. "I cannot believe you would speak to me like that, you ungrateful child."

Her surprise was understandable, for her daughter usually treated her with either amused patience or fond affection. Sometimes Flora rolled her eyes lavishly behind her mother's back, but she always kept her tone respectful.

Whatever bedeviled her now, Bea thought, left her cousin with little tolerance for Aunt Vera's antics.

Equally disconcerted by his sister's display, Russell pursued his lips and insisted sullenly, "*I* am the ungrateful child. This is *my* meeting, and nobody will change the subject until I have said my piece. I could have been sneaky about it, but I decided to be open and aboveboard and you will respect my maturity!"

Exhaling heavily, Aunt Vera assured him he had said quite enough. "And I have given my answer. You will not enter a public match."

"I don't want to!" Russell insisted.

"Then a private one," his mother replied dismissively. "You will engage in no more fights."

Russell sputtered angrily, his color high as well, and Kesgrave pressed closer to Bea to inform her that now was a good time to intercede. "I appreciate your forbearance in holding your tongue, but in a moment the discussion will descend into a squabble between your cousins."

It would, yes, inevitably.

Almost all conversations between the siblings ended in a spiteful exchange of insults. Their father had been very sparing with his approval during their childhood, and they were both almost desperate for his approbation. In recent months, Flora had earned it by displaying more intelligence than anyone had believed her capable of, scattering Latin phrases among her conversation. Russell had only recently acquired it by keeping a cool head in the immediate aftermath of a steam engine explosion. Emboldened by his father's esteem, he had announced he was taking lessons with Gentleman Jackson, then dared anyone in the household to stop him, even the housekeeper.

As his mother was in Cambridgeshire at the time, nobody did.

When Aunt Vera discovered what had transpired in her absence, she had shown unprecedented tact, withholding her disapproval so as not to undermine her husband's authority.

But she had been struggling for more than a week to restrain her anxiety and now it appeared to have corrupted her ability to reason.

Russell partaking in a title fight!

Aunt Vera's gross misunderstanding of the situation was more outlandish than anything Bea could ascribe to her.

It was for that reason she had no intention of interrupting. She could not conceive what her relative would do next.

"If you wish to avoid a quarrel, then I suggest you intervene," Bea replied as Russell threw himself back into the chair with a gloomy expression, as if his dream of winning a championship bout had indeed been thwarted. "I am too deeply engrossed in the unfolding drama to say a word."

Kesgrave demurred, citing his lack of standing. "I am not family."

"Coward," she observed softly.

He accepted the charge without comment.

Flora, displaying further impatience, told her mother she was making a ridiculous fuss over nothing. "Although I have seen few signs of intelligence in my brother, I am sure he is clever enough to avoid humiliation by displaying his meager skills in public."

Russell, straightening his posture in the chair, said his right hook was a prime rounder and that he would acquit himself quite well if he wanted to enter a mill on Highgate Common. Aunt Vera whimpered in distress, Flora cackled scornfully, and Uncle Horace remained silent.

Bea looked at the duke pointedly, as if to indicate that he could speak now if he so chose.

He did not.

Russell glowered ferociously and muttered that he had not intended to spar anywhere except at the salon, but if Flora continued to goad him, he might just change his mind.

"Ah, yes, there is his much-vaunted maturity," Flora murmured airily.

But in fact he did display a great deal of it by not responding to her taunt in kind. Instead, he smoothed his features and said his presentation had gone wildly off course. Seeking to correct that, he explained that he had not mentioned landing a facer on Ripley's nose to prove his bona fides as a boxer. "I was citing it as evidence of his temperament. He is an easygoing chap."

At the reminder that her son now punched the relatives

of marquesses, Aunt Vera winced, but it was not as deep as the flinch evinced by the word *chap*.

Truly, it was horrifying that her own flesh and blood could speak so nonchalantly about the nobility. Where was his overweening awe that made him ramble awkwardly in the presence of a better?

Unaware of his mother's discomfort, Russell continued. "Ripley is like that with everyone, you see, tolerant and good-natured. No matter how bruising the blow, he never loses his temper, which is how I know his family's understanding of the situation is off target. And that is the reason I have gathered you here today. As I said, I want to be aboveboard about the matter. There have been secrets in this family in the past and I do not want to perpetuate the cycle, most importantly because you, Bea, have been at the center of it."

Startled to find herself singled out, Bea wondered if Russell had discovered that the lowly law clerk with whom she had recently been infatuated was in fact a figment of her imagination.

It did not seem possible, for Russell displayed little interest in things that did not directly pertain to him and he would have no reason to launch his own investigation. Flora would not have told him either, for she delighted in knowing things her brother did not.

Most assuredly, Russell did not suspect the truth about Mr. Davies.

To what, then, was he referring?

Her investigative bent in general?

But that was widely known.

Satisfying her curiosity, he added that he thought it was reprehensible that his mother and father withheld vitally important information about her own parents from her. "I know how damaging that has been to your life."

Aunt Vera recoiled as if struck, but Uncle Horace advised

him not to comment on things he could not properly understand. "We made the best decisions we could based on the information we had at the time. I am not certain how this unfortunate history relates to your lessons with Gentleman Jackson, but I trust you will rectify that soon or risk losing them."

In recognition of his parent's authority, Russell acknowledged the complexity of the situation and even apologized for speaking out of turn. Vera, grateful that her son was still able to display some good sense, thanked him, then immediately cringed again when he reiterated his central thesis that secrets caused harm.

Identifying himself as unwilling to participate in clandestine behavior, he said, "That is why I am seeking my cousin's assistance in the presence of all of you. So that you may know what is going on."

"Yes, but what *is* going on?" Flora asked snappishly. "You have said nothing comprehensible and only succeeded in giving our mother vapors. If that was the purpose of this meeting, then next time you may hold it privately, for I have no need or desire to witness it."

Russell blinked at his sister in surprise, while Bea, who knew something was being asked of her even if she could not say what that was, marveled at Flora's malice. Although the girl frequently ridiculed her brother, her remarks were rarely so cutting. Whatever had put her in a churlish mood had made her mean as well.

"But it is obvious, is it not?" he replied, examining each of them in turn, a faint hint of disappointment clouding his eyes as he noted their lack of comprehension.

It was impossible not to bristle at his response, for the idea of being so lackwitted as to fail to meet Russell's expectations was a daunting one.

Naturally, Bea had her suspicions, for there were few

things with which one would reasonably seek her assistance, and help with solving a murder certainly topped the list. But if there was a dead body lurking somewhere in the background, Russell had done a poor job of identifying it. The only person he had mentioned was a viscount named Ripley, whom her cousin had discussed in the present tense, indicating he was alive.

Had someone else been killed at Gentleman Jackson's?

Surely not.

The salon was too well attended for an event of that nature not to be an on-dit, and there had been no mention of it in the *London Daily Gazette.* Of a certainty, Twaddle-Thum would have found some way to use a corpse in the famous boxing rooms to further deride Bea.

How is it possible, he might have wondered in one of his loathsome screeds, that her Outrageousness—because, yes, after several attempts at saddling her with an insulting sobriquet fell flat, he had finally settled on one that satisfied him—did not take lessons with Gentleman Jackson to complement her many other masculine traits?

Aunt Vera, her voice shrill with confusion, announced that nothing was obvious. "I do wish you would explain why we have been summoned here if not to be made aware of our forthcoming humiliation," she said, before nipping at her bottom lip in distress and apologizing to the duke for presuming to assign him to any group, let alone one so patently beneath him. "A man of your rank and breeding is immune to humiliation, for your participation immediately elevates the questionable behavior to acceptable conduct. It is why you did not pause to consider the consequences of marrying Beatrice, for which I am grateful."

But the source of her gratitude was not readily apparent, at least not to Vera, and she added that she was grateful for his confidence. "*Not* that you saved Bea from spinsterhood.

She was not a spinster yet and had many interested prospects. Indeed, a plan was in the works for her to marry a ... to marry a ... a ..."

Reluctant to say *law clerk* in the duke's presence just in case he had yet to realize just how dire the situation had been before he had kindly stepped in, she allowed the thought to trail off.

"Regarding Kesgrave's social sway, Mama," Flora said with cynical amusement, "does that mean Russell could fight publicly if the duke did it first?"

Aunt Vera turned bright red, and Uncle Horace ordered her to stop teasing her mother. Then he told his son to bring the meeting to a close because he was already late for an appointment. "I was supposed to meet Wilkinson at my club fifteen minutes ago."

"As I just finished explaining, there is no way Ripley could have done it," Russell said. "He is too genial to have even thought of anything like it."

Although Aunt Vera snapped that nobody knew what *it* was, the other occupants of the room in fact had a good idea of the viscount's situation and Flora irritably asked who was dead.

"His grandfather," Russell replied. "That is, the viscount's maternal grandfather, a cit called Roger Dugmore, who resided in St. James's Square. It is a very large house and Ripley is staying there with a parcel of cousins and one of his aunts. You see, the old man, who was in fact quite old, had a fall while climbing out of bed five days ago. It was dreadful. A deep cut along his forehead. And, well, he died—in the fall—but Ripley had had a vicious row with him about money only the day before *and* he was seen creeping out of the old man's room very early on the morning in question. And now everyone in his family thinks he is a depraved killer and he cannot bear the way they look at him, all scared and suspicious as if he might murder them next. So, knowing of my connection to Bea, he asked if I could ask *her* to do him the kindness of paying a call to the house and proving to his family that he did nothing wrong."

Finishing his explanation, he tilted his head forward to look beseechingly at his cousin. "I know the situation is a little unconventional and it is not the way you typically conduct an investigation, but you must understand how difficult it is for him. To have his own family suspect him of murder when he wouldn't hurt a fly!"

It was true, Bea thought, for it was unusual for her expertise to be sought. More frequently, she had to impose her presence on unwilling subjects and ask impertinent questions they did not want to answer. Although she had demonstrated an impressive proficiency at identifying murderers, she was nevertheless called upon repeatedly to prove her skill. The prospect of her interest being welcomed rather than resented appealed to her and she thought it might be a fitting last—

Ah, but no, she would not think of that either, she told herself sternly.

No assuming she knew what Aunt Vera was thinking.

No contemplating life after the cherub.

All that was permitted was staying focused on the event unfolding before her, which in this case was Russell's sparring partner's possible guilt.

Or, rather, his presumed innocence.

Deciding to accept the invitation, she straightened her shoulders and opened her mouth to gather more information just as Dawson entered to announce a visitor.

"Mr. Holcroft to see Miss Hyde-Clare," he said.

Author's Note

The *Bright Benny* is a Frankenstein's monster cobbled together from a variety of inventions over a period of time. Its two most significant contributors are Richard Trevithick's *Puffing Devil* and Matthew Murray's *Salamanca,* both of which are mentioned in the story in general terms so as not to draw attention to the inevitable overlaps in technology. Some contributions include the rack and pinion design from Murray and the fusible plug from Trevithick. (The fusible plug was, in fact, his response to the Greenwich tide mill explosion, thereby making Huzza's revolutionary innovation more than a decade out of date.) You can see the *Salamanca* in an 1813 watercolor by George Walker called *The Collier,* and you can watch a replica of the *Puffing Devil* puff through the streets of Camborne, England, on Trevithick Day, the last Saturday in April.

About the Author

Lynn Messina is the author of almost two dozen novels, including the Beatrice Hyde-Clare mysteries, a cozy series set in Regency-era England. Her first novel, *Fashionistas,* has been translated into sixteen languages and was briefly slated to be a movie starring Lindsay Lohan. Her essays have appeared in *Self, American Baby* and the *New York Times* Modern Love column, and she has been a regular contributor to the *Times* parenting blog. She lives in New York City with her sons.

Also by Lynn Messina

Verity Lark Mysteries Series

A Lark's Tale

A Lark's Flight

Beatrice Hyde-Clare Mysteries Series

A Brazen Curiosity

A Scandalous Deception

An Infamous Betrayal

A Nefarious Engagement

A Treacherous Performance

A Sinister Establishment

A Ghastly Spectacle

A Malevolent Connection

An Ominous Explosion

An Extravagant Duplicity

A Murderous Tryst

And Now a Spin-off from the BHC Mysteries Series:

A ~~Beatrice~~ Flora Hyde-Clare Novel

A Boldly Daring Scheme

Love Takes Root Series

Miss Fellingham's Rebellion (Prequel)

The Harlow Hoyden

The Other Harlow Girl

The Fellingham Minx

The Bolingbroke Chit

The Impertinent Miss Templeton

Stand Alones

Prejudice and Pride

The Girls' Guide to Dating Zombies

Savvy Girl

Winner Takes All

Little Vampire Women

Never on a Sundae

Troublemaker

Fashionista (Spanish Edition)

Violet Venom's Rules for Life

Henry and the Incredibly Incorrigible, Inconveniently Smart Human

Welcome to the Bea Hive

FUN STUFF FOR BEATRICE HYDE-CLARE FANS

The Bea Tee

Beatrice's favorite three warships not only in the wrong order but also from the wrong time period. (Take that, maritime tradition *and* historical accuracy!)

The Kesgrave Shirt

A tee bearing the Duke of Kesgrave's favorite warships in the order in which they appeared in the Battle of the Nile

Available in mugs too!

See all the options in Lynn's Store.